PRAISE FOR
the Blessings

sions that tie family members together...the reader leaves feeling lucky to have spent some time in their presence."

—*Publishers Weekly* (starred review)

"Fans of writers like Anne Tyler, Alice McDermott, and even Richard Yates will revel in Juska's resplendent novel detailing two decades in the life of the Blessing clan."

—BookReporter.com

"With a keen eye for detail and character, Juska shows us that, Tolstoy notwithstanding, a happy family can be happy in its own way and make for great storytelling...An exquisite portrait of a large family." —*Shelf Awareness*

"Throughout the novel, right up until the affecting final scene, Juska explores the paradox of family—how it is the thing that both stifles and sustains you, how it can be simultaneously predictable and unexpected, stable and fragile...the result is the best kind of family portrait—one in which you know each member's foibles and flaws and yet love them anyway."

—*BookBrowse* (Editor's Choice)

"It takes a writer with voice and depth to tell the story of a large Irish Catholic family's travails and make it feel fresh. Elise Juska succeeds with this novel set in Northeast Philly."

—*Philadelphia Magazine*

"Juska explores the collective experiences, traditions, and loyalties of a close-knit family...A multilayered, sympathetic account of its members' lives." —*Kirkus Reviews*

the Blessings

the Blessings

Elise Juska

GRAND CENTRAL
PUBLISHING

NEW YORK   BOSTON

Grand Central Publishing
Hachette Book Group
1290 Avenue of the Americas
New York, NY 10104

www.HachetteBookGroup.com

Printed in the United States of America

RRD-C

Originally published in hardcover by Hachette Book Group
First trade edition: May 2015
10 9 8 7 6 5 4 3 2 1

Grand Central Publishing is a division of Hachette Book Group, Inc.
The Grand Central Publishing name and logo is a trademark of Hachette Book Group, Inc.

The Hachette Speakers Bureau provides a wide range of authors for speaking events. To find out more, go to www.hachettespeakersbureau.com or call (866) 376-6591.

The publisher is not responsible for websites (or their content) that are not owned by the publisher.

Library of Congress Cataloging-in-Publication Data

Juska, Elise.
The blessings / Elise Juska. — First edition.
    pages cm
  ISBN 978-1-4555-7403-2 (hardcover) — ISBN 978-1-4555-7401-8 (ebook)
  1. Irish American families—Fiction. 2. Catholics—Fiction. 3. Domestic fiction. I. Title.
  PS3610.U87B54 2014
  813'.6—dc23
                                                2013019840

ISBN 978-1-4555-7402-5 (pbk)

For Catherine Pierce

Contents

the Blessings

Relief

It didn't take long for Abby to discover at college that most people did not have families like hers. Her roommates, Nicole and Mara, were amazed and amused by the letters cramming Abby's mailbox in the student union—notes from her aunts and twenty-dollar bills from her uncles, newspaper articles about the Phillies and the Eagles, her little sister's drawings of stick figures and houses—Philly row houses, tall and wobbly, crowned COME HOME SOON!—which Abby taped on the wall above her bed until it looked like one of her aunts' refrigerator doors. Her roommates laughed—*I didn't get this much mail at summer camp.* Abby had never gone to summer camp; she had never gone anywhere without her family, the entire clan, aunts and uncles and cousins renting houses within the same two blocks at the Jersey shore. They were a perennial mob at band concerts and Little League games, a discreet crowd of cameras in the living room before school dances. ("Are you serious?" Mara had paused here, a spoonful of cereal halfway to her mouth. "Were you *dying*?") None of this had struck Abby as remarkable before. But since going to college, she has begun to perceive her own uniqueness, to recognize her family as something apart from other families, with its own rhythm and code. *Epiphany*—it was a term she'd learned in her James Joyce seminar: the sudden realization of a larger truth.

On Sunday nights, Abby sank into the sound of her parents' voices, pressing the phone to her ear. It was 1992 and the hall phones were too public—the one time she'd talked to her mother there, voice trembling, she'd drawn sympathetic looks from the girls walking by holding flip-flops and plastic shower caddies—so she started going to the phone booth in the student union and sitting on the floor. Listening to her parents' measured voices, their talk of ordinary things—her new cousin Max's baptism, the eighteen points her cousin Joey scored in the basketball game against St. Cecilia's—she was overcome with a longing so great that it doubled her over, eyes full, knees drawn to her chin. The ruff from her new parka caught in her mouth. It was so cold in New England—why had she decided to go to college in New England? Something about the brochure—the picture of the quad in the snow, and the beginnings of a faint tug that would intensify as she got older, the sense that she belonged somewhere else.

But at eighteen, in the phone booth, Abby was so homesick that her stomach hurt. She reminded herself over and over that she would be home soon for Christmas break. For Thanksgiving, she'd accepted an invitation to Mara's house in Boston. Flights to Philadelphia were too expensive; it was a ten-hour drive, and she didn't have a ride. Her parents had wanted her to take a bus and train—her dad had even offered to drive up and get her—but Mara's was so much closer, and Abby was kind of pleased to have been invited. But as soon as Abby sat down to Thanksgiving dinner, she longed to be home. She missed her family, their unfancy stuffing and canned cranberry, the beat of calm silence when Pop said grace, the warm bluster of food passed around the long, crowded table, a plywood extender jammed in the middle so that one end nosed halfway across the kitchen floor. Dinner at Mara's was depressingly small (six people, including Abby) and formal. It had actually never occurred to Abby that other people's Thanksgivings might be like this. When she called home that night (collect, as her mother had instructed), every one of her aunts and uncles and cousins took a turn on the phone—baby Max held next to the receiver, crying, even her cousins Stephen and Joey mumbling, "Happy Thanksgiving"—and Abby chewed mercilessly on the inside of her cheek so she didn't cry herself.

For Christmas, Abby had found a girl on the ride board, a junior with a red Jeep who lived in Harrisburg and blared *The Joshua Tree* on an endless loop. She dropped Abby at a rest stop on the Pennsylvania Turnpike, where her dad picked her up to bring her the rest of the way home. And there it was: her old familiar neighborhood, old familiar street. Her driveway with its limp basketball net, her room with its pale yellow walls, the dried corsage from her senior prom drooping on her bulletin board. Her mom had stuffed the freezer with her favorite cinnamon-raisin bagels, and her little sister, Meghan, had made a sign for her bedroom door: WELCOME HOME ABBY! But to Abby's surprise, the ache was still there—a hollow feeling in her chest when she woke up the next morning and wandered through the quiet rooms alone. Her parents were at work, her brother and sister at school. As she roamed the house, Abby noticed for the first time the weirdly perfect symmetry of the curtains in the living room, the water rings on the end table in the den where her father watched TV at night, the hugeness of the stuffed panda collection on Meghan's bed. Within hours, she felt restless. She missed the dorm; she longed for noise. She missed the camaraderie of her roommates, the sleepy mornings piled in bed and gossiping about the night before, the clanging radiators and windows laced with frost. She felt a fleeting panic that college was all something she'd invented or dreamed, that maybe she'd never really gone. A few times, Abby dipped her nose into her suitcase, hoping to detect the scent of her dorm room or the New England cold, but she could smell only her house—impossible to define.

But tonight, ten days later, the entire family is together because Abby is about to leave again. In an hour she is driving to Nicole's house in New Jersey, and tomorrow the two of them are headed to Boston for New Year's Eve. Abby is wearing one of Nicole's sweaters, a baggy oatmeal-colored J.Crew roll-neck she's worn practically every day since she's been home. *Take it,* Nicole had said as they were packing, both of them sluggishly, pleasantly, hungover. *It's your good-luck charm!* The night before, Abby had worn the sweater to a party, where she'd kissed Eric Winn, an ice hockey player from Canada. He spoke with an accent: *So you know, you're one of the prettiest girls here.*

The memory brings a surge of heat to her cheeks, and Abby smiles, glances around the table, pushes her hair behind her ears. No one seems to notice. Her mom is clearing the dinner dishes as Aunt Margie brings out the desserts, the last of the plastic-wrapped Christmas leftovers: half a chocolate Bundt cake, a pumpkin loaf, and all the usual holiday cookies—the powdery white snowballs, the jellied thumbprints, the lumpy almond moons. Aunt Lauren puts on water for tea, cradling baby Max to her chest, while his two-year-old sister, Elena, scoots around under the table, crawling under people's knees and popping up in their laps: *Boo!*

Abby reaches for a cookie, something she would never eat in the dining hall, but at home with her family it's as though calories aren't real. The cookie is one Gran made, round with red-and-green sprinkles that look like crushed glass—Abby's known this cookie her whole life and it looks the same, tastes the same. Chewing, she catches Gran watching her, eyes watery behind her thick glasses. When Abby smiles at her, she winks.

If every family has a certain kind of music, Abby's is the murmur of sympathy around a dining room table. It starts in the pause after dinner and before dessert, when the men migrate to the living room and turn on sports and the women surround the wreckage, spilled crumbs and crumpled napkins and stained wineglasses. They pinch lids from sugar bowls and dip teabags in hot water, break cookies in half and chew slowly. They trade stories of other people's hardships. This is the melody, the measure, of her family: the response to sad things.

"Fifty-six years old," her mother is saying.

This story is one Abby already knows. One of their neighbors, Mr. Whelan, collapsed and died the day before Christmas Eve. A stroke. Fifty-six. Two sons in college. *Terrible.* They shake their heads. *A shame.*

Abby arranges her face into a sympathetic expression, but she is thinking about Eric Winn. Mara had heard that he might be in Boston tomorrow, at the party. It was at Chris Teppler's house; Eric and Chris both played on the JV hockey team. As

Abby watches her mother talking, she wonders if Eric Winn could be sitting around right now with his own family—in a house somewhere in Canada. Is he thinking about the party? Could he—possibly—be thinking about her?

Then her sister, Meghan, enters the room, and their mother stops talking about Mr. Whelan, because the night he died Meghan was so upset she couldn't sleep. "Football is stupid," Meghan announces, probably hurt that the boys aren't paying attention to her. She tags along with them relentlessly, especially Joey, the cool one.

"How about some dessert, Meg?" their mother says, extra brightly, just as Elena runs in and flings herself around Meghan's knees.

"Elena!" Meghan exclaims, scooping her up in both arms and hoisting her awkwardly onto one hip. "Do you want a cookie, Elena? Do you, cutie?" she says, doing her best imitation of a grown-up, and before Aunt Lauren can protest, one moment dissolves into the next—Elena taking a big bite of a snowball cookie, Meghan marching back downstairs with Elena in her arms, the kettle whistling, the baby beginning to cry.

"So," Aunt Margie says, and turns to Abby, wiping two powdery fingers on the napkin in her lap. "When are you heading back?" The party is at Aunt Margie's house tonight, hers and Uncle Joe's, and it's marked by all the usual Aunt Margie things: the chalky pink and green mints on the coffee table, the onion dip in the snowflake-shaped bowl, the wooden Jesus hanging on a cross above the toaster oven.

"Tonight," Abby says. "After this."

"Oh?" Aunt Margie reaches instinctively for the little gold

cross around her neck, worries it between two fingers. She has the same pink, freckled complexion as Abby's mother—as Abby herself—but where Abby's mother is tall, broad-shouldered, Aunt Margie is slight, tense and thin. "Tonight? Really?"

"But only to New Jersey," Abby explains. "One of my roommates lives in New Jersey. Tomorrow we're going to Boston. For New Year's Eve."

Her aunt is nodding, still rubbing the necklace. Abby doesn't mention the party, not after all her mother's questions—whose house and where does he live and will his parents be home? She'd had to lie about that last part (Mara had reported that Chris's parents would be out of town), though to mention Chris Teppler at all felt a little like lying, or at least pretending, Chris Teppler who Abby had never spoken to directly and who almost definitely didn't know her name.

"It's just two hours," Abby adds. "To New Jersey, I mean."

"And when are you coming home again?" Aunt Margie asks.

There will be other questions, but these will be the main questions, asked over and over tonight and for the next twenty years—*when are you leaving and when are you coming home again?*

"March," Abby says. "Spring break."

"Good," her aunt says, and Abby smiles. She knows they all expect she'll move back here after graduation. But Abby has always harbored a quiet, slightly worrying suspicion that the life her family adopts so effortlessly—meeting someone local, getting married and having babies and staying in Philadelphia, carrying on all the old traditions—won't happen for her, not so easily. Now that's she been to college, she feels even more sure. Yet to live anywhere else is unimaginable, too.

There is a commotion at the other end of the table—her cousins Stephen and Joey and her brother, Alex, crashing into the room. They descend on the desserts in a flurry of boyness—shiny jerseys, loud swishing athletic pants, giant hands, giant appetites. Abby watches her shy, skinny brother cram a snowball cookie into his mouth, and flip his shaggy hair from his face, eyes lowered. He is not as cool as his cousins, but he tries his hardest, hiding behind the mop of hair he thinks makes him invisible but actually makes him more conspicuous.

"Drink? Cake? Can I get you a piece of cake?"

The aunts are in motion, cutting the boys generous slabs and beaming as they head back to the living room, mouths full, sucking frosting off their thumbs—Stephen thick and slope-shouldered, Joey with his bristly crew cut and confident swagger, Alex hunched and bony—where they are absorbed back into the crowd of men around the TV. Abby can just hear her roommates: *You mean women in one room, men in the other?* This has never struck Abby as strange before; it's never struck her at all. In ten years, things will be different. People will have died or divorced; lines will have blurred. But for now the men are in one room, the women in the other, and this demarcation feels comforting, familiar.

From her seat at the table, Abby watches her grandfather. Pop is sitting where he always does at Aunt Margie's: the big, soft recliner in the living room with the brown tweed arms. It is Uncle Joe's chair, which he gives up whenever Pop is here. Tonight, on his blue sweater, Pop is wearing a sticker with a frog on it—IF YOU SMOKE, YOU CROAK! The frog dangles a cigarette from the corner of its mouth, like a waitress in a diner. A few weeks ago, Meghan had a school assembly about the dangers of smoking, and the school nurse had to call their mother because Meghan was crying so hard afterward she made herself throw up. *It was surprising*, Abby's mother had recounted calmly, but Abby heard the strain of concern in her voice. *It was surprising, how upset she was.* Abby didn't find it surprising. Meghan was always getting upset about things—whenever Abby went out with friends in high school, Meghan insisted she identify a "dedicated driver" (no matter that they were just going to the mall or the movies and Abby didn't even taste a beer until her senior year). Now there's Pop, wearing the sticker, curling on his blue sweater and losing its stick. But smoking is Pop's only vice, and one he can't be blamed for—they all know how he started by smoking the cigarettes in the Red Cross packages delivered to the POW camp in Germany—and he's always fed the habit quietly, slipping out onto porches and sidewalks, his jacket collar turned up against the wind. Now he's trying to quit, because of Meghan, though in less than two months it won't matter anymore. In early February, at five in the morning, Abby's hall phone will start to ring. At first she'll sleep right through it, waking only at the sound of the sharp knock—*Abby! Phone!*—and will find the receiver swinging from its thick silver cord, pointed at the floor. *Hi, honey.* Her throat will tighten instantly; her mother never calls her honey. *A heart attack. Come right home.* Abby will hang up and stand frozen in the hallway for several long minutes, blinking at the tattered flyers—*Live Music in the Pub!* and *Peer Counseling Hotline*—thinking: *This is how it feels to get one of these phone calls.* Back in her room, she'll study the sleeping body of Eric Winn, snoring under her cousin Elena's crayon

scribbles, which Aunt Lauren had translated in big block letters: TO ABBY, I MISS YOU! She will observe, numbly, the
strangeness of these worlds colliding—the phone call and the
drawings, Eric's ruddy chest and striped boxers—and how odd
it is that he will be attached to this memory forever. How, after this, things could never work out between them. How she
hopes Pop isn't up in heaven, watching. *This is really weird*, she
says, *but my grandfather just died*—and Eric will be bleary but
kind, and she'll manage to hold in her tears until he stumbles
out, shoes in hand, leaving a sloppy, markered SORRY on the
dry-erase board on her door.

But now, tonight, everyone is still here. The talk around the
table is getting slower. The women sigh, cut slivers of cake,
wipe children's noses. They ease their shoes off and flex their
stockinged feet beneath the table, squeezing the carpet between their toes. Aunt Lauren is sitting next to Abby, the new
baby squirming in her lap. She gave birth four months ago and
still looks extra soft, extra tired. *Isn't he cute?* everybody croons,
though Max is red and scrawny. *Too new to be cute*, Abby thinks,
then immediately regrets it, hoping she hasn't doomed herself
to having an uncute baby of her own.

"So when are you leaving, Abby?" Aunt Lauren asks, half
turning, tucking the baby against her shoulder. She's wearing a
loose pink blouse, a small diamond necklace resting in the tan
hollow of her throat. She has the kind of skin that's tan even in
winter, the kind Abby has always envied.

"Tonight," Abby says. "After this."

"Oh—tonight?"

"But I'm only going to New Jersey."

"Oh. Well. That's not so bad," she says. Lauren is distracted, nudging a pacifier into the baby's mouth. In Abby's family, babies are passed around constantly, casually, like serving bowls around a table, but Aunt Lauren likes to keep hers to herself. Aunt Lauren is an only child, Abby remembers, and it occurs to her then—the sort of awareness she may not have had before going away to college—that maybe Lauren isn't used to being around big families. She used to be Protestant, too, but converted to Catholicism when she married Uncle John.

From downstairs, there is a sudden gust of cheering, a few hard claps. Then Uncle Patrick comes jogging into the room. The women pause and look up, expectant.

"Fourteen-nothing us," he reports, and they nod—they don't watch the games but they want to know the score, to gauge the mood of the room, of the city in the morning.

"Good," Gran affirms, picking up her cup.

"More tea, Mother?" Aunt Margie says. The oldest siblings, Abby's mother and Margie, call Gran Mother; the younger ones, the boys, call her Mom. "Anyone? Tea?"

Uncle Patrick reaches over Abby to grab a brownie, rapping his knuckles on the top of her head. The Blessings all look Irish, fair-skinned and blue-eyed, but her youngest uncle is like a flag of Ireland, with red hair and freckles so thick that in places they're solid brown. "I hear you got some new wheels, Abs," he says.

It is the one thing Abby has accomplished over break—a used Volkswagen, three thousand dollars. Her parents paid half. Her father paced around the guy's driveway, picking at his fingernails, jingling change in his pocket. It wasn't like her parents to make big purchases, but it would be easier, they reasoned, for her to get home and back.

"You like it?"

Abby smiles. "I love it."

"Used?"

"Yeah. But not too used."

"Be careful driving," Uncle Patrick says. "Especially in that cold."

When she first arrived home, this was her family's primary question and greatest source of fascination: *How cold is it up there?* Then: *And you don't mind?*

"Just let the engine warm up first," Uncle Patrick is saying. Abby nods. She can feel her mother across the table, listening. She's concerned about Abby driving on highways, driving in snow, driving after dark, driving period. She doesn't want her leaving tonight, staying in Boston until intersession starts next week: This wasn't the plan. Of course, her mother has said none of this, but Abby can tell she's thinking it. Her mouth is drawn, her eyes sad. Even the way she's chewing that snow-ball cookie—how can chewing look so pained? It will be years before Abby's parents get divorced—not until Meghan is in college, after all her problems are out in the open—and only then will their lifelong quiet strike Abby as strange instead of soothing, and she and Alex will grow closer, out of necessity.

"Abs, is he bothering you?" Aunt Kate says, appearing at Uncle Patrick's side.

"Me?" Patrick says. "Never."

"Right." Kate laughs, swatting playfully at his arm.

Abby smiles. She knows this is not really about her—she's a means to an end, a reason to flirt—but doesn't mind because she likes Kate, now Aunt Kate. Kate and Lauren are the same age, only eight years older than Abby, though Kate seems younger. She and Uncle Patrick got married last summer and live in an apartment in Center City. Abby likes how affectionate they are. Once, she saw Kate sitting on Uncle Patrick's lap, his finger in her belt loop, an intimation of some private, physical ease. Her own parents never touched.

"So," says Aunt Kate, dropping into a chair beside Abby after Uncle Patrick has headed back to the game. She's wearing faded Levi's and long beaded earrings that swing forward as she inspects the desserts. "Got any New Year's Eve plans?"

Only Kate would ask. A year ago, the answer would have embarrassed Abby (she'd spent New Year's Eve watching movies she'd rented with her mother), but this year she can answer confidently. "Yeah. A party with some college friends. In Boston."

"Oh, I *love* Boston," Kate says, and sighs. She selects a cookie and leans back in her chair. "And you're loving school?"

"Yes." Abby nods. "Totally loving it."

"Savor every minute," Kate says, shaking her head wistfully as she chews. Kate went to Bryn Mawr, unlike Abby's mother and Aunt Margie, who didn't go to college—*It was a different time*, her mother always says—or even Aunt Lauren, who went to Drexel for two years, then dropped out when she met Uncle John. "When do you declare a major?"

"Next semester," Abby says. "I'll do English, I think. Or maybe art history."

"Or both?" Kate says, and Abby nods, appreciating this sense of possibility. Kate pops the rest of the cookie in her mouth and sweeps her hands together. "Have you met any nice guys yet?"

No one else in the family would venture to ask this either. Abby is grateful for the *yet*, as if her meeting them is one day inevitable.

"Kind of," Abby says. She glances at her mother, who is pretending not to listen as she presses her fingertip to a plate, collecting crumbs. "One."

She can't help herself. She knows it's a distortion of the truth, painting Eric Winn as anything more than a drunken hookup at a party, but who here will know the difference? All she needs to do is release a hint of him into the family and the rest will take care of itself, gather a life of its own as it gets passed around the table, accumulate legitimate weight and shape.

"Oh yeah?" Kate says. "What's his story?"

"He's from Canada," Abby says, adding, "Toronto. He's an ice hockey player." She feels weirdly proud as she offers up this profile, a person so different from the kinds they know at home. Since going to college, Abby has frequently found herself in thrall of such details—people with lives she's never considered, never known existed. Like Mara, who had spent Christmas skiing with her mother and stepfather. Or the girl in her dorm who has bulimia, who abruptly confided to Abby at a party that her esophagus was full of holes. Abby was alarmed and kind of excited at the same time.

Then Uncle John calls out from the living room—"Laur, can you grab her?"—just as Elena comes streaking into the room. She is wearing pink, footed pajamas and her mouth is smeared with confectioners' sugar. She pulls up short, as if startled to find herself there. Lauren is still holding the baby—"Can someone . . . ?" she says, a touch anxious—but Elena, lunging for a fruitcake, has already been scooped onto Aunt Kate's lap.

"Not so fast!" Kate says, tickling her. Elena shrieks with joy. The rest of the table beams, imagining Kate with a baby of her own.

Kate calls back: "I've got her, John!"

It is still nearly a year before Uncle John will get sick. Next Christmas, things will feel different, quiet and careful, fraught with unspoken and unspeakable things. But for now, the cancer in Uncle John's kidney is not yet there, or not yet known. *My uncle is really sick,* Abby will tell Nicole and Mara next November. *Aww,* they'll say, a quick frown, a poke of the bottom lip. It is not enough. She will repeat it to other people, inappropriate people—a professor during a conference about her Chaucer essay, a random girl in the bathroom at a bar. Every time, their reactions will disappoint her. She can tell it doesn't sound as important as it is. *Uncle*—in other families, it means less.

Dessert is winding down. The football game is over. The baby is tired, whimpering, a fuzzy little bundle packed into pajamas. The conversation gets slower, the pauses longer. Abby is thinking of tomorrow—of driving to Boston in her new Volkswagen with Nicole, of the jeans she bought with her Christmas money from Gran and Pop, jeans she's planning to wear to the party, of the possibility that Eric Winn will be there.

"Do you remember Matt McCabe?" Aunt Margie says. Abby hears the somber note in her voice. The table pauses, looks in her direction. "Joe's old friend? He played football for Saint B's?"

They nod, oriented—Joe, football, St. B's—and wait for the rest.

"His son just died."

"Died?"

"Died? How?"

"They don't know." Aunt Margie shakes her head slowly, almost reverently. "No reason. The doctors have no idea. They just found him dead in their backyard."

A note of disbelief, then murmurs of sadness around the table again, like the lapping of waves. Heads shake, spoons clink gently on teacup walls. Strange, how sadness can sound soothing. Abby remembers an experiment she learned about in Intro to Psych, about the relative improvement in the health of patients who were prayed for. She thinks about mentioning it but doesn't.

"How old?" they ask.

"Six."

"Six years old."

"Can you imagine?"

Slow shakes of the head. They can't. But would any age be less horrible than any other? Abby wonders. Is it worse to have known a child for six years, or is that extra time a gift? Instantly she regrets these thoughts. It makes her nervous to have even allowed them in, like tempting fate. Abby knows that being part of a family like hers carries with it a responsibility to be aware of those less fortunate. To be humble, to be grateful. To realize happiness is always edged with peril. As she stares at a stain on the tablecloth, Abby forces herself to think about the boy, six years old, the same way she forces herself to talk to God in church. She wonders what her family would think if they knew she'd gone to Mass only twice at college, back in September, and then only because she was lonely.

Abby feels loneliness now, pooling up inside her even as she sits among the people who have known her all her life. It is the beginning of what will become an unsolvable ache. When she's away, she'll miss her family; when she's with her family, she'll miss herself.

The coat pile is on the bed in her cousin Stephen's room—a rack of weights in the corner, posters of Kiss and Ozzy Osbourne on the walls. Abby thinks she smells pot, which seems unlikely. How old is Stephen? Fourteen? An aquarium bubbles in the dark. The fish look menacing and sharp. In ten years, Stephen's troubles will have grown so stark that Aunt Margie and Uncle Joe can no longer contain them. But now Abby locates her parka among the long wool coats on Stephen's bed, thinking of the furry pullovers that pile up in the corners of parties on campus, pawed through at night's end.

"You're not driving too far tonight, are you?" Aunt Margie says. She is standing at the bottom of the stairs, holding a glass of pink wine in one hand and rubbing her arm with the other, back and forth, as if she's cold.

"Nope," Abby reassures her. "Just to New Jersey." Then she waits for the rest—where in New Jersey, what route she'll take. But Aunt Margie has gone quiet, surveying the room. Her cheeks are flushed, eyes bright, maybe from the wine.

"It's a good moment," she says, "when everyone is okay."

At first Abby isn't sure Aunt Margie wasn't talking to herself.

Abby has her coat only half buttoned. Elena is scrambling past her knees, wrapped plates of leftovers are being passed from hand to hand. But her aunt looks at her with an extra modicum of gravity, and Abby sees that this was meant for her. That there will come a time when she looks at life this way, too: when, if everybody is okay, it is enough.

For now, though, Abby finishes buttoning her coat. She recognizes this point ahead, knows that someday she'll accept it as her measure of the world, but today, she's eighteen. Eighteen and in college, living away from home for the first time. Tomorrow is New Year's Eve.

"I better get on the road," she says, kissing her aunt's cheek. "Thank you for the party."

Then she starts her good-byes. Her parents stand by the front door, like the end of a receiving line, ensuring they are the last to say it. Abby makes her way across the living room, thanking Uncle Joe, touching Max's head, protesting as Gran hands her a plate of cookies—*for the drive*—nodding at parting advice from Uncle John about snow tires and antifreeze. *I'll see you soon*, she says to Pop. *March. Spring break.* He fumbles a twenty into her coat pocket, cups her face in his dry hands. She waves toward Alex, who is frowning at the postgame analysis, leaning forward with his hands on his knees, pretending to care. Meghan hugs her tightly, wrapping both arms around her waist and pressing a warm cheek to her side.

"Bye, bye, bye, bye," her family tells her—they never say *I love you*, but she knows it's true. A flurry of kisses, palms to cheeks, eyes pinched against the cold as the door is pulled open, jostling the jingle bells that hang from the knitted red cap on the knob. Her dad is hovering by the door, her mother clutching her sweatered elbows in her hands. Flakes are falling, but there's barely a dusting on the ground.

"It's snowing!" someone says.

"Snow! Is that really snow?"

"I didn't hear anything about snow, did you?"

A tremble of worry moves through the room, prompting departures to happen more quickly—kids wrapped into coats, shoes pushed onto feet. Her mother's expression has dissolved into concern.

"It's nothing," Abby tells her. "Look—it's just a few flakes."

Her mother looks outside, presses her lips together. Her hands are knotted at her chest, next to her bright Christmas pin. "Why don't you just leave in the morning?"

"I can't," Abby says, panic swelling inside her. She looks to her father, who looks at her mother. "If I leave in the morning—" But she can't bear to finish the thought, because any number of things could happen then: She might get snowed in, get to Nicole's house late or not at all, miss the party. Her mother looks so worried that Abby feels a spasm of annoyance—*it's not a big deal!*—then feels guilty, because she doesn't want to leave feeling annoyed, and because she knows how much her mother loves her, that there are people who would give anything to be loved that much.

"I'll be fine," she says.

"Be very careful, sweetheart," says her dad, the only one who calls her that.

"Call us when you get there," her mother says. "As soon as you get there."

"I know," Abby says, kisses them, and shuts the door.

In the snow, the neighborhood is strangely quiet. Abby's

footsteps shush along the sidewalk, leaving fresh prints. Flakes fall gently beneath the glow of the long-necked streetlights, the telephone poles strung with thick, sagging wires. Christmas lights pulse crazily, silently, on the narrow houses—lights twined around railings, Santas blinking on front porches, a red-nosed reindeer raising and lowering its head to a scrap of bald lawn. Abby unlocks her new used car. The smell of it is unfamiliar still, vaguely pinelike, the trace of an old air freshener. The air is cold, but she doesn't turn on the heat. Instead she shuts the door and watches the bright flakes drift onto the windshield, flashing red and green, landing and resting for a moment before disappearing into the glass. A mix tape waits in the cassette player, a bunch of songs Abby and her roommates recorded in a burst of feverish sentimentality the night before they left. She thinks about playing it but instead just sits, watching her breath bloom and dissolve, feeling a strange heaviness in her chest. Fog creeps in from the edges of the windshield. She looks at the street with all its blazing windows, and it occurs to her how strange it is that families live together in houses—how odd that some combination of fate and genetics brings these three or four or five people together to live, day in, day out, in the same small space.

It's another thought she might not have had before going to college, another of the kind her family might not understand. She looks at Aunt Margie's house, a brick row home with a green slate roof, attached to an almost identical one on either side. Gran and Pop live in a red-roofed version six blocks away. Abby studies the porch railing with its plastic braids of holly, the electric candles leaning in the windows, dark shapes moving inside. *Relief*—this was a term she learned in Intro to Art

History, the way part of a sculpture can stand out more sharply in relation to other parts. The way her family is not like other families, the way Abby is like her family and she isn't. The way the row homes of Philly look cramped and tiny compared with the houses of New England, separated by wide porches and snowy fields.

The door opens and out come Aunt Lauren and Uncle John, a slice of light widening on the porch behind them. They step carefully down the snow-dusted stairs. Lauren minces along the sidewalk, holding a casserole pan in her gloved hands. Uncle John, tall and handsome in his long gray coat, carries Max in the crook of one arm and holds Elena by the hand. Elena, mittens dangling from her coat sleeves, has her head turned, neck craned sideways. She is looking right at Abby—the only one who sees her sitting alone in her car—and Abby gives her a big smile and a furious wave, letting her know that *everything is fine, everything is okay.* Elena lifts one hand, uncertain or maybe just tired, a single droop of the wrist. Then she is scooped into the backseat, and the doors clap shut, and Uncle John slides behind the wheel, headlights on, snow falling softly through the beams.

Abby waits until they drive off before she turns the key. The dashboard glows. She sits and lets the engine warm, the way Uncle Patrick told her. When she looks up at the house one last time, she is startled to see her mother standing in an upstairs window. She's parting the curtain with one hand, the other palm resting on her middle. She's probably been watching Abby this entire time. The sadness this ignites in her is so acute it makes her eyes fill. She swipes quickly at her face. Now that her mother is watching, she needs to get moving. Abby rubs her palm on the windshield, clearing a circle in the glass. She can't see well, but well enough. As she turns the headlights on, she pictures the drive to Boston tomorrow morning—the way the landscape will decompress as she moves north, the buildings flattening and the sky opening, the pine trees gathering along the sides of the highway, the way the change will feel both slow and sudden.

Widows

I

What struck Lauren most at the funeral was how hard her niece Meghan was crying—long, shuddering sobs that echoed through the quiet cavern of St. Bonaventure's. Cheeks mottled, eyes swollen, her older sister Abby leaning down to whisper in her ear. It was alarming, Lauren thought. Not that it wasn't a sad thing, a terrible thing. Her grandfather, after all. The suddenness of it, and the open casket. It must be confusing for an eleven-year-old girl. Maybe Meghan, poor thing, thinks his death had something to do with his smoking. Lauren recalls how her sister-in-law Ann had described Meghan's reaction to the school assembly on cigarettes, crying so hard that she made herself sick. Lauren had nodded at Ann's story, hoping her face conveyed the proper mix of sympathy and understanding, but she was thinking: *That doesn't seem right.*

Now, at the luncheon, Lauren is watching as Meghan stands next to the buffet table, eating cheese and crackers. Her face is streaky, swollen, the aftermath of her sobbing at the cemetery when they all sprayed holy water on the coffin. Her ponytail, tight and smooth three hours before, is drooping, pieces falling loose from its sparkly neon band. Even when she was a little girl, back when John first started bringing Lauren around to family parties, Meghan had always seemed like a concern. She had a slightly feverish quality about her, chubby cheeks flushing with color as she flung herself into people's laps or clung to their knees. Lauren watches as Meghan swipes her bangs out of her eyes with one hand, reaches for a cracker with the other.

From her lap, a sigh. Lauren looks down to find the baby gazing up at her with his serene brown eyes. "Well, hello there." Lauren presses him closer, inhales him. "Are you getting hungry, little man?"

Lauren is relieved—pleased—about how her children are turning out. Both of them are easy babies, good sleepers. (Whoever said you don't get two easy ones was wrong.) Elena, two and a half, regularly draws compliments from strangers. *Isn't she well behaved? And gorgeous. Look at those big, big eyes!* Elena's are the kind of baby eyes that seem to absorb everything—long-lashed, inky, almost violet. She didn't get them from Lauren, with her brown Armenian features, and not from John, with his light blue eyes and clean, crisp face. (Was it possible for a face to actually look Catholic? If so, her husband's did.) The eyes, Lauren thought, belonged to her maternal grandmother. It pleased her that her small, scattered family had triumphed in some minor way over her husband's big, close-knit one.

She scans the room, finds John stationed by the door. He is shaking hands, receiving condolences, thanking people for coming. Old neighbors. Friends of the family. Colleagues of his, old co-workers of his father's. Young men in crisp black suits, stooped men in brown ones. Lauren watches him clasp an elderly man's hand, kiss his wife's cheek. Chivalrous and confident. John always was. It isn't arrogance—it's as if doubt simply doesn't exist for him, as if he doesn't know the feeling. This, more than any financial savvy, is the key to his success. In his dark suit, he looks terribly handsome—an inappropriate thing to think at her father-in-law's funeral, but Lauren can't help it. At the family parties, John sometimes recedes a little, gathering around the TV, accepting plates of butter cake, becoming the younger brother to his older sisters, who fuss over him and Patrick, assigning them some old helplessness they remember from childhood. Here, though, he is the strongest presence in the room. It comforts her. Lauren has never felt completely at ease around John's family—the bigness, the competence, the tight sphere of constant togetherness. But it doesn't matter because at the core of her life is this: her husband, their children. Their little family of four. The moments John says: *How did I get so lucky?* Or: *Do you know how much I love you?* Like feeding her babies, these are the hidden intimacies, the private exchanges, on which she builds her life.

The baby squirms. Lauren looks down, sees his little pink face working up to a cry. "Hang on," Lauren says. "I know, little one. You're hungry." She scans the room for someplace private to steal away. It's a large, multipurpose room, wood-paneled, the kind that can be modified to suit any occasion. Tables draped in starchy white tablecloths, now covered with balled-up napkins and discarded plates. A hearth adorned with tasteful sprays of flowers. On the far side, Lauren spots what looks like an unused coat closet. She'll have to wade through all these people to get there, but she has the baby—an excuse to keep moving. Lauren wraps a few cookies in a napkin and tucks them discreetly in her diaper bag. Then she fixes her face in a polite smile, shoulders the bag, and starts across the room. In an hour, she thinks, the babysitter will arrive with Elena, who John had agreed (thank God) was too young for the funeral. When Elena appears, she will lighten everybody's mood. She'll be wearing the puffy pink dress Lauren laid out for her this morning. She will recite her litany of new words—*happy*, *chicken*, *phone*. Early Monday morning, when they returned from John's parents' house and retrieved Elena from the neighbors', she had crawled right into her father's lap, as if sensing his sadness, and curled her head into his neck.

The call had come at one thirty in the morning. Mrs. Blessing had called Ann and Margie, who called Patrick and John. John's father had been asleep in bed, and somehow John's mother had heard—sensed—he wasn't breathing, the intuition from a lifetime of nights spent beside him. Everyone had rushed to the house, the children and the grandchildren, wearing their middle-of-the-night clothes, sneakers and sweatpants, plastic hair clips and eyeglasses. John took charge, calling the paramedics, and later Mike Leary, an old high school classmate, now co-owner of the local funeral home. Patrick and Kate sat together at one end of the couch, holding hands. Kate looked remarkably put together for the hour—jeans, a sweater, even makeup and earrings. Maybe they'd just gotten home from somewhere when they got the call? (Lauren's nights were now devoted entirely to nursing. She couldn't fathom being out that late anymore, and didn't miss it.) But despite this, Kate looked genuinely upset—she always wore the right expression and always seemed to mean it, both traits Lauren envied—as she rubbed Patrick's wrist with her thumb. Patrick was crying, his shoulders slumped and shaking. The teenage boys stood around uncomfortably, looking stunned and uneasy in their hooded sweatshirts and huge plaid flannel pants. It was like some alternate, late-night version of a family party, twisted and vulnerable and strange.

John's father was still in bed. John had told the Learys to wait an hour before coming so everyone had the chance to see the body. In small groups, they filed in to see him in his blue-striped pajamas, a wooden rosary twined around the bedpost, his arms by his sides. (Had someone moved his arms, to place them there so neatly? Was this the duty of the wife?) Lauren stood slightly behind John, saying nothing, feeling her pulse beat in her cheeks. The glowing arms of the bedside clock pointed to two forty-five. She kept one hand on John's back, as if bracing him, or maybe herself, and held the baby in the other. Mr. Blessing looked colorless, frozen, his mouth agape. One eye was open, one half-closed. Rigor mortis. Somehow she hadn't anticipated this. But more shocking than the body of John's father was the presence of John's mother, keeping vigil over this terrible tableau. Lauren was almost afraid to look at her, but when she did, Mrs. Blessing was startling in her composure: eyes two tidy pools of water, spine ramrod straight. It was as if she'd been preparing for this moment all her life.

When Lauren followed John back to the living room, she felt dizzy. The Learys had pulled up outside, headlights shining in the dark. They were approaching the house. They were both wearing suits. Someone was sobbing, a hoarse, deep sound—Stephen, of all people, a stocky fifteen-year-old in sweatpants and big sneakers, crying raggedly. Margie went to touch her son's shoulder, but Stephen shook her off, stepping onto the porch and slamming the door, the long shade shivering against the glass. Then Meghan started to cry again, and the baby began whimpering in Lauren's arms—oh, thank God.

She stole off to the spare bedroom and quietly closed the door. It was John and Patrick's old room: two twin beds with blue bedspreads, a small rabbit-eared TV, a rocking chair with a flat braided mat on the seat. A simple wooden cross hung above the door. Lauren sat and rocked as she nursed the baby. Then she worried the others might hear the floorboards creaking, so she sat perfectly still. She watched the dark sky out the window. She heard activity in the room next door. The low rumble of voices, the squeak of a metal hinge—or a zipper? She shut her eyes. She just wanted this strange, awful night to be over. She thought about how it was something they would all remember forever. How this was family: to own such moments together. To experience them in all their raw shock and sadness, then get the food from the refrigerator, unwrap the crackers and fill the glasses, keep the gears turning, the grand existing beside the routine, the ordinary.

The Learys drove away. For the next two hours, they all stayed. It was nearly five when they convinced John's mother to try to get some sleep—would she get back in that bed? Lauren couldn't help wondering—and five thirty when she and John pulled into their driveway, the first faint pink glimmer of dawn coloring the sky. John turned the engine off and put his head in his hands. It was only then that he cried. Lauren had never heard her husband cry before. It was an awful sound, halting, awkward, as if his body weren't sure how. He moaned. Lauren touched him lightly, tentatively, on the shoulder. She couldn't imagine what he was feeling. Both her parents were alive and in good health, living in a retirement village in Florida. In twenty-six years, real tragedy had not touched her life at all. She rubbed John's wrist—a gesture, she realized, she'd stolen from Kate—and murmured some things about getting through it, calling out of work, eating something, getting some sleep. Imperfect, but it seemed to calm him somewhat, and as she slid into bed an hour later, having collected Elena from the neighbors' and put both her children back in their cribs, Lauren felt relieved—even a touch proud—that they were surviving this sad thing.

Lauren peers out from behind the thick curtain of the empty coat closet. From this vantage point, she can nurse the baby and observe the entire room unseen. "Come on," she whispers to him. "I know you're hungry." Max cranes his neck, twisting his head, distracted by his new surroundings. Lauren touches his cheek, steadying him. "Up here," she says, and he looks up at her, blinking slowly, and latches on.

If Lauren could, she would breast-feed forever. Part of it is the closeness, the almost magical intimacy. The way her milk lets down when she hears her children cry—it still happens even with Elena, who switched to formula before Max was born. But breast-feeding has also become her escape. It allows her to step away from the family without penalty, to go collect herself in a spare room. Because she isn't like Kate, who socializes with everyone so effortlessly. She isn't like

John's sisters—look at them standing by the hearth in their muted dresses, dark blue with discreet gold earrings, gracefully accepting condolences. John's mother stands beside them, equally composed, eyes brimming but never spilling over. All of the Blessings excel at this: looking right, acting right. At the wake, they had been tirelessly gracious, which was no easy feat—John's family seemed to know half of Northeast Philadelphia. (When Lauren first told them she'd grown up in Upper Darby, they had paused—*the other side of City Line*, one said, and the rest nodded, as if orienting her on the other side of the moon.) The wake had lasted four hours, the line stretching down two city blocks in the biting February cold. For the past week, the entire family had been together constantly, shifting from house to house at night. Only the setting changed, and the food, which seemed to appear as if from nowhere, all of it appropriately subdued. Nothing decadent, not too much spice or frosting. Nothing delicious. Plain and practical, just sustenance: pound cakes, cold salads, casseroles, triangles of ham and cheese.

A sharp cry—Max is peering up at her with a furrowed brow, as if sensing her inattention. "I'm sorry, bug," she says, cajoling him to latch back on. She hikes up one side of her bra and switches sides, repositions his rosy mouth, then reaches into her bag for a cookie. When she looks up again, biting into it, Kate is standing in her line of sight. She is impossible to miss—tall and blond, with a daringly short bob. She's wearing a short, satiny jacket and wide gray trousers. Fashionable even at a funeral. An hour earlier, when Lauren went to the car for the diaper bag, she'd run into Kate in the parking lot, smoking furtively. "Oh, I know!" Kate had said. Her voice always had the slight rasp of someone who'd been yelling over loud music all night. "It's terrible," she'd said, dropping the cigarette, grinding it out with her sharp heel. "It's so incredibly inappropriate—especially here. Please don't tell on me."

"Don't worry," Lauren had said, though she did find it disrespectful, considering. She had hugged Max to her chest, fumbling for her keys, as Kate pulled a little tin of mints from her purse.

Now Kate is standing by the drinks station, chatting easily with the nephews: Stephen and Joey and Alex. The boys look stiff, drawn, awkward in their black or brown suits, holding dimpled plastic cups of Coke. Lauren never would have approached the boys, especially not all together. From time to time she manages a conversation with Alex, who will offer a few polite details about school. Joey is friendly enough, but always in motion. But Kate is at ease talking to anyone—even Stephen, who Lauren finds intimidating, with his dour expression and broad shoulders and whiskered upper lip.

It would all be much easier if she and Kate were close, Lauren thinks. They're the same age, but Kate is entirely different from her—stylish, outgoing, an exception to everything. She went to Bryn Mawr and has no children. She calls Patrick *babe*. To family parties, she brings frozen appetizers you warm in the oven or those giant chocolate-chip cookies they sell in malls, and somehow, from Kate, this seems charming, understandable, as if she has more important things to do than cook. Lauren wouldn't dare. She slaves over coleslaw and three-bean salads, following the recipes she was given in a pretty flowered binder at her wedding shower—*The Blessing Family Cookbook*—along with a food processor, an electric mixer. For Kate's shower, they'd all pitched in to send her and Patrick on a long weekend down the shore.

It doesn't matter, John likes to say. *It's not a contest.*

He enjoys teasing her, finds her discomfort endearing. He knows his own family too well to appreciate how they make her feel: like standing so close to a mirror you can't see your own face. Because how could she *not* feel inferior around them? Between the supremely capable sisters and the supremely confident sister-in-law, she has every right—though in truth, Lauren has always been prone to feeling this way. When she was eleven, the one time she agreed to try overnight camp, she had refused to do the trust fall, the one where you flop backward blindly into strangers' arms. The other kids were pressuring her and Lauren became so adamant, so agitated, that the blood rushed to her head, and she started to faint, so they caught her anyway.

II

When John first felt the pain in his back, they assumed it was a pulled muscle. A strain from all the swimming. They'd had the in-ground pool dug over the summer and he'd been doing twenty laps each day before work. This was John: determined, disciplined. He set his mind to something and he did it. He stretched his muscles, took Extra Strength Tylenol. At night, watching TV, he pressed a heating pad against his side.

It was October then, not a particularly remarkable October, though later Lauren would remember its every moment as if gilded in gold. The dinner party they hosted for some of

John's friends from the brokerage. The compliments she received on the stuffed peppers (her own family's recipe). Max taking his first steps. The Phillies making it all the way to the World Series, then losing in game six. Dropping Elena off at preschool, ripping Lauren's heart out three mornings a week.

Then one morning, a Saturday, John said: *Lauren. Something isn't right.*

The appointment with Dr. Gwynn had been inconclusive, John said. He wanted John to go to the hospital for tests. *Tests?* Lauren said, a tick of alarm. *What kind of tests?* John wasn't worried. Ed Gwynn was his old family doctor, the one they'd all gone to since they were children. He probably wasn't equipped to deal with more than flus and fevers, skinned knees. They would wait and see what a real doctor had to say.

Aggressive, the oncologist called it—that was the first word that stuck. They were sitting in his office side by side, facing the vast shining expanse of his desk, deep enough to buffer him from the people receiving bad news. *Cancer in the kidney.* Lauren watched the doctor's mouth moving but couldn't absorb what he was saying. Other words drifted by. She heard a few—*fatty tissue, renal cells.* Beside her, John's hands gripped the leather arms of the chair. He nodded, kept nodding, as the doctor showed them the CT scan, pointed to a gray blur. It looked like a smudge, something she could erase with a dab of spit on her thumb. *Lymph nodes*, he said. The sun was coming through the blinds on a slant, striping the desk. Lauren stared at a picture of the doctor's family: his wife and three children, waving from a dock. They were all wearing life preservers. Did the parents usually wear life preservers? The doctor wanted to order more tests—*chest X-ray, bone scan.* He handed them a Kleenex and shook their hands. They left the office in numb silence, rode the elevator with two chatting receptionists, and stepped into the cool, oily dark of the parking garage. Her hands were tingling. She held John's arm to keep from falling. They walked quickly toward the car, as if they'd mutually agreed to just keep moving, get into the car and out of sight. John opened her door, as always, and she took comfort in this small act of consistency, in the businesslike clap of his shoes as they rounded the bumper. But when he slid into the seat beside her, she saw the fear on his face. Something snapped in her brain, and she started sobbing. "It'll be fine," John said. "It'll be fine. We'll be fine." But his voice was stunned. He turned on the car. "We need gas," he said, and Lauren remembered the tank was low, that they'd discussed filling it on the way but had been running late. It seemed inconceivable that this was the same car they were sitting in an hour ago, the same life with its same trivial problems. But the evidence was all there: the two car seats strapped in the back, the saltine crackers ground into the carpet, the needle on the dashboard hovering near E. How could the car need gas in a moment like this? "We'll get through this," John told her. "We will." They stopped at the Hess station and John pumped the gas and drove home.

Once, shortly after they were engaged, Lauren and John had gone to the wedding of one of his high school friends. John was nearly thirty then, Lauren only twenty-two. *Sure you don't mind being with an older man?* John often teased her. She didn't. In fact, she liked that John was so much older, the same way she liked that he was so much taller; it made her feel safe. Toward the end of the reception, when John was refilling their drinks, a guy started hitting on her. He was loose and red-faced, one hand on her elbow, his drunken grin too broad and too close. John walked up to him, smiled, and said: *I see you like looking at my wife?* It was so out of character, like a line from a gangster movie. It thrilled her, especially because they weren't married yet. *Wife.* She loved just hearing him say it. She had let her mind run wildly, girlishly, imagining the word in different contexts.

My wife and I have an eight o'clock reservation.

Oh, I'm sorry—have you met my wife?

But in the oncology ward of Holy Redeemer, the word carries a different weight. The wife is the one whom the nurses question, the one to whom doctors deliver the sobering news, the one who talks to insurance companies and signs forms. The wife begins learning a new language—*radical nephrectomy*, which the first oncologist recommended. The second one agreed. *Full removal of kidney and nearby lymph nodes.* "I'm the wife," Lauren tells them, countless times, the transition from *his* to *the* happening without her noticing.

John is in the hospital for a week. His family is there every day, some in the morning and some the afternoon. They trade off taking care of the children. Neighbors, family. Abby, home for Thanksgiving. When Lauren misses Thanksgiving dinner, Ann drives over with a lukewarm plate. At home at night, Lauren pumps her milk for the next day and stores it in the refrigerator and holds the baby, who cries for some loneliness he doesn't understand. She eats late at night, whatever she can find. She can't bear being in their bed alone, so she sleeps on the couch. Staring at the darkened ceiling, she thinks that she should have pressed harder for John to see a doctor. Should have made him go when he first mentioned the pain. Everybody knows men are stubborn about seeing doctors, admitting weakness, John especially. His sisters, mother—any of them would have gotten him there sooner. This was her job—the wife's job. What difference, she wonders over and over, might those weeks have made?

John insists on coming to Christmas even though he's started chemo and has been vomiting for four days. Everyone moves carefully, quietly, as if not wanting to awaken the sickness. Even the children are uncharacteristically subdued. John has assumed the spot in the brown tweed recliner, the position once occupied by his father, who died only in February—shouldn't that have been their greatest trial this year? But the family carries on with all the usual traditions. Almond crescents, powdered snowballs, Mrs. Blessing's potato soup. If anything, they adhere to these things even more closely. They stay in motion. The men gather around the TV, the women around the dining room table, telling stories—a friend of Stephen's, a boy Mark, whose father up and left the family, *a shame*—but it feels different with so much sadness right here in the room. Twice Kate gives Lauren's arm a sympathetic squeeze, and Lauren feels a burst of resentment—pure, unmitigated, unjustified. Then John is standing in the doorway, signaling her with his eyes. Her anger leaves her. He is horribly pale. They refuse leftovers, moving quickly—Elena crying because she doesn't want to go yet and Meghan petting her arm consolingly, only making it worse. *Why don't we drop her off later?* Ann offers, but Lauren shakes her head firmly, no. *But thank you*, she manages before hustling them out the door, fastening Max into one car seat and Elena into the other. John leans his forehead against the dashboard as Elena starts kicking the back of his seat with her hard patent leather heels. Then John opens the door and vomits on the sidewalk, and Elena stops kicking, and Lauren drives them all home.

New Year's Day: It feels significant this year. John is plodding through the chemo treatments, determined to get back to normal. But there is no normal, Lauren thinks. The hair in the sink, sweat on his face. Like a fool, she was surprised. She wouldn't have believed, didn't believe until she saw it, that her husband was as vulnerable as anybody else.

Sunday mornings, they go to Our Lady of Ransom. Though Lauren converted when they got married, she still feels self-conscious in Catholic churches. At least no one here knows her; John's mother and sisters all go to their old parish, St. B's. Lauren recites the prayers but doesn't really think about the words, too preoccupied with trying to remember what to do and say and when. Secretly, the only thing she likes about church is how they look as a family in their nice Sunday clothes. Now, when people look, Lauren sees sympathy on their faces: the sick husband, the two young children. *A shame.*

John is determined to attend a work event: a black-tie dinner, for charity. Lauren worries out loud that it's not a good idea, though secretly she wants to go. She buys a new dress, gets her hair done. John wears his tuxedo, though it hangs loose everywhere. At the dinner, people speak to them too kindly, too carefully. She sees the tension creeping into John's face. After an hour, Lauren's mouth aches from smiling. In the auction, they win two tickets to a B&B in New England: *Romantic Getaway*. They are in the car twenty minutes later, John punching the dashboard. The next day, his knuckles are bruised.

Lauren no longer hides in spare bedrooms at family parties; she couldn't if she tried. If she had no clear role in John's family before, she does now: liaison, informant, nurse, repository for everyone's questions and concerns. Her life is public now, available, turned inside out. The phone rings off the hook. *How can I help? What can I do?* They are a family that responds by doing. *What do you need?* Lauren bats away their offers, politely, because what she needs is for them to leave her be. What she needs is for the chemo to be over, for their lives to go back to normal. What she needs is for her husband to get better, which he does—but only briefly, a clean scan, a spasm of unfair hope, before the illness takes a swift turn for the worse.

Metastasized. Another word that sticks.

The family stops asking permission. Help just appears. Casseroles in the freezer. Margie's boys, to cut the lawn. When John is recovering from chemo, someone might show up to take Elena to the mall or to the roller rink, the movies. Lauren wishes they would leave her alone. *We were fine before*, she thinks, smiling furiously. *Just leave her here! Leave us be!* She is so worried about their little girl. If anyone is going to explain to Elena what's going on, it should be her mother. It should be her father—it should be her mother *and* her father. God knows what a sensitive child like Meghan might say. Recently, Elena has had a defiant streak about her. Maybe it's her age. Maybe it's a response to the tumult, the constant visitors, the time spent with her older cousins, the disruptions to her usual routine—all the things she quietly absorbs with those big violet eyes.

Lauren feels ungrateful. She should be glad for the help from John's family, even if it makes her feel inadequate. Other times, gratitude overwhelms her, and she takes comfort in their constancy, in the reliability of small things.

She devotes herself to doing: monitoring medication, cleaning the bathroom, the kitchen, disinfecting the tub, taking care of the children, who need diapers changed and baths drawn and bottles made. She is beginning to understand the comfort in it. How these small tasks keep you busy, focused, make you feel not entirely helpless. Keep your mind from thinking unbearable thoughts. *How can I help? What do you need?*

When his wedding band falls off, John sets it on the dresser beside an army of pill bottles, hand sanitizers, anti-itch creams. Lauren remembers how he proposed, down on one knee—*Will you do me the honor?* He'd bought her a dozen roses, asked her father first—*I promised him I'd take good care of you*, he told her. It had all been just how she'd imagined it would be.

*   *   *

She talks occasionally to friends from high school. *How are you doing, Lauren?* They pause, the silence stretching on the line. *With everything?* They don't mention cancer; maybe they think you're not supposed to. They have no experience with a thing like this. Lauren was the first of them to get married, and they helped her plan the wedding, gushing over the dresses and bouquets. Now they're all catching up to her. Having their first babies, buying their first houses, modest twins with postage-stamp backyards. When Lauren and John moved into their house in Chestnut Hill, the girls had come to see it, awed by the size of it, envious of her new adult life.

John goes in to work, half days. Twice a week, or once. A gesture. Then nothing. He shaves off what's left of his hair. He wears a knit Eagles hat every day. He's grown so thin—Lauren is startled by the contrast, her thigh next to his. The thermostat is cranked to seventy-five. Max scrambles around in just a diaper, hair damp and curling. Outside, it is early April, and when Lauren drags the trash to the curb, the nights are cool and sweet, but the house is always the same temperature, its own climate. A world apart.

Friends come—John's friends from high school, a few of his co-workers. A guy who, at their dinner party in October, had done a loud, drunken impression of their boss. Now he refuses the beer that Lauren offers. He makes jokes—business jokes. *Couldn't you market this thing as a diet plan?* he says, and John offers the obligatory laugh. Lauren almost can't bear to look at the guy's face, the terror in his eyes: *A guy like me, reduced to this.*

On warm afternoons, if John is feeling strong enough, the four of them sit by the pool. John dressed in layers, Lauren holding the baby, Elena carefully dunking her feet. When they had the pool dug last summer, John had imagined all the family barbecues they would be hosting. *It'll be fun for the kids,* he'd said, and Lauren had cringed inwardly at the thought of their house becoming the locus of all John's family gatherings for the rest of their lives. Now she makes a promise to herself: to keep hosting, no matter what.

Mrs. Blessing is there every other day, like clockwork. Fixing meals, doing laundry, washing dishes. Lauren is too exhausted to refuse. She knows John likes having her there, and there is something steadying about John's mother: the dependability of her habits, the flowered half apron she keeps folded neatly in a kitchen drawer, the warm, simple dishes she pulls from the oven. Macaroni and cheese, potato soup, vats of rice pudding. Another promise Lauren makes to herself: She will never eat rice pudding again.

Lauren's mother flies up from Florida and stays for six days. *My poor little girl,* she says, stepping from the cab in the driveway, as Lauren collapses in her arms. Her mother lines up her travel-size shampoos and lotions on the dresser in the guest bedroom. She coos over the baby, teaches Elena to play Go Fish and Old Maid. Sitting on the couch beside John, she is so tan that it seems an affront. John's mother surrenders the kitchen for the week, but Lauren's mother makes grape leaves, which are too difficult for John to eat. At night, when the rest of the house is sleeping, she quizzes Lauren about things: life insurance, health insurance, items on a list prepared by her dad. *We don't talk about that yet*, Lauren snaps. She thinks she'll be glad to see her mother go until the moment her cab pulls away.

When John is too weak to leave the house, Lauren takes the children to church alone. She feels like a fake martyr, folding her hands, bowing her head to pray. *Say the word and I shall be healed*, she recites along with everybody else. But there is nothing in her head, just words in space. On her knees, she concentrates. *God, please help us. Please.* Still, she feels nothing. Maybe she is just not a religious person; maybe she's doing it wrong. Walking to the car, she notices people's sorry smiles and realizes they must be wondering if John isn't there because he's dead.

I wish there were more we could do, the doctor says.

Lauren wants to pull Elena out of preschool, but John insists on keeping things as normal as possible, as long as possible. To bring her home would be conceding something. *Not yet*, he says.

When the baby is running a temperature, he is whisked away, quarantined at Ann and Dave's house until the fever goes down.

★   ★   ★

Around John, Elena is careful. She can't sit on Daddy's lap because it hurts his bones, so she plays by his feet. She can't
kiss him because of germs. Instead, they touch heads. She
does these things gently, without complaining. Whatever other
emotions are building inside her are reserved for Lauren alone.
One day in the Thriftway, as Lauren is shopping for things
John can eat—nothing hard or chewy, nothing spicy—Elena
throws a box of Oreos on the floor. "Elena!" Lauren exclaims.
Elena stares back at her, unmoved. She throws another box,
sending it skidding across the floor, and starts to laugh. "Elena!
Stop that!" Lauren says, shocked, thinking: *This is not my
daughter. This is not my life!* Elena keeps throwing boxes, one
after the other, laughing, until Lauren takes her by the elbow.
The spell breaks, Elena's face crumples, and she starts to shriek.
People look at Lauren, surely thinking she's a terrible mother.
She yanks Max out of the half-full cart, grabs Elena by the
hand, and leaves the store.

When I'm not here, you can talk to me anytime.

Lauren is listening from outside Elena's bedroom door. She
is struck by how weak John's voice is, weaker because she can't
see him.

But where are you going?

Heaven.

Can I come?

I'm afraid not, sweetheart.

But why?

It's not the kind of place you can visit, John says solemnly. He has answers at the ready. Lauren has to push her hands in her mouth to keep from screaming.

But where is it?

It's all around, he tells her. *It's in the air. In the sky.*

Outside the house, everyday things have a quality of unreality. The beep of the grocery belt in the Thriftway. The cashier with the blotchy skin asking in a bored tone: *Would you like to donate a dollar to UNICEF today?* The car in the parking lot, the fearless teenagers inside it, music blaring from its windows. Sometimes it startles her, the world. How bright and sharp and loud things are.

Lauren knows she shouldn't keep breast-feeding but can't make herself stop. Probably she's using Max to comfort herself, embedding some attachment issues that will cripple him when he's older. It will be a struggle, getting him on a bottle later. But there is no later. Nursing her baby, pressing his warm skin against hers, gazing out the window of the nursery at the backyard, is the only time she doesn't feel abject terror—the dew on the grass in the mornings, the unkempt purple flowers, the pool cover strewn with leaves, and in late spring, the wild growth of daffodils and tulips, bursting up in bunches, untended.

Two days to two weeks, the doctor says.

Lauren. Something isn't right. She will always recall every facet of this moment, like turning a diamond in the light: how John looked standing there in the bedroom doorway, hand pressed against his back. How he called her Lauren, not Laur, which meant that it was serious. How for a split second she thought he was unhappy with *her*—that the *something* was about their marriage—sending a geyser of panic up her middle. But then she saw his face and knew it was something else, something worse. His expression was so vulnerable—she will always remember this, too—and it occurred to her then that maybe his family had known something about him she didn't, that John did have a strain of helplessness that Lauren had just never seen before, never needed to. And she would remember thinking, despite the quickening of her pulse, how handsome he looked, and how sweet life seemed just then, her husband standing in the light streaming through the bedroom window, Max nestled in her lap, Elena calling upstairs from the kitchen where she was finishing her waffle: *Daddy! I'm done!*

The Lookout

Stephen didn't want to go through with it but there he is, standing in the parking lot behind the Wendy's on Rhawn Street. Lately, everything in his life felt like this. He doesn't want to do something, knows he shouldn't, but suddenly there he is, doing it anyway. It's like something just goes slack inside him, the way he lets his right eye wander when he's tired. In the end, his friends start hassling him or cheering him on and it seems like too much work to resist, and he thinks, *Fuck it.*

They're standing by the Dumpster next to the red Chevy Impala. The air is warm and smells like trash. At eight o'clock on a Sunday night, the Wendy's parking lot is less than half-full, the sky above the roof the deep yellow of a deviled egg. Pigeons stalk the Dumpster lid.

"Where the fuck is he," Mark says.

"Fuck if I know."

Mark toes a burger box on the ground, nudging it with his Chucks. Stephen has known Mark Rourke since they were in kindergarten at St. Bonaventure's and swears the kid gets uglier with each passing year. Mark has a square head, eyes set too close, and serious acne peppering his sideburns, which are black and flecked, like ants. One of those guys so ugly that his best bet is to play it up and go uglier, be so ugly that it turns into something else, like cool or scary.

"Sure we shouldn't wait until it's less crowded?" Stephen says.

"No, asshole," Mark says. "That's part of it."

"What's part of it?"

"You know. The risk."

"Right," Stephen says, smirking at Mark for taking it all so seriously, though in fact this is what makes Mark a good partner for things like this.

"Here," Stephen says, and passes Mark the sticky, near empty bottle of Jameson he stole from his parents' liquor cabinet. Mark grabs it, takes a deep swallow, and swipes at his chin. At least, Stephen thinks, guys like Mark have reasons for doing stupid shit like this. No one in the world cares what happens to Mark Rourke. His dad took off when they were in ninth grade, his mother drinks too much. Stephen has no such excuse. His is a big family, a nice family that taught him right from wrong. Maybe that *is* his excuse—they have enough good kids already. His brother, Joey, working up a shelf of basketball trophies. His cousin Alex, some kind of nerd superstar at his public high school out in the suburbs. He'd be better off in Catholic school, where they'd make him cut his hair. He looks like a tool.

"Give me that," Stephen says, grabbing the bottle back and taking a swig.

Stephen feels rattled tonight, jittery. For dinner, he and his dad ate pizza in front of the TV. Lately his mom has been visiting his uncle every night, which means his dad is in charge of dinner, which means that nine times out of ten they have pizza in front of the TV. Joey is usually out playing ball, so it's just the two of them. At six fifteen, his dad gets home from work at the ShopRite, smelling like the deli counter, and drops into his big brown tweed chair. Stephen makes the call. At seven, his father watches the lottery numbers while Stephen carries in the pizza and two plates. Tonight it was sausage and pepperoni and *America's Funniest Home Videos* when his father said: *You know John is gonna die, right?*

Stephen froze with a half-chewed glob of pizza in his mouth.

His father added, *Your uncle.*

I know that, Stephen managed, swallowing, but didn't clarify which part. He knew, obviously, that John was his uncle. And knew that he was sick. *Uncle John is very, very sick,* his mother said constantly, eyes teary, rubbing her locket like she was praying on a rosary. But being very, very sick wasn't the same thing as dying. Earlier that day, Stephen had visited his uncle—his mother drove him and Joey over to Uncle John and Aunt Lauren's, and it seemed like a good sign that Uncle John was home. If you're that sick, hospitals don't just let you go home. But his uncle looked terrible. Bony, with sunken cheeks and yellow skin. He was bald under his Eagles hat, and his voice sounded thin. Later, talking to his father, Stephen understood this was what dying looked like, but in the moment he was shocked. The joint he'd smoked before he left the house was starting to wear off and he was sweating. It felt like something was crawling on his skin. Uncle John had always been a good-looking guy—how could a good-looking guy end up like this? Their house was warm, too warm, because Uncle John was always cold. Uncle John had started asking Joey about basketball in that thin voice, eyes bulging in his head. Harry Kalas was calling the Phillies game on the radio while they watched it with the sound turned down on the TV. His mom was holding Max, jiggling him and making these kind of desperate cooing noises, while Aunt Lauren hovered over everything and Elena brushed her doll's hair. *Pretty dolly!* she kept saying. Stephen needed to get the fuck out of there. *Eat anything you can find!* Aunt Lauren called after him as he headed for the kitchen. Stephen wished she weren't so nice to him. Lately, he felt like some kind of impostor with his family; they gave him too much credit. None of them knew about all the dumb shit he'd been getting into, and what his parents knew they were too ashamed to tell. Last Thursday, the day of the locker room "incident," Father Malcahy had called his dad at home. *Vandalism*, his father had repeated after he hung up, his big face flushing red. *Obscenities of a religious and sexual nature.* His mother had looked at Stephen with tears in her eyes. He'd thought she might cry, but instead she spoke through clenched teeth. "Now, Stephen?" Her voice was hissing, shaking with fury. *"Now?"* Then she'd left the room. Even his father, who Stephen could usually count on to go easy on him—even seem a little bit proud if he was caught drinking or fighting, chalk it up to normal kid stuff, guy stuff—looked angry. More than angry: disgusted. *Cut the shit*, his father had said. And that was it. They never spoke of it again. It was worse than being punished.

Standing in Uncle John's kitchen, Stephen felt weirdly nervous. He found a can of orange soda rolling around the cheese drawer, chugged half, then stared out into the backyard. He used to look forward to coming to Uncle John and Aunt Lauren's. It was quiet here, and kind of shielded from the neighbors. The backyard was five times the size of their square of burnt grass in Northeast Philly and backed up onto a little grove of trees.

They had a pool, too—a real one, in-ground, put in last summer. A basketball hoop, a deck. But now it all had a sad look about it. The soft basketball planted in the driveway, the things that looked like flowers but he knew were really weeds. His mom had made Joey and him come mow their lawn a few times, but that was weeks ago, and now the grass was shaggy, the ivy growing wild. The entire place felt like sickness, inside and out. At the back of the yard, the trees swayed softly, though it wasn't windy. Stephen's pulse hammered in his throat. He was convinced suddenly that this fringe of woods was haunted, that there was something—not something stupid like a werewolf or a zombie, but something real, like death—lurking in those trees. His hands shook a little, like they had when he sprayed the lockers, and suddenly he needed to not be alone. He drank down the rest of the soda and went back to the living room, where he and Uncle John shot the shit about the Phillies for a minute—*Looks like they're going to be contenders again*, Stephen said; for the rest of his life, he would remember this as a particularly fucking stupid thing to say—and as they walked back to the car, his mother looked at him with those teary eyes, as if seeing—what? a young person? a not-sick person? Was she remembering how Stephen broke down crying the night Pop died? Was she feeling bad that Uncle John was dying and nobody had told him? That he wouldn't be a mentor for poor Stephen, get him back on the right path? Fuck knows.

"What?" he snapped, slumping low in the front seat, his brother's knees digging into his back.

★   ★   ★

It's a warm night, too warm for a hooded sweatshirt, but Stephen's palms are damp and cold. "Where the fuck is he," Mark mutters, giving the burger box a hard kick. It flies open and half a bun falls out. The pigeons go nuts. Of course Timmy is late; he's the one who started this whole thing. Timmy's always late, always the one who starts things. He's also dumb. Mark might be the world's ugliest human being, but at least he isn't stupid. In fact, Mark's combination of ugliness and intelligence and general lack of morals would probably make him an excellent criminal in the real world. Timmy's just a loose cannon, a dishwasher at Wendy's with the same long, loping stride he's had since the first grade, pants always an inch too short, that stupid hemp necklace. He always has a crush on a girl he's convinced he has a shot with. Mark has no luck with girls, even ugly ones, but he doesn't pretend to. In this department, Stephen is their hero. He's had sex with three girls and is currently screwing Molly Healy, who isn't especially pretty but is nice, and comes over whenever he calls.

"There he is," Mark says, and sure enough, Timmy is slouching across the parking lot, backpack hooked over one shoulder, grinning as he heads toward them. He angles his head toward the Impala, as if to say, *What did I tell you?*

"Yeah, yeah, yeah." Mark exhales, annoyed.

Timmy had promised them the red Impala would be parked by the Dumpster. It was always there on Sundays, he swore; he saw it whenever he worked Sunday nights, went out back to dump the trash and smoke a joint. This one, apparently, had some kind of high-end stereo system, a piece of information Timmy got from some guy named Bruno, an ex–pro wrestler who works the French fry station and who

Stephen suspects is half-invented. Whatever. He just wants to get this over with.

"See?" Timmy grins. "Here it is. What did I tell you?"

"We get it," Mark says. "Do you want a medal?" He scratches hard at his chin.

Stephen looks at the ground, at the pigeons swarming the ketchup-stained bun. He's done plenty of dumb shit before and sometimes gotten in trouble for it—for the locker room, he got a week's detention and (worse) had to talk to the school shrink—but that was just school. He's never done anything in real life, nothing beyond shoplifting or buying pot off his neighbor. He's never done anything so personal and planned. But he reminds himself this isn't personal; he doesn't know the car's owner. It isn't about people, just stuff. The locker room incident wasn't personal either, despite what the shrink was driving at—*Your brother is a very good athlete, isn't he, Stephen?* Yes, yes, he is. He's fucking Dr. J. But Stephen didn't vandalize the locker room because he's jealous of his brother. Timmy had the spray paint, his friends were hassling him to do it, and he got pissed off, so he did it—*Fuck you, assholes!!* streaming from the nozzle. This got a laugh. Then, there was the other stuff. The shrink just smiled and sat there, letting the silence drag on and on, thinking it would break him. Stephen didn't say a word. If she thought he was going to make it easy, she was nuts. Finally she asked: *Is there anything going on at home?*

"Okay," Mark says, looking both ways. The parking lot is about half-full, cars inching toward the drive-through window. "Take your positions."

Stephen might have chuckled at this, but he knew Mark was dead serious. Earlier that day, Mark had doled out their assignments. Timmy's popping the lock, because he claims to know how. Mark is covering Timmy's back. Stephen is the lookout—standing by the bumper, watching for oncoming trouble—and, if necessary, the muscle. That's how Mark put it: *if necessary, the muscle.* Stephen wasn't thrilled about this, but of the three of them, he made the most sense in the role. He's the biggest, and can bench-press 250. Sometimes he practices keeping his face perfectly still.

Timmy and Mark move to the driver's-side door. Stephen steps up next to the bumper, yanking up his sweatshirt hood and tightening the cords under his chin. Behind him, he hears the backpack unzipping and then Timmy's loud breathing as he jams the hanger into the crack at the top of the window. The sun is setting, the orange edged with bright pink. It looks almost pretty, even though Stephen knows it's just pollution from the oil refineries near 95. A fan on top of Wendy's starts to crank and whir, blowing the smell of stale grease in his direction. The back of his neck is sweating. He thinks about Molly Healy, sitting on the edge of his bed yesterday, fully dressed, the way she twisted a single strand of hair around her thumb. She was asking him about the stuff he'd sprayed on the lockers. She'd heard some crazy things, she said, with a little laugh. *Fuck God?* she said nervously. *Jesus loves pussy?* Stephen could barely remember—it wasn't like he thought about it first. He aimed the can and that's just what came out. But hearing the words spoken in Molly Healy's small voice, Stephen winced. He hated himself for making her say those things. *I mean, that's kind of really weird, isn't it?* Molly said. Then she told him her stomach hurt and she better go home.

"What are you *doing*, Tim?" Mark hisses. "Hurry the fuck up."

Stephen looks over his shoulder. Both of them are hunched over the lock, Timmy guiding the bent hanger, metal scraping the inside of the glass.

"Hang on," Timmy says. "It's stuck."

"You asshole," Mark whispers. "I thought you said you knew—"

"I do. Just give me a minute. Jesus."

Stephen faces forward again. Cars are rolling slowly past them, toward the drive-through lane, glancing over and away. They don't want to know.

Behind him, Timmy's breathing is getting louder. "Shit."

"What?"

Stephen looks back, sees Timmy's face reddening as he fishes with the hanger, trying to grab the button. "I almost had it."

"Hey!" somebody shouts. "Hey, you!"

Stephen turns around and sees the old man, halfway across the lot. He's at least seventy, maybe older, and wearing plaid pants and a windbreaker. It's Stephen the man is yelling at, Stephen he can see. "That's my car!"

"Guys," Stephen says. "He's coming."

"Hurry!" Mark snaps. "Jesus, Timmy, what the fuck?"

The old guy is trying to hurry toward them but can move only so quickly. He has a limp—maybe he was in the war. "Get away from that car, boys!"

"Steve, how close is he?" Mark says.

"Close," says Stephen, glancing again over his shoulder. Timmy is hunched over the lock, whispering, "Fuck, fuck, fuck." The old man yells, "Step away from there!" Then Mark straightens up and looks pointedly at Stephen. His ugly face is hard as a rock. He says, "You got this, Steve?"

This, after all, is what Stephen is there for—*if necessary, the muscle*. He just hadn't considered what would happen if it actually came to this.

"He's old," Stephen says.

"And?"

The guy is so close, Stephen can see the bulge of the cigarette pack in his jacket pocket, banging against his ribs as he walks. His hair is silver, combed backward in neat metallic lines. He looks like somebody who might go to St. Bonaventure's. Stephen would bet money this guy knows somebody in his family. His family knows everybody.

"Get away from my car!" the old man is shouting, fumbling in his pocket for his keys. "I'll call the cops!"

Stephen takes a breath and steps forward. It's then that he sees the hat. Sitting in the back window of the Impala, facing outward, not tossed there but propped deliberately. *Local 691*. His grandfather had kept a hat in the back window of his Buick, a black-and-yellow cap that said *World War II Veteran*, and something about the proud way this hat is displayed makes Stephen want to bolt from the parking lot and run home. But then the old guy shoves past him, knocking hard into his shoulder, barking, "Get away from there!" just as Stephen hears the door slam and Timmy crowing, "I'm in! Guys, I'm in!"

Mark sprints around to the passenger side. The motor guns, tires rip backward, and Timmy yells out the window, "Steve! Let's go!"

But Stephen is frozen. The old guy is reaching for the door, yanking at the locked handle. "Steve! What the fuck, man?" Mark is annoyed, Timmy laughing like a maniac. The old guy is trying to poke his key in the lock as his car rolls back out of his reach, a few inches each time, like a game of chicken. Stephen's face fills with heat. He's angry at his friends for being such assholes, angry at the old guy for being unable to stop them. His hands are trembling and the next thing he knows he's swinging, fist connecting with the loose skin of the old man's cheek. The guy's head flies to one side and he staggers a few steps backward but stays standing. He hits Stephen back, knocking him square in the nose. He's surprisingly strong. A vet for sure. Timmy is now laughing hysterically. Mark is incredulous, saying, "Really, Steve?" But now Stephen is in it and can't stop. He's punching and getting punched, feeling the blows land haphazardly on the old man's face and chest. Vaguely he senses cars stopping but he's just throwing his fist, sometimes getting nothing but air, arm sailing weightless through the empty space, other times feeling his knuckles connect with bone. He hears the guy grunting, breathing hard, and then a menacing growl—*You're done, Steve.* Stephen hits the guy in the stomach and hears a low moan. The guy stumbles onto his knees, bracing himself with his old spotty hands, and a wallet falls from his pocket, flopping on the pavement like a dead brown fish. Stephen grabs it. "Steve!" Mark yells. "*Jesus! Get in!*" There is a note of something—true panic—in his voice that Stephen has never heard before. Stephen stands up, but slowly. He feels huge, untouchable, capable of anything. He doesn't want to look at the old guy, but he does: curled on the ground, knees pulled to his chest, a thin line of blood trickling from his nose. He shoves the wallet in his pocket and gets in the backseat and is carried away.

Stephen is dumped in front of his house on Tyson fifteen bucks richer. The Impala's stereo system was a piece of junk—not even a stereo, just a tape deck with a bunch of old-man cassettes. Tony Bennett, Fats Domino. Why Tim ever thought this guy would have a high-end stereo was anybody's guess. Even the wallet had just thirty-five bucks inside. They each got ten, with Stephen getting the extra five for doing the stealing.

He slumps on the curb in front of his porch. It's nearly dark. His mom's car is still gone. Stephen assesses the damage. His left knee hurts, knuckles are sore. He feels a black eye forming, but nothing's broken. He sits and he waits, listening for the sound of cop cars, but the street is quiet, or as quiet as it ever is. A gang of kids is playing stickball near the corner, extra charged up from the nearness of summer vacation. In neighbors' houses, TVs blare from open windows. Cheap electric fans crank and spin. It feels like summer, sounds like summer, the lazy chirp of crickets, the smells of dinners clinging to the humid night air.

When the streetlamps snap on and the kids are called in, Stephen decides that the police aren't coming. It doesn't surprise him. In fact, it makes sense: Because if his uncle is dying, really dying, nothing truly bad can happen to Stephen. The chance of two things happening in one family, in one week—the odds are impossible. As long as his uncle is dying, Stephen is safe.

Still, there's a knot of fear inside him. The same feeling he had looking at the trees in Uncle John's backyard. It's not a fear of getting caught, but the feeling that he's waiting for something else, something bigger, worse than the police. Usually when Stephen gets in trouble, he asks for it. He invites it. But this other thing, this unknown darkness, is abstract, formless, and approaching with a certainty Stephen can't shake.

When he hears the dribble of a basketball, Stephen quickly pushes himself to his feet. He can't deal with his brother right now, asking what happened to his face. Not because he's jealous that Joey is so *extraordinary*—the shrink had that completely backward. It's that his brother is so totally fucking normal. He has normal friends, thinks normal thoughts. Stephen walks in the opposite direction, limping a little on the knee. He crosses Longshore, heading toward Rising Sun, goes into the Wawa, and spends the old guy's ten on a hoagie, a bag of chips, and a Coke. Then he sits on the curb and eats. At least it tastes better than pizza. In the car today, his mother said that Uncle John could barely eat anymore—the chemo caused sores in his mouth, so he could handle only soft things. When he's hungry, he watches cooking shows. Stephen pauses, the food stuck in his throat. He thinks what an asshole he is, fucking around with his life while his uncle is trying just to stay alive, then pushes the thought back down and stands up, shoving the rest of his sandwich in the trash.

His mother's car is parked outside by the time Stephen gets home. As he opens the front door, he braces himself, but everything seems normal. Joey is playing *Mortal Kombat*, the sounds of fake video fighting spilling under his bedroom door. His father is exactly where Stephen left him, watching TV and drinking a beer. "Mark called," he says without taking his eyes off the screen. Stephen goes to his room and shuts the door, shoves his sneakers off, and kicks them across the floor. He stretches out gingerly on the bed and props his head on the pillows. Through the wall behind his head, he can hear his mother on the phone. If she's home, she's always on the phone.

He can't make out all the words, but he knows the sound: the muffled rise and fall of it, the nervous pauses, the sad one-note answers, as she talks about Uncle John. *Mm-hm. I know. It will.*

Stephen's right eye is throbbing. He places a hand over it, as if the darkness might keep the swelling down. He thinks of the old joke: *Does your face hurt? Because it's killing me!* A corny joke, the kind uncles tell at parties. It occurs to him that if Uncle John dies tonight, he'll have a black eye at his funeral—the thought makes him sick. He can't even imagine what his mother would say. *Now, Stephen? Now?* He presses both hands over his eyes. In the darkness, he pictures that red Impala. Not the car itself—now dumped in the back of the Clover parking lot—but the back window, the hat. He wonders what became of the World War II cap his grandfather always kept in his Buick. Last winter when Pop died, they all went over in the middle of the night and filed into the bedroom to say good-bye. Stephen had lost it that night in front of everyone. It wasn't the rigor mortis, which he had expected from biology class, but the other stuff, the little stuff. The stubble on his cheeks, the dab of toothpaste on his chin, signs that an hour ago he had still been alive.

At least he died in his sleep, Stephen thinks. At least he was old. He lifts his hands from his eyes and stares at the ceiling. His upper lip is sweating. From the other side of the wall, he hears a click as the receiver is returned to its cradle. Then the eternal grind of numbers as his mother dials the next person. Slow, heavy, as if just placing the call is an effort. *It's Margie,* she says. *Two days to two weeks.*

Stephen's heart is throbbing in his chest. He tries to empty his mind, focus on the bubbling of his fish tank to distract

himself from the sound of his mother's voice. It's the tank
his parents gave him for his ninth birthday, along with a bag
of blue gravel and two goldfish he named Nuts and Bolts.
Stephen was really into the tank back then. He saved up his
allowance to buy a bunch of other junk for it. A little ceramic bridge, plastic plants, a dorky sign that said NO FISHING
ALLOWED. He stuck a kitchen place mat behind the glass, an
ocean scene with a lighthouse and waves. He was thinking he
might become a deep-sea diver. That summer, when his family
was all down the shore together, he'd told Uncle John about his
plan. Uncle John always took his ideas seriously, unlike his dad,
who chuckled—*Aren't you afraid of swimming?* But Uncle John
asked Stephen a bunch of questions, the two of them leaning
against the deck railing like they were businessmen discussing
some proposition, or he was interviewing Stephen for a very
important job. *Do you have a backup plan?* Uncle John said, and
Stephen thought about it before answering: *Astronaut.*

When they got back from the shore, Nuts and Bolts were
dead. The dissolving food pellets hadn't dissolved fast enough
and the bodies floated on the surface of the water, already
partway decomposed. The clumps of uneaten food looked
gray and wet, like brain matter. *They're dead*, his father told
him, and Stephen said nothing, watching his father scoop
them out with the measuring cup his mother used for baking
cakes. A minute later he heard the flush of the toilet, pictured
his dead fish flying through the pipes inside his bedroom wall.
The next day he trashed the NO FISHING sign, the place mat,
the bridge. For years the tank sat empty, a few gray pebbles
of gravel in the bottom. A year ago, when he got a job at Pet
World, the new fish he picked out were silver, sharp-finned,

with teeth and whiskers; they looked like miniature sharks. He didn't give them names. He rigged black lights to the tank so when the fish swam through, they glowed. *Freaky*, said Molly Healy the first time she came over, lying beside him, partway naked, the covers pulled to her chin in the semidark.

Stephen's blood pounds thickly in his ears. He pulls the five from his pocket and stares at it, the one from the old man's wallet. The bill is wrinkled and damp, torn at one corner. He opens the tank lid and drops it in. He watches it float like a lily pad, soaking up water, then start to sink. *Isn't that kind of really weird?* The five drowns slowly before settling on the bottom, the fish swimming obliviously around it. Stephen thinks of the old man, curled on the parking lot, and wonders what happened after they left. Could the man have died? Could Stephen have killed him? *You're done, Steve*—had the man actually said that? He must have been hearing things. Or maybe the old man was a messenger, the thing that had been haunting Uncle John's backyard, rustling in the trees.

From the other side of the wall, his mother's voice rises suddenly and Stephen feels a twinge of panic—then it drops back down to the lower register, murmuring. He grabs the pillow from behind his head, angling himself so he's leaning directly against the tank, picturing the fish's teeth just inches from his ear. He hopes the motor will drown out the sound of her voice, but the tank only amplifies it, like a glass pressed to a wall, sharpening every word. *I know*, his mother says. Stephen closes his eyes and for a minute just rests there, listening. *He is. It could come at any time.*

Sadness Is a Factor

Kate had been prepared for the scene in the waiting room, for she's grown accustomed to the fact that babies have taken over the world. The streets are teeming with them. Coffee shops, hair salons, a recent lunch meeting at Le Bec-Fin. Every ad in every catalog, every commercial on TV. In the waiting room at Dr. Steiner's office, Kate was privy to every version: the pregnant mothers with their bubbled stomachs and trendy maternity dresses, the collage of newborn photos and thank-you notes on the wall, the parenting magazines in the rack, and the success stories playing happily on the floor. But she hadn't been prepared for the back door.

"It's just another exit," Dr. Steiner told her. She waited a tactful pause, gauging whether or not Kate needed further explanation. "For patients who would rather avoid the waiting room."

It took a minute to sink in. Dr. Steiner was tall, with a neat bob, naturally gray. The room was clean and cold. A poster of a waterfall hung above the exam table, rows of Anne Geddes babies in flowerpots, a basket of kittens. Then it clicked: This exit was for the women who couldn't get pregnant, so they could avoid walking back out through all the new-baby joy. Kate was stunned that such a thing existed. Horrified that she'd been offered it. Did they extend the invitation to all the fertility-challenged women, or did you have to be a particularly unhinged case?

"Oh!" she said breezily, chummily, as if she and Dr. Steiner were on the same side of a shared joke. "I get it. Because walking through the waiting room is too traumatic? Because of all the happiness?"

She was trying to be funny—really, what could a person do in this situation but be funny?

"A baby-free zone!" Kate laughed, too loudly, wondering why she'd told Patrick it was okay to skip today's appointment. Surely Dr. Steiner wouldn't have said it with him there. "Good to know! Although, let's be honest—aren't I kind of living in a baby-free zone already?"

Dr. Steiner gave her a neutral smile. "Some women find it more comfortable."

"Oh, I'm fine! Sorry if I seemed—it's just the hormones, I promise. I'm fine, certainly fine enough to walk through a waiting room. The back door—I mean, to take it almost seems like admitting defeat, don't you think?" Kate looked at the wall, at the babies in flowerpots, most of them screaming. Then she looked down at the paper gown draped across her bare knees. "My husband's brother died in May," she said.

"I'm sorry to hear that," said Dr. Steiner, a woman used to hearing sad things.

"He's been very sad," Kate said. "Just so—*sad*."

She looked up, expectant, only to find that Dr. Steiner's smile had recalibrated slightly: still kind, but firm. "I know this is difficult, Kate," the doctor said. "But I would caution you against thinking it's anyone's fault." Then she touched Kate's knee and left the room, leaving her to put on her clothes.

Hormones, yes. Thank God for hormones. Kate is taking a hefty dose of Clomid and relies on it on a daily basis to excuse her bad behavior. Lately she is a steaming cauldron of ugly emotions. Jealousy, naturally, of all the new mothers. Of all the bad mothers who don't deserve to raise children. Of all the teenagers who got pregnant accidentally. Of her friends from Bryn Mawr, who are all simultaneously having babies. They all got married over the same two-year span—Kate included—but now she is veering distressingly off course. She attends their showers, visits their newborns, listens to them discuss things like baby sunscreen and organic peaches with the seriousness of an international peace summit. Are these the same girls she used to get stoned with in college? They're all so *earnest*. "No sunscreen before six months," they say with an air that is satisfied—more than satisfied, almost desperately pleased with themselves, because if they don't assure themselves that knowledge like this is vitally important, what then? She recognizes it as an unappealing new strain in herself, this bitterness. Still, she's jealous of them, all of them. She's even jealous of Lauren—poor Lauren, a widow at twenty-seven—for her adorable little girl and boy.

Kate clutches the wheel, squinting into the sunlight, bright even through her new, too-expensive shades. She hasn't told Patrick what she spent on them (not that he's even noticed them) and feels a twinge of guilt, but she reasons that she deserved to treat herself. She's the one earning money, after all. She inches the car forward, behind a belching city bus, and wrenches the sun visor down. Only two blocks from their apartment and the traffic is ungodly, crawling along for no apparent reason. Life would be so much easier in general if only there were reasons. But the doctors have concluded nothing's wrong—nothing *technically* wrong, Dr. Steiner always says, as if to imply some other realm of abstractions. Karmic retribution, maybe. Sin and punishment—she married a Catholic, after all! Kate's theory, which she has been forming in secret, is that Patrick's grief is making it impossible for them to conceive. Since May, he's been so sad—immovably sad. Kate remembers what the hippie gynecologist at Bryn Mawr used to tell the girls: *Never underestimate the emotional disorders of the crotch!* She and her friends had quoted the line, mirthfully, for years.

Kate hadn't told anyone her sadness theory, in part because there are so few people she could tell. Not Patrick, certainly. Not Patrick's family, who are all grieving themselves. Her new work friends she doesn't know well enough yet. It was hard—oddly hard, really—to find someone to talk to about certain things at a certain age. In retrospect, it may be the thing she took most for granted in college, when she couldn't walk to the bathroom without tripping over another girl's bared soul. Finally, yesterday, she'd run her theory by her old college roommate Liz.

"I just think it could be that his, you know, sadness is a factor," Kate said.

"Mm," Liz replied. They were eating lunch at an Italian place near Rittenhouse Square, Liz's four-month-old in a sling on her lap. Liz was eating quickly while the baby slept. Ever since her friends started having babies, lunches went like this. Kate had part of them, half of them at most.

"Keep talking," Liz said, stabbing at her Caprese salad. "I'm listening."

"It's just, I mean, there's nothing else wrong. Medically."

"But, sweetie, sometimes there just *isn't*," Liz said. "Sometimes that's just true."

"Well, right. I know that," Kate said irritably. "Still, though. I'm thinking this could be affecting his virility. You know, keeping him from knocking me up." Talking to her college friends, Kate sometimes felt herself becoming more coarse, glib, reverting to a younger, truer version of herself.

"It might help if you could stop worrying about it," Liz offered. "Have a glass of wine at night. Don't focus on it so much."

Easy for her to say, Kate thought. She ripped a piece of bread in half and mashed it in the little dish of olive oil. "All I meant is," she said, "in the absence of anything else, this might help explain it. The sadness, I mean. You know—an emotional disorder of the crotch," she joked, and Liz's head snapped up. Maybe you weren't supposed to say *crotch* around babies, even sleeping babies.

But Liz recovered herself and laughed. "Could be." She smiled and shook her head. "I'd forgotten all about that."

The luxury! If only Kate had a life where advice doled out by gynecologists at the campus health center ten years ago no longer felt so relevant. It was just one more way her life had deviated from her friends'. They used to talk bluntly about sex with boyfriends, but it was different, she supposed, with husbands. Maybe it would sound too critical; maybe they just had nothing to talk about anymore. Kate used to regale them with tales of her exploits—when she and Patrick were first dating, the stories were legendary, and she wore them like a flag—and now she longed to tell her old friend how sex with Patrick had become so regimented, so humorless and goal-driven. How sex, for him, seemed less like pleasure and more like just not-sadness.

Then the baby started squirming. Liz immediately put her fork down and peered inside the sling.

"I just think," Kate said, "if I could cheer him up, it could happen."

"And how do you propose to do that?" Liz said, digging in her diaper bag.

Kate was stung. She wasn't being serious—at least not *how do you propose* serious. Liz had once been a cynic, too, but motherhood seemed to have sapped her cynicism. A mother and a cynic—maybe you can't be both.

"I guess if I knew that, I wouldn't be telling you, would I?" Kate said with more bite than she'd intended. "I mean, I know there's nothing I can really do about it. Because there's nothing I can do about any of it. Because it's all a giant mystery. Somehow, I managed to marry the one Irish Catholic in all of Philadelphia who can't reproduce!"

Liz procured a pacifier from the bag and poked it in the baby's mouth, then looked at Kate. She wasn't laughing. Maybe it wasn't funny? Kate had thought it was funny, at least a little bit funny.

"I'm worried about you," Liz said, and Kate felt suddenly like bursting into tears. Instead she said, "Join the club."

"I'm serious, Katie. You're different."

"How?"

"You're becoming...I don't know. Hard."

Well, don't I have a right? Kate felt like shouting. She didn't have a baby to melt into, to allow her to drift away from adult conversations and go all motherly and soft. Not to mention she had a full-time job doing mindless market research to support her med student husband, not that these former Bryn Mawr feminists ever asked.

Instead Kate said, "I'm sorry," and meant it. "It's hormones," she added.

Liz had looked at her then with the same worried expression, Kate realizes now, squeezing her car into a parking spot, that Dr. Steiner had that morning. And this, she understands, was the moment that had tipped her over the edge: from brave, fertility-challenged would-be mother to desperate, blaming wife. This was the reason she'd been offered the back exit—not to protect her from the happy moms-to-be, but to keep the happy moms from being exposed to her. She locks the car and runs up the stairs to their sweltering fourth-floor walk-up, where she dials Patrick's pager from the phone in the kitchen, then waits, forehead pressed to the warm refrigerator door. "Babe?" she says when the phone rings. "Can you come home? Please?"

Kate was Catholic, but not really. *Raised Catholic*, she always said. Catholic enough to go to Mass on Easter and Christmas (which was mostly about babies dressed in cute outfits—more babies!) and Catholic enough to get married in a church (though she insisted on generous editing privileges over Bible readings—deleting any mention of God, man's image, young stags). When she and Patrick first started dating, she'd teased him that meeting a good Catholic was like hitting the sexual jackpot—all those repressed urges, the unindulged desires to break rules. And in the beginning, it was true. They couldn't keep their hands off each other, and Patrick was game for whatever thing Kate proposed. Sex in the ocean, in a coat closet, an elevator. Once, in the tacky pastel bathroom at his sister's rental down the shore. At his family parties, Kate liked to squeeze Patrick's leg under the table, thinking of things that would shock his reserved family. Patrick and Kate were the exception to the rule—younger, looser, more liberal than the others. Lately, though, Patrick had been delivering lines right out of the Catholic playbook. *Things happen for a reason*, he might say, waiting for toast to pop. *What doesn't kill you . . .*

"Kate?" Patrick calls, slamming the front door.

"In here!"

She listens to him moving through the apartment, all fifty feet of it—the tiny living room, the kitchen alcove with the washer but no dryer—as she kneels at the foot of their bed. It must be a hundred degrees in the bedroom, and she's sweating in just her bra and underwear, slightly racy pink ones she dug out of the back of a drawer. Listening to his footsteps get closer, she pushes her shoulders back and rakes her fingers through her hair. She feels oddly nervous, trying to look seductive, trying to remember how.

"What's wrong?" Patrick says then, appearing in the doorway. He looks mussed, slightly winded, in his sneakers, jeans, and white coat.

"This"—she smiles—"is a booty call."

"What?" He laughs, looks confused. But at least he laughs.

"A booty call—remember? Like in college?"

"I don't think I ever had one of those," he says, scratching his cheek, running a palm over his red hair. His freckles look even brighter from the sun. "I thought something happened at the doctor's."

"Well, it did. Kind of."

"Is everything okay?" He looks around the room, as if he might find the answer. "Are you ovulating?"

There is something so absolutely awful, unsexy, and—*Bryn Mawr, forgive me!*—emasculating about the word *ovulating* slipping so easily off her husband's tongue.

"Nope," she says, flashing a smile. "This is just sex. Just fucking. No ulterior motive." Which isn't true, of course. Because she's thinking it will be good for them. A little spontaneity, a shake-up of the routine.

When she sees the hesitation on his face, she reaches for his hand—if he rejects her right now, she thinks, she may never recover—and pulls him toward her as he says, "Aren't you supposed to be at work?"

"I called out."

"You did?"

"I already took the morning," she says, kissing his neck.

"It's just, I have rounds at one—"

But she is pressed against him now, moving her mouth to his chest. Knowing that he's going back to the hospital, that they have only this brief window, makes it somehow more exciting—sort of like having an affair. She strokes his crotch, lightly at first—imagining he's someone else's husband, a rich, distracted lawyer, maybe, stopping by her house on her lunch break—and feels him rising under her hand. He fumbles with his belt, then lifts her off the bed and they have sex standing up, his hands gripping her hips and her back pressed against the closet door. He comes quickly, with a loud, long moan.

Then he flops to the bed and whistles through his teeth. Kate joins him, curling on top of the unmade sheets. He gropes one limp hand in her direction, but she says, "It's okay, I'm good," and kisses his cheek. Her former self would have been insulted. It used to be a point of pride that they both have orgasms every time—*equal opportunity sex life!*—but today she has bigger goals in mind. She glances at her husband's face, and it looks soft. Happy, Kate thinks. She lets her eyes close, satisfied. Through the open window, she listens to the sounds of life rising from the street. A blast of hip-hop from a passing car, a motorcycle engine gunning. She feels him dribble down her thigh and thinks: *All those babies.* Then: *I'll have to wash the sheets.* It's no small undertaking—she pictures the damp sheets draped to dry all over the apartment—but it was worth it, she thinks, as Patrick heaves a heavy sigh. Kate opens her eyes. She finds him staring at the ceiling, all contentment drained from his face, and realizes then that she has no idea where he is. Her husband is right beside her, and she has no clue what he's thinking. Being in bed together in the middle of a Friday, listening to the world outside the window, should feel stolen, special, but it feels lonely.

She puts her hand on his chest, tracing circles with her fingernail. He speaks to the ceiling. "Are you picking up something for the party?"

"Party?"

"Max's birthday party," he says, turning toward her on the pillow. "Tomorrow. You didn't remember?"

"Of course I remembered," she says, bristling, and she did. She just can't believe he's talking about it right now.

"Maybe you could go over a little early—"

Her hand stops moving. "Why?"

"To help," he says, an emphatic note in his voice. "In case Lauren needs help."

I need help, she thinks. *We need help.* She sits up and picks her shirt off the floor. "Not a problem," she says, and for the second time in an hour, she starts putting on her clothes.

It is Max's second birthday and of course there's a party, though this particular celebration feels insanely difficult and soon. But it's important, Kate knows, to keep acknowledging these things. Especially in Patrick's family: Every event is celebrated, big or small. Holidays, Little League games, the all-family August vacation to the Jersey shore, where even this year they dragged themselves through the motions, eyes watering, staring out at the ocean and blinking, passing John's children back and forth. They are committed to keeping these family traditions alive, as if to abandon one would grind the entire machine to a halt. But since John's death, every little thing is loaded: recalibrated to accommodate his absence, experienced without him for the first time.

Kate stops at the little grocery on the corner, selects a few tubs of ice cream from their meager selection, then drives to John and Lauren's—now just Lauren's—out in Chestnut Hill. Kate has never really clicked with John's wife; it's hard to imagine them being friends in real life, to see Lauren hanging out with the Bryn Mawr girls. But who knows? At this point, Kate's college friends might have more in common with Lauren than with her. When she and Patrick first started dating, sorting out the who's who of his family, she was amazed to learn Lauren had converted when she married John. "You mean, converted *for* him?" Kate said, incredulous. It seemed so subservient—so *wifey*. "You would never want that, would you?" she teased. Patrick swore to her he wouldn't. He said he wanted a more modern marriage, didn't mind that Kate wasn't a good cook like his mother and his sisters, but sometimes Kate detects a look of disappointment, or just plain confusion, when she serves him another plate of takeout Chinese.

Kate turns off Germantown Avenue and starts winding through the leafy green streets. She dredges up an ignored, unsolicited piece of advice her mom once gave her: *You want to know what a man expects from his wife, look at his mother.* The kind of line Kate would have dismissed as regressive, ridiculous, at the time. She starts down Lauren's block: the sloping lawns and electric fences, the big houses made of glass and stone. Just a half hour outside the city, but it's like another world. At least these are the tasteful suburbs, Kate thinks, not the depressing cookie-cutter ones made of clapboard and strip malls. Although really, aren't all suburbs depressing? Unoriginal, lacking in character? She would hate to live in a place like this.

Kate pulls into the long, horseshoe-shaped driveway and parks by the door, shifting her sunglasses to the top of her head. She grabs the ice cream, gone slightly soft in the heat. It's a perfect day for a party, sunny with a breeze, but the house looks closed. On the porch, a tricycle is lying on its side, dirty pink-and-white streamers drooping from the handlebars, and the welcome mat is crooked, the mailbox crammed with coupon circulars and junk mail.

"Oh!" Lauren says when she answers the door, holding Max on her hip. "Hi." She glances over Kate's shoulder, as if expecting the entire party to file in behind her. She's wearing a purple terrycloth bathrobe, way too bulky for a day like this. Her face is bare, her uncombed hair pinched back in a plastic clip. Patrick had advised Kate not to call first—Lauren was known to refuse help, sometimes not even answer the phone—but seeing her now, Kate wishes that she had.

"Just me," Kate says breezily. "I came a little early to help you get ready—not that you need it, I'm sure!"

She isn't sure. In fact, something about Lauren seems unnervingly fragile, like a vase with tiny fissures running just beneath the surface. One that had been splintered into pieces and reglued—one wrong tap and the whole thing could come apart.

"How's the birthday boy?" Kate says, giving Max a poke. He is sucking on two fingers, wearing only a diaper, bright purple juice staining his chin. Lauren just stands there, as if unsure what to do next, so Kate says briskly, "Where's my girl Elena?" and takes a step inside.

Lauren trails behind her through the living room, barefoot, murmuring, "It's a mess in here. I know."

"Oh, please!" Kate says, taking quick stock of the place. The TV is playing *Beauty and the Beast*. Cheerios are sprinkled on the coffee table, toys splayed on the floor, a sparkly tiara and an armless doll. It feels too dark, too cold, for a sunny summer Saturday. The air-conditioning is blasting, the shutters closed. And there's a smell—a baby smell, but not a good one. Stale and damp, like wet saltines. As she walks through the house, Kate feels concern, but at the same time a corresponding sense of purpose. She glances into John's office, the desk of gleaming mahogany, and wonders if it's been touched since the night he died. Patrick had described the scene to her later, as well as he was able: how John took him inside, shut the door, and explained his family's financial plan for the next twenty years: stocks and investments, Catholic school tuitions, funds for college, for Elena's wedding. The desk is still covered with neat stacks of papers, a gold pen on the green blotter, as if frozen under glass.

In the kitchen, Kate shoves the ice cream in the freezer. The dishwasher is gaping and there is a juice carton sitting open on the table, three sticky place mats, burnt toast crusts, a bag of limp blue balloons: *Party Pak!*

"Aunt Kate!" Elena yells, racing through the back door, and flings herself around Kate's legs, face pressed into her knees.

"Hi there, cutie," Kate says, scooping her into her arms. Elena is a gorgeous little girl, with dark hair and big violet eyes. She has Lauren's coloring—enviably tan, unlike the rest of the family, Kate included, who are pale and prone to sunburns. Elena starts fondling Kate's jewelry, a raft of slender gold bangles shivering on her wrist.

"We're swimming," Elena says. She is the only one dressed for a party, in a pink dress and jellied sandals.

"Really?" Kate says.

"Not swimming," Lauren says. "Cleaning the pool."

"We're cleaning the pool," Elena dutifully repeats.

"Oh, *are* you," Kate says, thinking: At least that might explain the bathrobe. Max starts whimpering to be put down. "Let's go see what you're up to, shall we?" Kate says, and they all troop out of the kitchen and through the back door, an ungainly procession, Max squirming in Lauren's arms and Elena with hands wrapped tightly around Kate's neck, digging into her thighs with her hard plastic heels.

Their backyard, Kate has to admit, is heaven. A deck for entertaining, an in-ground pool. A row of shade trees lines the back of the property, fluttering gently in the breeze. This is the upside of life in the suburbs, she concedes: the space. Lately the apartment on Spruce Street has begun to feel even more cramped and small, too small for married people who are dealing with difficult things. A small apartment works only if you're purely happy, Kate decides. Fertility drugs, ovulation predictor kits, sympathy cards—you need a whole house to accommodate things like these.

Lauren sets Max down on the lawn and he starts racing around in circles in his bare feet. "Not too close to the pool," Lauren says. Her voice is toneless, on autopilot.

"Not too close, Maxy!" Elena yells, still clinging to Kate's neck.

Kate squints at the pool, assessing the situation. A metal pole with a net on the end rests on a lounge chair, but the cleaning appears not to have begun. The entire yard is looking neglected. The grass is long, the flower beds ragged. The pool water looks slightly green, the surface of it strewn with things—dead leaves and bugs and God knows what else.

"This looks like a royal pain," Kate says. "Are you sure you want to bother, Lauren? The summer's almost over. Why don't you just cover it up?"

"I can't," Lauren says. "I mean, I have to. It'll be fun for the kids."

Kate watches her gaze drift from the pool, to the deck, to

the unkempt yard, all the things that had once been exciting now a worry, a burden.

"Plus it's hot," Lauren says, touching her brow, as if saying it reminded her to feel it. "They'll bring their suits."

On the lawn, Max is still running in circles. Elena is trying to pry Kate's sunglasses off, breathing warmly on her cheek. Lauren just stares at the water.

"Well, okay," Kate says resolutely. "In that case." She turns and looks at Elena. "Let's do this."

"Let's do this," Elena repeats.

Kate plops the little girl down on a lounger, places the sunglasses on her face. "Here—you be the lifeguard," Kate says, feeling every bit the part of the breezy, take-charge aunt. She picks up the metal pole and holds it away from her body, trying not to smudge her white capris, and starts skimming it along the surface of the water, guiding debris into the net. Brown leaves, a candy wrapper, bits of paper. She dumps a small pile of trash on the side of the pool and Elena applauds.

Lauren is still staring vacantly at the water; Kate wonders how to tactfully suggest she go straighten up inside. "What else needs to be done, Lauren?" she says. "I've got this covered, if you need to deal with the food—"

Lauren shrugs. "I don't, really. Everyone's bringing something."

"Right," Kate says. She dips the net back in, catches a soaked brown feather. "What are you having?" she asks, just to keep her talking. She's reminded of how you're supposed to deal with people who have had concussions, keep them from falling asleep.

"Oh, you know," Lauren says, and in the same flat tone

runs through the menu: lunch meat and rolls, macaroni salad, pink fluff, deviled eggs. Kate can picture every bit. The ham rolled into glistening pink scrolls, eggs sprinkled with paprika, the pink fluff—which looks exactly as it sounds, a bright concoction of fruit and marshmallows that the entire family inexplicably loves. All the usual things, the summertime things. She had to admire this about the Blessings: They were consistent.

Kate dumps another pile of wet slog on the side of the pool. Elena cheers again. Kate hasn't felt this useful in weeks. Then Max veers off the lawn and goes running toward Lauren, flinging himself around her knees. She reaches down absently, picks him up, and drops onto a lounger, holding Max on her lap. Then she loosens the top of her robe and, without looking at Kate, says: "Don't judge."

"Oh!" Kate says, taken aback. "Oh, it's fine! No judgment."

But it's strange. Max looks way too big to be nursing, his two-year-old head at Lauren's breast, bare limbs draped over her lap like a sloppy pietà. Kate averts her eyes. She focuses on the pool, gliding the net through the water, while Elena wanders over to the trash pile and kneels beside it, Kate's expensive white sunglasses sliding down her nose.

"Thank you," Lauren says then, and Kate isn't sure what she's being thanked for. She glances at Lauren, who nods at the pool.

"Oh, please," Kate says. "Not a problem."

"It's good that you're so independent," Lauren adds.

"Is it?" Kate laughs.

"I've been staring at this pool for days. I couldn't do it."

"Oh, sure you could have."

"I've never done it before."

"Well," Kate says, "there's a first time for everything, right?"

Elena is peering closely at the pile of wet trash, poking at it with one hand. Kate has the urge to stop her—is that even sanitary?—but it's not her place.

"You know what else I never did?" Lauren says. "Pumped gas."

"Well." Kate chuckles. "That's easy enough."

"I never put air in tires, either. Or changed the batteries in the smoke alarm—it started beeping the other night and I couldn't find it. It beeped for over two hours. I guess this is why you don't let yourself become too dependent on your husband. Because he might die."

Kate stops with the pole and stares at Lauren. Lauren isn't crying; she doesn't even look close to crying. Her expression is flat. Maybe sadness has become so much her baseline that sad things don't even register as sad anymore.

"Oh, Lauren," Kate says.

Lauren looks out over the pool, the trees. Her bathrobe is hanging open, Max draped across her thighs. Her diamond necklace, the one John gave her, glints in the core of her throat. "I'm not up to this."

"Of course you are."

"I'm not . . . made for this."

"Well, Jesus Christ, who is?"

Lauren shakes her head. "I'm just not a strong person."

"Oh, Lauren. Sure you are."

"No. Really. Some people are and some people aren't. Some people are just more capable. Like you."

If only she knew. That Kate had spent the last twenty-four

hours making pathetic attempts to seduce her own husband, being shuttled down her gynecologist's back stairs. Neither of those things would ever happen to Lauren, not in a million years.

Elena flings one arm up, triumphant, waving wet silver foil from a candy bar, shouting, "Look what I got!"

"Great, honey," Lauren says as Max lifts his head. He clambers down to the ground and scampers toward Elena, diaper sagging almost to his knees. Suddenly everything—Lauren's gaping robe, Max's legs across her lap, Elena picking happily through the trash—makes Kate's eyes fill with tears. She pats the top of her head, looking for sunglasses that aren't there.

"Kate?" Lauren says. She is squinting. "Are you all right?"

"Sorry," Kate says, swiping a finger beneath each eye. "It's nothing."

Elena looks up then, too, alert to some shift in the air, watching Kate with those big, long-lashed eyes. "Are you crying, Aunt Kate?"

"A little," Kate says. "But I'm fine, honey."

"Are you sad?"

Sad—a word this little girl must have heard a lot of lately. Three years old. What could she possibly understand it to mean?

"I'm a little bit sad," Kate tells her, forcing a smile, feels it tremble dangerously on her face. "But don't worry." She looks back at Lauren. "It's nothing, Lauren. Honestly. Just hormones—" She catches herself a second too late. The excuse has become such a reflex that she forgot who she was talking to. Kate had no intention of foisting her problems on poor Lauren. "Sorry," she says with a short laugh. "Strike that from the record." But her sister-in-law does not look fazed. In fact, she looks slightly energized, as if the intimation of someone else's trouble has awakened something in her, some new tick of life.

"Are you and Patrick trying?"

Trying—the term has always made Kate cringe. But Lauren is just the type who would say it. The ones who say it are the ones who get pregnant, Kate thinks.

"Well, you know. Trying is the operative word," Kate allows. She touches the corner of each eye. "It hasn't been going so well."

"I'm sorry."

"Don't be," Kate says, wanting to add: *You can't feel sorry for me. Your life is so much worse!*

"What does your OB say?"

Kate shrugs. "She doesn't know. No one knows. There's nothing really wrong—nothing *technically* wrong, I mean." She is talking quickly now, and Lauren looks as though she's really listening to her, as though she actually *understands* her, and Kate has to suppress the urge to tell her everything—the rote sex, the embarrassing seduction attempt, the sadness theory. But she can't tell Lauren the sadness theory, not when Lauren's life is the sadness.

"Anyway," Kate says, with another awkward laugh. "That's the deal. But we're not telling people, really. The family, I mean. Because, you know, once it's out there..."

"Oh, I know." Lauren smiles then, a genuine smile. "Believe me. I won't say a word."

It occurs to Kate that maybe she doesn't really know Lauren—has her sister-in-law always been so blunt? She's always struck Kate as so upright and proper, but maybe grief has altered her, reshaped her. Maybe, in the same way Kate's college friends have become more soft and circumspect, the profoundness of Lauren's loss has made her more candid, brought other, truer parts of her to light.

"Thanks," Kate says. She surveys the pool. The water looks cleaner, even bluer somehow. The breeze makes slight ripples in the surface. The kids are still playing in the trash pile, Elena making piles of the piles, instructing Max on where things go. *Bugs. Leaves. Paper.*

"Listen," Kate says then, propping the pole at her side. "I want to help you, Lauren."

"You already have."

"No, no, not just today," Kate says. "Not the pool. I mean, in general."

Lauren shakes her head quickly. "That's okay."

"Truly, I want to—*we* want to. Patrick and I could take the kids off your hands once a week," Kate says, warming to the idea. "How about we pick a day and make it a regular thing? How about Sundays?"

Thinking: This might be good for Patrick, for both of them. Get them out of their cramped apartment, draw Patrick out of himself. Isn't that what kids can do?

"Really," Lauren says. "You don't have to."

"No, I insist! You could have time to yourself once a week. Clean the house or—no, something better. Something decadent. Treat yourself. Have a spa day! Get a pedicure."

Lauren looks at her feet, her bare toenails. "I'm a mess, I know."

"No, no, that's not what I meant. I just think you deserve a break," Kate says. "Let me help you. Please."

But Lauren shakes her head again, more firmly. "No," she says, and she pulls her robe closed with one hand. "But thank you."

"Oh." Kate fixes her eyes on the pool. "Okay," she says, but feels chastened, rejected—the feeling sprawls through her body, blooming in her gut. She wishes she had never asked. Wishes she had her sunglasses to hide her face. She looks over at Elena, who is still wearing them, giggling as she sprinkles grass into Max's hair.

"I just like to keep them here," Lauren explains. "With me."

"No, no, it's fine. Totally fine. I understand."

Lauren looks down at her bare wrist, as if for a watch that isn't there. "I better go get dressed. They'll be here."

"Right," Kate says. As she sets the pole down on the edge of the pool, she notices the left knee of her capris is smudged with dirt.

Elena giggles again, louder, drizzling grass on Max, glancing up to see if anyone will stop her. Then Max lunges for the trash pile and flings a fistful in the air. "Maxy, no!" Elena shrieks, and slaps him across the face.

"Elena!" Lauren jumps to her feet. Elena ignores her, pushing Max to the ground with both hands. Kate is shocked— she's never seen Elena act this way. "Elena! Stop that!" Lauren shouts as Max begins to cry. Lauren starts rushing toward Elena, who looks at her and lets out a loud shriek, then dashes toward the pool.

"Elena, no!" Lauren screams, her tone shifting instantly from anger to panic. Elena is racing toward the five-foot end, her jellied shoes clapping on the wet cement. "Stop! No, Elena! Not near the pool!" But Elena doesn't hesitate for a second, running straight for the water and jumping off the side. Kate's heart stops beating. Elena's brown face bobs to the surface and then drifts under. Lauren leaps in after her, sending up a great splash, and for a moment there is an unearthly silence—Max watching too, fingers in his mouth, standing a safe distance from the edge—as Lauren's purple robe billows beneath the churning water, like a sprawling sea creature, the silence long and terrible, until finally Lauren surfaces with Elena in her arms.

It is not until they touch the side that Elena starts to cry. Kate has never heard a child cry like this before. The sound is more like wailing, like keening—the sound of anguish itself. Kate feels paralyzed as Lauren rises slowly from the water, climbing up the metal ladder with Elena held tightly in both arms. Her purple robe has fallen open to reveal her naked body, her legs sturdy and brown. Without pausing, she walks toward the house, lips pressed to Elena's temple. The heavy robe is streaming water, the wet sash dragging at her sides, but her stride is even and calm. Elena is still wailing, and Max is crying now too, the backyard a whirlpool of grief. Kate watches as Elena buries her chin in Lauren's shoulder, water dripping from her pink party dress, sandaled feet limp at her sides. When her eyes meet Kate's, they are wide and terrified and slide right over her, not even seeing her. Lauren keeps her lips pressed firmly to Elena's hair. She doesn't turn as she opens the back door, saying over her shoulder, "You'll watch him, Kate?"

Kate nods, unable to speak. Lauren's ferocity startles her, reduces her. She watches as they disappear inside. When the back door shuts, the yard goes abruptly quiet, Elena's cries swallowed by the huge, airtight house. Even Max's whimpering tapers off quickly, now that his mother isn't there. Kate looks at the baby and the baby looks at her, then wanders back to the grass. A bird chirps sweetly in the trees. The surface of the pool is calm again, the tumult already forgotten. Kate's white sunglasses quiver on the bottom. When she looks again at Max, he has returned to playing in the trash pile, tearing leaves into pieces. She can do nothing but stand there, watching him, until a thick wind stirs, scattering the pile and blowing the trash back into the pool.

Town Watch

Driving to Mister Wok at quarter to midnight on a rainy Tuesday, Dave curses under his breath. Mister Wok is a shabby suburban Chinese restaurant that probably does no business after nine on weekdays and closes in fifteen minutes and he's the guy who just called for a single carton of moo shu pork. On the phone, Dave couldn't understand a word the guy was saying, but he sounded justifiably annoyed. "Appreciate it," Dave said, and left the house immediately so as not to keep the guy waiting. Now he's hitting every red light. "Goddamn it," he says. This is new, the cursing. At fifty, Dave has finally discovered its appeal.

He parks in the deserted lot by the strip mall and runs for the Chinese place. The door is locked. He signals the guy vacuuming, who ambles through the empty restaurant to let him in. "Thanks, buddy," Dave says, rain dripping down his glasses. The guy returns to his vacuum. After-hours rock music is blasting through the speakers. The cashier, a teenage girl with a shy smile, appears from the back to hand him the stapled brown paper bag. Dave wants to tell her it's not what it looks like, that he's not some lonely middle-aged guy ordering takeout to eat alone in front of the TV. He doesn't even *like* Chinese food. "Eleven fifty," she says, and he hands her a twenty, saying, "Keep the change." An absurd tip—Ann would kill him.

As he hurries home, wipers flapping, the car filling with the smell of greasy pork, Dave tries to remember if he's ever even seen Meghan eat Chinese. His daughter has always had weird eating habits, but lately she's been choosy about when and if she eats at all. She refuses to eat in public but doesn't like to eat at home, either, at least at any normal times, like meals. She'll sit at the table with him and Ann and complain about her stomach hurting, then excuse herself and disappear to her room. Later, though, she might eat a frozen pizza. Or the next morning, he'll find an empty ice-cream tub in the trash. It isn't healthy, all that junk food, but it's better than nothing, Dave thinks. This is his rationale when Meghan announces some urgent craving at eleven thirty on a Tuesday, when he's settled in front of the TV in the den with a bowl of chips and a beer. "Daddy?" she calls. "I'm starving. Can you go get me a..." Is she testing him? Wanting to see if he'll go? If there's anything he wouldn't do for her? His little girl, the baby of the family. The one who loves him unreservedly. He can't say no to Meghan, especially if it means seeing her eat something. *I'm starving*, she tells him. He goes.

Dave tears through the sleeping streets, wanting to get the food home before Meghan has a change of heart. At the stop signs, he jams on the brakes. The car jerks forward. A little thing, but it feels good to do it. Most of the neighbors' houses are dark now, their porch lights on, kids tucked safely in their beds. TOWN WATCH, say the signs pinned to the front lawns.

The signs are shaped like eyeballs, red with black pupils, so the entire neighborhood looks like a crowd of staring eyes. Dave volunteered to do a shift, eight to ten every third Saturday. They became a Town Watch community last year, an attempt to feel safer. There had been a few incidents—a burglary, some smashed car windows. You wouldn't think it of this neighborhood, just by looking. The houses are all kept up, from modest middle-income ones like Dave's to the giant ones in the cul-de-sac on Trafalgar. But they're only a mile from the city and sometimes, lately, the danger spills over.

Dave pulls into the driveway, hurries through the rain and in the front door. His daughter is exactly where he left her, on the couch in a nest of fuzzy blankets, empty Diet Coke cans crowding the end table beside her. His wife sits in the rocking chair, a stack of fourth graders' spelling tests in her lap. With Abby living in New York and Alex at college, this is the nightly tableau: Meghan on the couch, Ann in the chair.

"One moo shu pork, coming up!" Dave says brightly, whipping the takeout box from the paper bag, dangling by its metal handle.

"I'm not really hungry anymore," Meghan says without glancing up from the TV.

His heart sinks. She's watching a movie she's seen a million times, a teenage comedy about an unpopular girl who becomes cool.

"Not hungry?"

She shakes her head, just barely.

"Why not?"

She shrugs. "I'm just not."

"Well, did you eat something else?" he says, a tick of annoyance in his voice. Ann detects it immediately and shoots him a look—quiet but firm, warning him to shut down this line of questioning. But how does this make any sense? How the hell do you go from hungry to not hungry if you don't eat anything? Neither of them is looking at him now, their faces pointed at the TV.

"Dad, that really smells," Meghan says. She pulls one of her blankets up over her mouth. "Oh, my God. I'm going to be sick."

Dave walks into the kitchen, holding the carton by the handle like a tiny purse. He throws it into the fridge and slams the door, then retreats to the den.

To Dave, it's simple: You're hungry, you eat. But apparently this is not the case with his daughter, for reasons that elude him. They've taken her to the pediatrician, who referred her to a gastroenterologist, who said nothing was wrong with her. But Meghan keeps complaining. Her stomach hurts. She's not hungry. As a little girl, she was a big eater—she would request Dave's pancakes on Sunday mornings, invite her friends over for pizza night on Fridays (now, on the rare occasion she's seen eating pizza, she blots it over and over until there's a pile of oily orange napkins beside her plate). She used to have a little baby fat but in the past year has gotten noticeably thinner. A growth spurt, Dave reasons. Fifteen. Don't most girls thin out at fifteen? And aren't most fifteen-year-olds temperamental? Lately Meghan will have bursts of energy—chattering away on the phone, screaming cheers from the sidelines at her field hockey games, blasting music in her room—but then, just as suddenly, become quiet, irritable, giving flat one- and two-word an-

swers, curled up on the couch. With just the three of them
at home now, her moods dictate the temper of their house
like storm systems sweeping in and out. Or maybe they're just
more obvious without Abby and Alex there. Because Meghan's
always been moody, Dave reminds himself, sensitive, dissolving into tears when she wasn't invited to a classmate's party, or
watched a movie that was sad or scary, or at the funeral for
Ann's brother, who died of cancer three years ago. Only three
years—could that be affecting her still? Every time Dave thinks
his way through the problem, it feels like plodding through a
thicket of evidence, considering and discounting, like tidying
columns of checks and balances at work.

He can't talk to his wife about it. Lately, he and Ann seem
to be drifting toward opposite poles—as Dave gets increasingly agitated, Ann grows more measured and composed. It
wasn't so long ago they actually *did* things together on occasion—a movie, dinner at the pub around the corner—but after
more than twenty years, his marriage has been reduced to this:
a bond of worry about their children. They come together,
trade observations, retreat to their respective corners. It's tax
season, a time Dave has traditionally dreaded, but this year he
welcomes the excuse to work late. *Did she eat?* he asks when
he gets home. *Some,* Ann reports. *A little.* They don't argue;
they've never argued. They barely touch, unless by accident.
His wife used to be curvy, but in recent years her body seems
to have withdrawn along with the rest of her, her shape soft-
ening, losing its definition. She stopped dyeing her hair. At
night, she watches TV in the living room with Meghan, and
Dave watches *Letterman* in the den, with chips and a few beers.
Sometimes he just sleeps in the chair.

⋆   ⋆   ⋆

This weekend, all three of Dave's kids will be home for almost twenty-four hours. It doesn't happen often, not outside of holidays and the Jersey shore trip every August, which both involve Ann's entire family. But this Saturday, all five of them will be under one roof, and Dave feels its approach as excitedly as a vacation. Alex they had known was coming; it was his spring break from Penn. Abby was the surprise, calling to say she'd broken up with her boyfriend, Leo, and needed a "break from real life." Dave was overjoyed—both that he'd get to see her and that Leo was out of the picture. He'd met Leo only once and told Abby he seemed like an interesting guy (*interesting*—he'd chosen the word carefully; not positive, not untrue), but Dave had instantly disliked him: a skinny twenty-three-year-old with a mangy ponytail and the brooding intensity of a kid who's never actually experienced a hard thing in his life.

He seemed like a punk, honey, Dave told her on the phone, which at least made her laugh. *A punk? Really, Dad?*

Abby was arriving Friday night and heading back late on Saturday. Dave tried to convince her to stay at least until Sunday morning, but Abby started protesting about this thing she really had to get back for, so he dropped it. They'd take what they could get. By Friday evening, Ann has stocked the kitchen with all of Abby's favorites—cinnamon-raisin bagels and root beer and a spinach lasagna, which sits cooling on the stove as they wait for the sound of her car, glancing at the oven clock, telling Meghan to stay off the phone to keep the line free in case Abby calls from the road.

"This is why we need call waiting!" Meghan cries. It's her

most recent crusade: Meghan desperately needs call waiting, Ann doesn't want the unnecessary expense. For his part, Dave just has no desire for any more phone calls. They already gave in on the cordless, so Meghan could talk privately in her room, but apparently now all her friends have call waiting—and in the end, what's more important? The promise of an uptick in Meghan's mood? A glimpse of her old, cheerful self? For this alone, he knows they'll eventually cave.

At nine fifteen, Dave hears the Volkswagen zip into the driveway—a smart buy four years ago, one hundred thousand miles on the odometer then and still going—and Abby comes through the back door, dumps her laundry-bloated duffel on the floor. She kisses them both on the cheeks and collapses on the couch. "What a drive," she says, holding out her hands before her, palms up. "I'm vibrating."

"Bad traffic, huh?" Dave asks.

Ann is still standing, hands clasped in front of her chest. Her smile is tight and small, but Dave knows she's overjoyed that Abby's home. Abby, who surprised and saddened them by wanting to go to college in New England, who used to call them tearfully when she first got there but now seems to have acclimated to living somewhere else. Four years in Maine, a move to Brooklyn. She looks like someone who lives in Brooklyn, Dave thinks. More angular and confident. Her eyes are lined with black, jeans ripped at one knee. She rakes one hand through her hair, long and messy and tangled in her long silver earrings. In her left ear alone, he counts three. "Where is everyone?"

"Alex is coming home tomorrow," Ann says.

"Tomorrow morning," adds Dave.

"And Meghan's watching a movie—"

"Meg!" Dave yells. "Where are you? Your sister's here!"

Meghan slouches into the kitchen, cocooned in a blanket, with her sweatshirt hood pulled up. "Hey," she says flatly.

"Hey yourself," Abby says, and laughs.

"What?"

"What's wrong with you?"

"What do you mean?"

"Could you sound any less excited to see me?"

"I'm excited," she says. "I've just been waiting for the phone." She gives Abby a quick hug, then picks up the cordless and leaves the room.

Abby looks at them, waiting for an explanation, but Ann says, "Are you hungry?"

"Hungry?" Abby scratches her cheek. "Maybe."

"I made a spinach lasagna..."

Abby opens the fridge and pulls out the Chinese takeout carton. "What's this?"

"Moo shu pork," Dave says.

"Moo shu?" she says, prying open the box flaps. "Since when does anyone in this house eat moo shu? Are we getting more culinarily adventurous?"

"It's Meghan's," Dave says.

She peers inside. "It's full."

"She asked for it. But then she wasn't hungry."

Abby closes the box and stares into the fridge.

"What can I get you?" Ann presses. "A sandwich? Lasagna?"

"Whatever," Abby says, shoving the box back in. "Lasagna's good."

★   ★   ★

Saturday morning, Dave proposes they all drive to Penn to pick up Alex. They can walk around the campus, then go to breakfast at the American, a classic diner Dave's own father used to take him to when he was a kid.

"I really don't feel good," Meghan says as they're putting on their coats.

Dave turns to her, keys clutched in his fist. She's standing in the kitchen doorway, wearing an enormous PENN sweatshirt and baggy black running pants with white stripes down the sides. "What's wrong?" he says.

"I think I have a fever."

"Well, did you take your temperature?"

"I don't have to. I can just tell."

"Here, let me feel," Ann says, and moves a hand toward Meghan's forehead, but she ducks out of her reach. Ann freezes.

"I have a fever," Meghan mumbles, looking at the floor.

"Well, maybe you just need some Tylenol," Dave says, appealing to Ann for backup. "Shouldn't she take some Tylenol? Advil? Why doesn't she take something?"

"I don't need Tylenol," Meghan says.

Ann says nothing. Abby stands up abruptly and walks onto the back deck, clomping heavily in her tall red boots.

"Why don't you go up and take a nap, Meg?" Ann says.

"I can't take naps," she says. "And anyway, I'm not tired."

"Why don't you just try," Ann says. "Just lie down." She pauses then and looks at Dave. "We should call Lauren. If she's sick, she can't be near the children—"

"I'll be fine," Meghan says. "That's like hours from now," she adds, grabbing the phone and heading for the stairs.

Meghan is babysitting that night for John's kids, Max and Elena—*my favorite little people*, she calls them. Dave knows it would take wild horses to keep her away.

Upstairs, Meghan shuts her door, and seconds later music comes pouring through the walls, the depressing Jewel CD that plays on a seemingly endless loop.

Ann turns to Dave. She says decisively, "I'll stay." Her tone, as always, is that perfect balance of light and firm: casual on the surface, but underneath tense as steel cable. There is no room for discussion. Defeated, Dave goes outside, where Abby is waiting by the car. They get in without a word. They buckle their seat belts and Dave fusses briefly with the mirrors, which are always slightly out of whack after Ann drives, until Abby says, "What's going on with her?"

Dave blinks out at the yard—the lawn that badly needs mowing, the onion grass bursting up in patches of dense, dark green. The basketball hoop he'd put in, hopefully, when Alex shot up past six feet. The back of Abby's car, the Colby sticker in the window. The New York plate. She's never here, he thinks; she doesn't know how it is.

Finally he says, "She's always been this way, sweetheart," and starts the car. As they drive toward the city, Abby faces the window, picking at the hole in the knee of her jeans. Dave drives quickly, braking hard at red lights, as the orderly, tended yards of the suburbs yield to the gray neighborhoods of West Philadelphia, the cramped houses and narrow streets.

Dave would actually enjoy his Town Watch shift—in fact, might welcome the chance to be alone in the car for two hours—except that he isn't alone. His partner (they're actually referred to as "partners," as if this is real law enforcement) is Dean Kramer, who lives in one of the mansions on Trafalgar. Dean is the kind of guy Dave makes a point of avoiding at parties. He's in sports marketing and loves to talk about being in sports marketing. When he tires of bragging about his clients, he brags about his kids. Josh, a senior lacrosse player. Jeremy, a junior, lead in the school play.

Dean is picking Dave up at eight sharp, and Meghan is scheduled to babysit at seven thirty, which is why Dave has planned for the family to go to dinner early. Five o'clock. The Olive Garden. Everybody's favorite. "I won't take no for an answer," he said lightly, not looking at Meghan.

But ever since they got home from breakfast, Meghan has seemed in better spirits. "Love you, Daddy!" she said, bouncing up to her room after going to the mall with her friend Jess. The fever wasn't mentioned again.

Dave checks his watch—five on the dot. He and Alex are waiting on the back deck. Dave's paging through the *Inquirer*. It's a cool night, with a hint of spring. Up on Spry Boulevard, the traffic goes zooming by, loud music splashing from the cracked car windows. Alex is reading a textbook, shoulders bowed over his skinny knees, chomping on a bag of chips. Dave grabs a handful gratefully, tossing them in his mouth. "What are these things?"

"Munchos," his son replies, his mouth full.

"Huh," Dave says, chewing. He is supposed to be watching his cholesterol—at his last physical, the doctor said he should lose fifteen pounds—but lately, all he does is eat. "What's that you're reading, Al?"

"Organic chemistry," his son says. He pushes his hair off

his brow, the last vestiges of his teenage mop, and turns the page. Alex has never offered up much about himself; he never seemed to need to. He studied hard, liked school. If he had girlfriends, Dave never heard about them. He went to his senior prom with a girl named Debbie who wore a tight, shiny red dress. Ann's family had come over to take pictures and murmured after the limo pulled away: *That was a mature dress, wasn't it?*

Alex grabs another handful of chips. Dave shakes open the sports section and does the same. In some fundamental way, Dave's wife and daughters will always be a mystery to him—clothes and bras, periods and boys, boys like the awful Leo—but with Alex, it's different. It's easy. He and his son can sit comfortably in a room together, just the two of them, and not say much at all.

Then the back door slides open. When Dave looks up at his wife, his heart sinks into his gut. He knows her look. Her face is still, near serene, but her eyes have taken on a distant cast, retreating to some more worried place inside her. "I think Meg and I are going to stay here," Ann says.

"What?" Dave says, swiping crumbs from his shirt. "Why?"

"I can't go," Meghan says. She's standing slightly behind Ann, her face drawn, wearing sweats and big puffy slippers with puppy faces on the toes.

"What do you mean, can't go? This is our family dinner—"

"I still don't feel good, Daddy."

Dave looks at Ann, her fingers laced across her middle. "It's fine," she says with her unfailing calmness. "If she's not up to babysitting, I'll go over to Lauren's."

"But what about dinner?"

"You three go," she says. "I'll stay."

Alex still has his book open but is looking at the floor. Abby is staring toward her car, as if fantasizing already about going back to New York.

Dave tosses the paper down and stands up. "No," he says. "This is a family dinner." He doesn't look at Ann. He looks at Meghan and makes himself say it. "You're going, honey. Even if you don't eat anything. You're going to sit there with the rest of us."

Meghan's eyes flood with tears, and the sight of it nearly breaks Dave's resolve, but he stands firm, watching her face pool and crumple. And it works. Sometimes, he thinks, a little push is all it takes. Meghan kicks her slippers off and slides on her running sneakers, squashing the backs with her heels. She shuffles to the car without a word, arms crossed, face closed, and slumps down in the backseat. Abby and Alex pile in around her. Ann sits stiffly in the passenger seat, hands clasped in her lap. Driving away, Dave feels, for a moment, triumphant.

At the Olive Garden, Meghan orders nothing. "Just water, please," she tells the waitress.

"Water? That's all?"

"Uh-huh," she says, giving her a small, pained smile. "I'm not hungry."

"You sure? Not even an appetizer? We have some great new appetizers—"

"No, thank you," Meghan says politely, and Dave is relieved when the waitress drops her pitch. The rest of them order and a busboy zips by, tossing down a basket of breadsticks.

"So," Dave says with forced enthusiasm. He turns to Abby. "You're over this Leo guy, right, Abs?"

"Yeah," she says with a one-shouldered shrug. "Basically."

Out of the corner of his eye, he sees Meghan tear a breadstick into pieces and start eating. Dave keeps on talking. If anybody draws attention to it, she might stop. "Any other prospects up in Brooklyn?"

"Sort of," Abby says, glancing at Meghan. "One, maybe."

"Oh yeah? Who's the lucky guy?"

Abby coughs up a few details—friend of a friend, a DJ (Christ) who's spinning tonight in Brooklyn (*this* was the thing she was rushing back for?)—but Dave doesn't have time to feel offended. Meghan is now ripping apart breadstick after breadstick. When the basket is empty, she licks her salty fingers. "Hang on," Dave interrupts Abby, waving at the waitress. "Miss?"

"Dave," Ann murmurs, but he ignores her.

"Excuse me? Miss!"

"Dave!" Ann snaps.

"What?" He looks at his wife. Her face, above her turtleneck sweater, is tight-lipped and pink. Do they not want more bread as quickly as possible? Since their daughter who never eats anything is actually eating something, don't they want her to keep on doing it?

It's all a moot point because their dinners appear, four big steaming plates. "Change your mind?" the waitress says to Meghan, smiling at the crumbs on the table before her.

Meghan looks down at the empty basket, the waxed paper translucent with grease. "No," she says, in a whisper.

"Don't be shy," the waitress says, and she grabs a busboy,

who plunks down another basket. Meghan reaches for the shaker of red pepper flakes and showers it on top.

"Meg!" Abby says. "What the hell?"

"I just ate like a hundred of them," Meghan says, sounding stricken.

"But that's good!" Dave says. "Nothing wrong with a few breadsticks." He hears his tone, jocular and large. Meghan doesn't respond, now studying her fingertips. "So," Dave says, and turns to his son. "Al. Tell us, what's new at school?"

It's unfair, he knows, to make his children keep talking, but Dave is determined to keep this meal from capsizing. Dinner with his goddamn family in the goddamn Olive Garden—is it so much to ask? Alex obliges him with a few details about classes and midterms, but his eyes keep shifting to Meghan, who abruptly stands and leaves.

With Meghan gone, everybody shuts up. Canned Italian opera soars through the speakers. Abby tosses her napkin down. "I'll be back," she says. In her daughters' absence, Ann doesn't touch her plate. Alex picks at his ravioli. Dave isn't even hungry but can't stop eating, wolfing down his entire plate of lasagna and half of Ann's chicken Florentine.

When Meghan returns, Abby is walking behind her, face stolid like a parole officer's. Meghan is pale, her eyes teary. Dave tenses, hoping she doesn't make a scene. He tosses his napkin on his plate and half stands to flag down the waitress. "Check, please!" he says, miming writing on his palm.

"Dave!" Ann says, chagrined.

He looks at her hard. "What?" he says. "What, Ann? What?" As if his ordering is the problem. As if *he* is the goddamn problem. He's just trying to take action, do something, get his family out of here.

"Saved room for the dessert?" the waitress says.

"We'll just take the check," Dave says.

"Was everything all right?" the waitress asks, cheerfully confused, looking around the table at the mostly untouched plates.

"Everything's fine," Dave says, and tells her no, they won't need anything wrapped.

Dave waits on the back deck for Dean to pick him up. They switch off driving every shift. Tonight, they'll case the neighborhood in Dean's obnoxious new Hummer. Dave is dressed for two idle hours in the passenger seat: jeans and an old sweatshirt, moccasins with toes worn shiny as cue balls. In two hours they'll cover the circuit six times—Spry all the way up to Hastings, then down Oak Road to Keene and back again—looking for "suspicious activity," though they have yet to see anything that qualifies. Once they found an old woman wandering the sidewalk searching for her cat, and Dave had ended up shimmying under her porch on his stomach while Dean held the flashlight. The cat was in her kitchen the whole time.

The night is growing cold, but Dave can smell the first few intrepid flowers, the bright yellow forsythia blooming by the curb, the purple crocuses bursting by the garage where the kids used to play freeze tag. He surveys his yard, the familiar shapes in the dark, and feels a distant ache in his chest. The rusted swing set the kids have long outgrown. The basketball hoop Alex used one summer, obsessively shooting foul shots, and never again. Dave fishes an antacid from his pocket and crunches it, leaning his elbows on the deck railing. The deck they had built almost a decade ago, when Ann went back to work. Abby had just turned thirteen. There's a picture of her posing with the carpenters, flexing her muscles. Alex was nine, Meghan five. All six handprints were pressed into the wet varnish of the deck floor. Now the paint on the railing is chipping. The center of the top step sags, soft from years of moisture and trampling feet. Dave looks at Abby's car in the driveway, remembers when they went to buy it together her freshman year of college. He's already said good-bye; she'll be gone before he gets home.

"Dad?"

Dave turns, surprised. "Hey, honey." Abby is standing in the kitchen, behind the shadowy mesh of the screen door. "What's up?"

"Can I talk to you a minute?" she says, and Dave feels a needle of worry. Something in the stiff fold of her arms, the forced lightness in her voice.

"Change your mind about leaving?" he asks with a hopeful laugh.

She indulges him with a small, sympathetic smile. "In the living room?" she says, and Dave is about to remind her that his shift starts at eight, that his ride will be here any second, but she's already walking back inside. He scrapes back the screen door and trails his daughter through the empty kitchen. Past the greasy lasagna pan soaking in the sink, the duffel bag full of clean laundry waiting by the door. His feet are heavy, despite the moccasins. The house feels still, deeply quiet. Meghan is babysitting. Alex went to Joey's game. Ann is in the living room, sitting in the chair she always does, her eyes on the floor.

"You should sit, Dave," Ann says, but her voice sounds weak and strange, like an echo in a tunnel.

He remains standing just inside the doorway, one hand braced lightly against the wall. "What?" he says. "What is it?"

Abby sits on the edge of the couch, hunched over her knees. Ann looks at her and nods. "Tell Dad what you told me."

Dave is suddenly terrified. Ann's eyes are glassy. But it's Abby's expression that alarms him most: the look of apology on her face. Quietly, she starts to catalog the things she's noticed about Meghan since she's been home. The dry lips. The watery eyes. The feet facing backward in the Olive Garden stall. The tiny cuts on the backs of her hands: tooth marks, Abby says, from putting her hand down her throat. Dave listens numbly as the details pile up before him and around him, feeling bewildered. Betrayed. How does Abby even know these things? How to do them, and to diagnose them? As if there's some other world his daughters live in, dangerous and cryptic and submerged somewhere beneath his own—but how the hell is he supposed to protect them from what he doesn't even know is there? As Abby keeps talking, the details grow more sordid and strange—the smell of vomit in Meghan's bedroom, a backyard trash can stuffed with wrappers from the Sbarro in the mall. It doesn't seem possible, Dave thinks. It *isn't* possible. All of this going on here? In his own house? He refuses to believe that Meghan would lie to them, take such pains to deceive them—*Love you, Daddy!* How could she say that not six hours ago if all of this were true?

"This is nuts," Dave snaps, cutting Abby off midsentence.

Ann looks up quickly, her face a crushed pink moon. "Dave," she says. Her eyes are wide, but her lips barely move.

"You've been here, what, honey?" Dave says to Abby. "One day? Less than a day?"

Abby looks at her knees, says under her breath, "Oh my God, get me out of here."

"Dave," Ann says louder, a notch of pleading in her voice.

"I mean, we're with her all the time, Ann," Dave says. "There's no way."

"It's kind of textbook, Dad," Abby says. She adds that she knew some girls in college with eating disorders. *Eating disorder*— it's like a punch to the throat.

Ann is staring at the floor. She looks stunned, small, as if absorbing this has made her shrink. "Abby thinks she needs a therapist," she says.

"I mean, I don't know," Abby says. "A therapist, a nutritionist. I mean—" She looks at Ann. "This is why I didn't want to tell you. Should I have told you?"

"Yes," Ann says. "Yes. Yes, of course."

From outside, Dave hears a burst of honking up on Spry Boulevard. His brain is pounding, ears swarming with white noise. He needs to get out of there. He looks at the couch, the fuzzy nest of Meghan's blankets. His wife's face, flushed to bursting, his older daughter teary-eyed, pinching at the ripped hole in her jeans. The mug of hot cocoa Meghan made last night, still sitting full on the end table, powdery chocolate streaking down the sides like dried entrails. Then the honking comes into focus—three sharp, aggravated blasts. "That's my ride," Dave says, and relief surges through his bones. He steps toward Abby, kisses the top of her head. "I love you, honey. Drive safely," he says, and starts for the door.

"You're not leaving," Ann says, but Dave keeps moving. He

feels life returning to his limbs. "You're *leaving?*" she repeats, her voice rising abruptly, high and loose, almost a shriek. Dave continues through the foyer and onto the front porch, letting the front door slam behind him. He crosses the shaggy front lawn to where Dean and his Hummer sit chugging by the curb.

"Sorry," Dave says, climbing in and shutting the door hard, but the car is too expensive to slam properly. It closes with a puny click.

"New car?" Dean says.

Dave's heart is banging in his chest. "What?"

"The Volkswagen," Dean says, nodding at the driveway.

"Oh," Dave says. "That's Abby's. My oldest. She's just home for a few days."

Dean nods, a thick fold of pink flesh rolling over his shirt collar, as he puts the car in drive. "New England, right?"

"Brooklyn now."

"These kids," Dean says, shaking his head. "Who can keep track. They move around so much. It's goddamn nuts."

"She's leaving tonight," Dave adds, as Dean pulls away from the curb.

As they start their assigned loop, Spry up to Hastings, Dave's chest hurts. Blood pounds in his ears. He stares at the neighbors' houses breezing past the window, a long march of glowing porch lights, trimmed front lawns, and eyeballs on sticks. Dean is flipping through the radio channels, talking about how Jeremy, his younger boy, told them he wants to move to L.A. after high school. Try to make it as an actor. "I told him, I'll be damned," Dean says. "You're staying here and getting a degree. I'm not going to let you fuck up your life on my watch."

Dave lets out a choked laugh, but he's thinking that Dean

is made for this patrol—a guy who's vigilant, who keeps his kids in line, keeps them from going down the wrong path. His throat is tightening, the pressure building in his chest. Then the dashboard emits a gentle ping. "That's you," Dean says.

Dave blinks at him.

"Seat belt, partner."

"Oh," Dave breathes. "Righty-o, partner," he adds, pulling the belt sharply across his middle, jamming it in the buckle. He balls his damp palms into fists. Dry heat is pouring silently from the vents. The Rolling Stones thrash faintly on the radio. The dashboard is shiny, wide as an airplane cockpit, and Dave feels a surge of anger—at the belt, the car, Dean himself.

"I told him, I don't care what your friends are doing or what bullshit you heard from the guidance counselor," Dean is saying. Dave cranks his window down. His brow is filmed with sweat, his belted gut so tight it might implode. As Dean approaches the corner of Keene and Hastings, still inconceivably talking about his stupid son, Dave imagines bolting from the car, diving for the corner yard. The house on the corner is a colonial, brick, twice the size of his own. A tall, tidy hedge shields the lawn from the street. Dean is fiddling now with the heat, tweaking the glowing dials—"I try to get my wife to back me up, but she likes to let me do the dirty work," he says—when Dave spots a shadow in the yard: a movement toward the back of the high hedge. Was it a person? He squints hard into the darkness. The house is unlit, except for a single window upstairs.

"Hold on," Dave says, knocking one fist on the dashboard. "Stop it. Stop driving."

"What?"

He slaps the dashboard with his palm. "Stop the car!"

"Jesus!" Dean says, jerking to a stop at the corner. "What's the problem?"

"I saw something."

"Saw something?"

"In the bushes." Dave points. "Over there."

"What, like a robber?" Dean chuckles.

"Yeah," Dave says, unbuckling his seat belt.

"Seriously?" Dean says, but there's a note of uncertainty in his voice. He glances in the rearview mirror. "So, what? Do we think we should call it in or something?"

"I'm going to have a look," Dave says, thrusting the door open. The dashboard pings again in feeble protest.

"Seriously?" Dean repeats as Dave steps onto the sidewalk and slams the door. He inhales sharply, letting his lungs inflate. The night is colder, but the air smells fresh, like newly mown grass. As he strides across the neighbor's lawn, his breath comes in hard, clean puffs. Past the red eyeball staked in the clipped grass, past the long porch with its matching chairs and potted plants. Marching down the narrow path at the side of the house, Dave feels expansive, churning with adrenaline. The ground is slick with mud and he trips once, soaking his pants from the knees down, but clambers up and keeps going, swiping his palms on his jeans. When he emerges in the backyard, he finds it lit only by a single streetlamp. A newish Subaru is parked by the garage. The yard is empty except for the traces of a baseball game, a flung bat, some makeshift bases. There are no intruders here—none that Dave can see, at least. But a person could easily be crouched behind the car or lurking on the far side of the garage. Dave picks up the baseball bat—it's surprisingly light, near weightless—and stalks across the lawn. But when he steps within ten feet of the garage door, the sensor light blazes on, flooding the yard with light. He freezes, just as the back door slams.

"Hey!" shouts a voice from the porch. "What the fuck!"

The guy standing on the back porch looks younger than Dave, though not by much. His hair is still dark but starting to recede at the temples. He's wearing flip-flops, plaid pajama bottoms, a Temple Owls T-shirt.

"What the hell are you doing on my property?"

"It's okay," Dave says, squinting in the sudden brightness, breaths heaving. "Take it easy—"

"Step away from my car."

"I'm on Town Watch," Dave says.

"Will you step the hell away from my car, please?"

"I'm Town Watch!" Dave shouts, but he takes a conciliatory step onto the grass. "I saw something," he says. "In your yard."

"You what?" The guy pauses, peering at him. The gold dome of the porch light shines above his head. "You saw something in my yard?"

"In that hedge," Dave says, pointing, still sucking air. "I saw somebody."

"Somebody?" the guy says. "Like what? A person?"

"Right." Dave nods. "Yes." He drops his hand to his side. His lungs are burning. Cold mud has seeped through his moccasins, oozed between his toes. In the glow of the porch, he can make out a pair of small pink sneakers, a hula hoop, a Little Mermaid backpack—a family younger than his, he thinks, and is hit with a blast of sadness.

The guy folds his arms across his chest. "What exactly did you see?"

Dave tries to focus, to call up the memory, but suddenly the details are deserting him. Was it an actual figure he saw moving in the bushes? Or just a shadow, a rustling of leaves? "I'm not sure," he admits.

"Well, what did it look like?" the guy presses.

"I don't know," Dave says. "It's hard to describe. I just—I had the sense of something."

"The sense of something?"

Dave closes his eyes, but his mind is a vast blankness. He saw no intruder, he thinks. He saw nothing. *It's kind of textbook, Dad*—the line returns to him like a blow.

"You said you're with Town Watch?"

Dave opens his eyes to find the guy scrutinizing him again, more closely. He considers what he looks like—the soaked moccasins, the muddy jeans, the old sweatshirt at least a size too small. "Dave," he tells him, straightening his glasses. "Townsend. I live at 258 Waverly—you can ask my partner. He's right out front in the Hummer—"

As if on cue, there's the sound of a branch snapping from the side of the house. Dean steps into the yard, wearing a broad, easy smile. "Everything okay back here?" He walks right up to the guy, hand extended. "Dean Kramer, 401 Trafalgar. Really sorry about all this."

"Scott," the guy says. "Cassidy." He sounds less wary: Maybe it's Dean's collared shirt, maybe his address. "You're Town Watch, too?"

"Afraid so," Dean says. "My partner here just went all gangbusters on me."

They share a laugh together at Dave's expense: a laugh that seems united in its ease, its suburban normality.

"He saw something, but now he can't remember what it was," Scott says, as if Dave isn't standing there. "Did you see it, too?"

"Afraid not," Dean says, but allows, "I was driving, though." He's standing on the bottom step, rocking on the balls of his feet. Scott squints into the middle distance, shaking his head slowly, in disappointment or disbelief. Talking together in the light of the porch, they look like actors on a stage.

Then, to Dave's surprise, Scott says, "If it's him again, I'll kill the punk."

"Who's that?" Dean says with an appreciative laugh.

"My daughter's goddamn boyfriend."

"Oh yeah?" Dean chuckles and slides his hands into his pockets, settling in. "How old?"

"Sixteen."

"Uh-oh. He have a car?"

"Yeah. Luckily, he's too much of an idiot to pass the test," Scott says. "He already failed twice. But it hasn't stopped him from sneaking her out of the house after curfew. Last week, they ran off to the 7-Eleven," he says, still shaking his head. Then he returns his attention to Dave. "Did this thing you saw look sixteen?"

The two fathers are both looking at him now, arms folded across their chests, waiting for an answer. But Dave can't bring himself to speak. He is paralyzed with jealousy, with grief—a daughter breaking curfew, sneaking out to the 7-Eleven. It sounds like the best problem in the world.

"Hey, man," Dean says, sounding startled. "Hey, partner. You okay?"

The yard has gone blurry. Dave realizes then that he's crying, his glasses two smeared pools of fog. He drops the baseball bat and it lands on the grass with a soft, almost soundless plunk.

"It's no big deal," Dean says uncomfortably. "Honest mistake. Could have happened to either one of us."

With shaky fingers, Dave fumbles his glasses off and drops them to the lawn. The porch light is dissolving, the yard swimming in his tears. "I need to go home," he manages as his voice breaks, and he covers his face with both hands.

"No problem," Dean says. "Whatever you say, partner." His voice is touched with concern. But the two men stand on the porch a moment longer, eyes averted, because they're embarrassed for him, or want to preserve his dignity, or they just can't bear to look.

Her Last Great Act

After her son died of cancer at thirty-five, Helen decided she wasn't attending any more funerals. A year later, she told the family she was no longer making potato soup. In December, she wouldn't be baking her Christmas cookies but would pass along the recipes to anyone who was interested. After a lifetime of doing for others, she was done.

Her new address, Apartment 16D in St. Mary's Senior Living Community, is the place she's lived for the past two years and eight months, but it isn't her home. Her children did their best trying to replicate the house on Oxford Avenue, choosing her most meaningful possessions and compressing them into a quarter of the space. The twin brass lamps with the horses for bases. The blue couch and matching wingback chair that was John's, her husband's, favorite seat. The candy dish, cream and green, shaped like a four-leaf clover. The Sears portrait of her six grandchildren, taken seven years ago. Elena was a baby then, Max not yet born; a picture of him had since been tucked into the corner of the frame.

The apartment has an odd smell, synthetic, like hotel carpet.

The walls are so thick that Helen hears nothing from outside. She knows this is meant to be a selling point—*Your privacy is our priority*, the brochure said—but Helen always liked to know what people were up to, to step out onto the stoop and chat with her neighbors, look out a window and see what's happening on the street. In 16D, the window is so high that all she can see is the roof of a Rite Aid, telephone wires, and clouds.

Her children had decided that she should move someplace smaller, which made sense after John, her husband, died. To pare down. Simplify. *It'll be easier*, they told her, and Helen trusted it was true. She'd raised her children right. But when the call came that the apartment was available, it was just nine months after John, her son—her *son*; it still made her heart stop—and Helen didn't want to move. She didn't want any more upheaval, any more loss or change, but the spot had opened up, and spots were hard to get, her children said, so she went.

It amazed her, how life went on. A birth, a death, and all without her husband there. People from the parish, from the old neighborhood. Their own son. After a lifetime experiencing everything together, now these things were hers alone. She took them in, found one more place to put them. Good news, bad. All with that hollowed-out place inside her, that deep emptiness that no one could see.

Helen remembers nothing about the move itself except the day her grandsons, Stevie and Alex and Joey, came to assemble the new bureau. Her old wooden one wouldn't fit through the bedroom door. While they worked, Helen cooked a feast—roast beef, twice-baked potatoes, a chocolate cake, a full meal in the middle of a Saturday—and when the dresser was upright, the three of them piled around her square table, smaller now without the leaf in the middle, wedged in the narrow space between her kitchen and TV. She loved having them there, elbows sprawling, knees banging. Joey ate three helpings of everything. A basketball star—he needed it. Helen wished she could have gone on feeding them forever. Before they left, she introduced them to her neighbors. *My grandsons*, she said, beaming, Joey's long arm slung around her shoulders. Alex politely shaking their hands. Stevie nodding, shuffling his feet the way he always did. Good boys.

There had been other things to get used to at St. Mary's: the stove, which was electric, after forty years of adjustable blue flames. The refrigerator with the freezer on the bottom instead of the top, with a pullout handle, like a drawer. The faucet in the bathroom, two spouts instead of one. The sudden urgency of sirens flashing in front of the building in the middle of the night.

After John, her son, died, Helen devoted herself to his wife and children. She went to their house every afternoon. She made dinners and tidied the kitchen, fed Elena and read her stories, gave Max his bath. Her daughters, Ann and Margie, had cautioned her that her daughter-in-law could be hard to help—*sometimes you have to push it*, they said—but with Helen, Lauren was never that way. Helen simply showed up and started doing things, sliding a few chicken breasts in the oven or washing off the sticky place mats, folding a load of laundry and putting another in the machine. *Thank you*, Lauren said with a tired smile, at the end of each day. Helen could tell that it helped, having her there. And Helen liked to be in her son's house. It made her feel closer to him. She kissed Elena. She held the baby, saw his face.

Helen doesn't make a habit of remembering. To sit and dwell on sad things—she doesn't see the point. But sometimes she can't help returning to that afternoon John and Lauren showed up on her porch on Oxford Avenue. Her husband had died just nine months before. *We have something we need to tell you, Mom*, her son said, and Helen knew right away the news wasn't good. The set of his jaw, the absence of the children. Her first thought was Lauren—she looked so stunned as they sat beside each other on the couch, holding hands. Right here, on that same couch.

In Apartment 16D, the weeks feel formless. Easy to forget which day it is, even with the calendar on the closet door: a pumpkin patch, October, 1997. Helen keeps up with small things. Getting her hair done every other Wednesday, balancing her bankbook, going to the Rite Aid for M&M's to keep the candy dish filled in case one of the grandchildren comes. She goes to Lauren's only once a week now. Max is in kindergarten, Elena in second grade. They have their own life, their own family. Helen doesn't want to be in the way. She marks her visits on the calendar, so she doesn't lose track of when she's been there. On weekends, she's picked up and taken away—a birthday party, a school concert, one of Joey's games—but the weekdays are all the same: church in the morning, coffee and the paper. Cans of soup, cups of tea, a chocolate after dinner (one). *Jeopardy!* and *Wheel of Fortune*, the final minutes of the Phillies game, just to get the score. The first few minutes of the news. Phone calls from her daughters, both or sometimes just one. The rosary, and a fitful night's sleep. Then church again, coffee again, the paper.

One evening, a Wednesday, her granddaughter Meghan calls. *Gran? I have a favor.* A historical interview, a project for her social studies class. Could she come interview her this weekend? It seems improbable that Helen has anything interesting to say, but she'll do it, of course. Anything they ask.

They show up on Saturday afternoon, Ann and Meghan, who is clutching a little recorder in her hand. A pretty Irish girl, her freckled face pink from the cold. She hugs Helen, as she always does. "Can I fix you something?" Helen says, and wishes she'd made a late lunch, an early dinner. Her granddaughter looks thin.

Ann looks at Meghan, who shakes her head and folds herself into a ball on the couch, spreading one of Helen's afghans over her knees. "No thanks," she says. "I'm not hungry."

"Well," Helen says. "At least have some candy." She sets the bowl on the coffee table, then takes a seat in the blue chair.

Meghan slides the candy to the very corner of the table and unscrolls a long paper time line. All the important historical junctures in Helen's lifetime are marked with big black dots. *The Roaring Twenties. World War II. The Great Depression.* Helen tells her the year she was born, 1918, and Meghan marks it with a red star. Then she pushes the button on the recorder. "Give me some wisdom, Gran," she says, a joke.

Helen looks at the recorder. "What should I say?"

"Anything," Meghan says. "I mean, your whole life is history."

"Is it?" Helen laughs.

"Why don't you tell her about a typical day," Ann suggests. "Back in the old neighborhood."

"It's nothing too interesting."

"That's okay. Just your daily routine. Little things."

Little things? That's all it was, little things. Cooking, cleaning, minding the babies. Dinner for six people, seven nights a week. The dinners weren't fancy, but they were good and warm. There was always a vegetable. And color—John liked color on a plate. They ate every bite, not a wasted mouthful. At this, Meghan laughs. "No wonder my family is so food-centric," she says.

Food-centric? Helen thinks.

Meghan begins picking at the M&M's as they talk of other things—clothes and music, the prices of eggs and milk and gasoline. It's easier than Helen expected, once she gets started, even though it's all a bunch of nothing—ordinary details, ordinary days. Her granddaughter takes notes with one hand, eats M&M's with the other. It isn't the way the boys eat them, in big handfuls. She ferries them to her mouth one by one like a little machine.

"What important things do you know now about life that you didn't when you were my age?" Meghan asks at the end, crunching candy. She is reading from her notes.

"Oh, well," Helen says. What to say? The truth is that life

in the end—even a long life, especially a long life—amounts to a handful of a very few things. The longer you live, the shorter the story. *Lived in Philadelphia her entire life. Moved twice: into the house on Oxford Avenue, out of the house on Oxford Avenue. Had seven grandchildren and four children. One died.*

"At your age?" Helen says with a laugh. "That was a long time ago."

Meghan says, "That's okay," and clicks the recorder off. The candy dish is empty.

"How about I make you some lunch?" Helen tries again, but Meghan shakes her head, rolling up her time line.

"Are you sure, Meg?" Ann says.

"I'm stuffed," Meghan says. Then she goes into the bathroom, and when Helen turns to her daughter, she is startled by the look of concern on Ann's face—about what, Helen has no idea. She's always worried about Ann, her first child. Even as a girl, she was so quiet and contained. When Meghan emerges, Ann quickly packs their things, and Meghan gives Helen a hug good-bye. Helen stands in the doorway waving until they're out of sight.

In November—December?—Helen notices the spot in her eye. Small and hazy, like watching the news when one of the faces is blurred. At first she thinks it's a smudge on her glasses, an eyelash, something she can rub off the lens or blink away. She waits a few days for it to disappear, but every morning wakes to find it there, floating on her bedroom ceiling, in the same place.

★　　★　　★

She remembers the night Lauren called her, just before midnight. *John's asking for you*, she said. *He wants you to come now. He wants you here.* They didn't want Helen driving herself so late, so she stood on her stoop, waiting to be picked up, aware of the precious minutes wasting as her son lay dying and she waited for a car she recognized. These were the longest, loneliest moments of her life. Finally, Margie's husband, Joe, appeared—he was driving too slowly, she remembers thinking, considering—and she hugged a sweater around her shoulders as she hurried down the steps. It was her white sweater—she knows this because she wore it for the next two days. When she arrived at the house, John was speaking to Elena. He told her that he loved her, and she was carried off to a neighbor's. Then her son got into bed and did not get back up again. He writhed in pain. The nurse arrived with morphine and for the next six hours, Ann and Margie and Patrick and Lauren sat around him, encircled him, hands on him. Watching him destroyed Helen, broke her forever. But in the moment she withstood it, wanting his final image of her to be of comfort, determined to be strong for her son.

She knows she should tell Patrick about the blur in her eye. Not only is he training to be a doctor, but an eye doctor. Silly that she hasn't asked. But Helen also knows that once she does, it will be out there. Could she be declared unfit to drive? To live on her own? St. Mary's is not a place for people who need assistance. *An active senior living community*, the brochure said. She's too afraid of what could happen next.

★   ★   ★

The Blessings

In December, there is gossip at St. Mary's: Two residents, Stan and Lila, have fallen in love. Both widowed, of course. They are now moving in together, consolidating their two small rooms into one. Helen is bothered. It isn't right, isn't fair, to their former spouses. It doesn't seem kind to the other residents, either, all of them people who lost their other halves. Helen says hello to them in the lounge, but that's it.

News comes. Abby, her oldest grandchild, has moved again—still Brooklyn, Ann explains, but a different part of Brooklyn. *Is it safe?* It's safe.

Patrick's wife, Kate, has a miscarriage. Helen hadn't known she was pregnant; the news breaks her heart. *It just wasn't meant to be,* Helen tells her, and Kate smiles lightly. Helen knows she doesn't agree. Kate isn't really Catholic—*raised Catholic,* is how she puts it. They've been doing fertility treatments, about which Helen keeps her mouth shut. "Thanks, Helen," Kate says; it's a title that happened without discussion. The others call her Mrs. Blessing, which she prefers.

Christmas lights appear in the lobby, wreaths on apartment doors. There's a sing-along one afternoon in the lounge—*all your holiday favorites!*—that Helen avoids. She goes to the bank and counts out thirty dollars for each grandchild, puts the money in envelopes, and writes their names on the fronts. She'll give them to their parents to buy a gift and sign her name.

On Christmas Day, her daughters make all her old cookies: the snowballs and jelly thumbprints and almond moons. Meghan gives everyone a gift—*something really special*, she announces, a stack of red binders in her arms. Bound copies of the historical interview. *A Journey with Gran*, it's called, on a sticker decorated with berries and holly. Helen feels embarrassed for her story to be given so much fanfare, even more embarrassed when she begins to read: *According to my mom, taking care of my uncle was Helen Blessing's last great act. But in my grandmother's lifetime, there were many . . .*

It goes on to talk about all the great things Helen's done—raising her children, taking care of a baby when John was off fighting in Germany. As if they were paying her tribute. Where had all this come from? Had Helen even said these things? All she remembers talking about were little things, dinners and bus tokens, but this paints her in grand, heroic strokes. Raising a family, caring for her dying son. *Great acts.* Is that how they saw it? These things aren't great. It was what you did, was what family did. Dangerous to see it as something noble.

January is cold and quiet, largely eventless. Alex turns twenty and goes back to Penn, a sophomore. Another blur appears, and another, like drops of rain on glass. Once, when Margie is visiting, Helen notices her looking closely at the silverware. She rewashes a handful of forks.

There are activities on the calendar at St. Mary's, which looks just like the school cafeteria menu stuck to Lauren's refrigerator door. *Exercise Class! Day Trip to Atlantic City!* Helen finds them slipped under her door and throws them in the trash. *One of the most important advantages of our communities is the opportunity for socialization,* the brochure said. But these activities are for people whose lives are empty, whose children never come to visit. Helen doesn't need that kind of thing. She has her family: She needs nothing else.

One evening, Ann drops by unannounced. Helen knows she's come about her eyes. The dirty forks, the half-gallon of milk that Margie discovered past its expiration date—who knows what else. Helen sits in the blue wingback chair, hands folded tightly in her lap. She is ready to concede to whatever humiliation comes next, but as Ann sits on the couch, she says: "Mother, I have to tell you something." Her voice is calm, but Helen sees the deep lines on her face. "It's about Meghan."

"Meghan?" Helen says—a bolt of alarm.

"She's sick... well, no, not sick," Ann says, pausing. "She has an eating disorder. Bulimia."

Helen has heard of such things before, food things. Ann explains how it works, the eating and the throwing up. They're seeing doctors, Ann assures her; they're getting it fixed. Helen doesn't know what it all means exactly, but she starts saying an extra rosary for Meghan every night.

Church, coffee, the paper. There is no baseball now, no football. Her legs hurt, but she keeps this to herself.

One night, three in the morning, an ambulance comes racing up to St. Mary's. Helen sees the red lights flashing on the Rite Aid across the street. Stan, she hears the next morning. A heart attack in his sleep. Probably Lila was there in bed beside him. Helen goes to the Rite Aid and buys a sympathy card, slips it under her door. She feels sorry for her, having to go through it twice.

She remembers the night that John, her husband, died. How she knew immediately that he was gone. She felt the air change in the room, the sudden stillness. She gave herself one hour: the last hour it would be just the two of them. She talked to him, prayed for him, cried and smoothed his hair and straightened his clothes. Then she picked up the phone.

On a Tuesday in late March, she drives to Lauren's. She hasn't been there in nearly a week. She drives slowly, squinting into the sharp, late-afternoon sun. At first, when the police car appears behind her, lights going, it doesn't even occur to Helen that it could be meant for her. She sees the car fill her mirror and slows down to get out of his way, then is shocked when the policeman gets out and approaches her window, taps a knuckle on the glass.

"License and registration."

The officer looks young, and not particularly kind. Disappointed, maybe, to be dealing with an old lady. Helen is trembling as she tries to pry the license from her wallet.

"Just a minute," she says, shaking, but finally manages to dislodge it. "Just a minute, Officer, please." She pushes through the glove compartment, looking for the registration, wishing John were here—*it isn't fair, without him here!* She rifles through the papers, starting to panic, when there it is, bless him, clearly marked in her husband's lovely penmanship: *Registration, Auto.*

"Do you know you ran a stop sign back there?"

Had she?

"No," she says. "I didn't see it."

It was probably the wrong thing, to admit it. The young policeman looks at the car, walking slowly around the front bumper, examining it as if she's some sort of escaped criminal. What on earth is he looking for?

Finally he returns to his police car. Helen can only wait. It is the worst part, the most excruciating part, sitting there on display. She is aware of the other cars slowing down and glancing over. She keeps her head down, turned to the side. Her window is still open and she's cold, but to close it would mean turning the engine on, which she probably isn't allowed to do. So she sits, shivering and trying to blink away the blurred patches, her eyes pooling repeatedly with tears. Will he figure out that she shouldn't be driving? Make her get out and do an eye test on the spot?

When the policeman comes back, he hands her a ticket for eighty dollars—eighty!—and Helen thanks him. Then he returns to his car, and she prays he'll just drive away, but he sits and watches until she's forced to pull away first.

Helen drives twenty miles an hour the rest of the way to Lauren's. Her hands are tingling on the wheel. Cars honk at her for going so slowly, but she can't make her foot press any harder. When finally she pulls into Lauren's driveway, crosses her porch, and steps inside her warm house, she feels as though she's washed ashore.

"Gran!" Elena waves. She's on the couch under a blanket, holding a bowl of Goldfish crackers and watching a cartoon on TV. Helen sits beside her, puts a hand on her knee.

Lauren pops out of the kitchen to say hello as Max comes running toward her. "Gran's here!" he shouts.

"Easy, Max," Lauren says. "Are you feeling okay, Mrs. Blessing?"

"I'm fine," Helen says as Max jumps into her lap.

"Max, let Gran catch her breath," Lauren says, studying her. "Can I get you a drink?"

"Well, maybe. I am a little thirsty. I'll get it—"

But Lauren has already disappeared. Helen blinks around the living room. Her pulse is still beating fast. Clouds float on the wall, on the hearth, which is decorated for Easter, with pictures of bunnies and Jesuses the children made. On the mantel, a photo of her handsome son, holding his children on his knees. Lauren appears with a glass of iced tea. "Thank you," Helen says, and takes a sip.

"Another!" Max cries as the show ends.

"Just one more, then dinner," Lauren says, and the children bicker about which episode to watch, but Lauren says, "It's Max's turn," and the argument subsides, and they sit watching, limbs flopped over one another, Max sucking on his fingers the way he always does.

Helen moves to get up, but Lauren waves her off. "Stay put and relax," she says. "Really. It's just spaghetti." Then she heads back to the kitchen to finish with dinner and Helen can't help herself—she stays. She is so relieved to just sit there, so overcome with exhaustion and gratitude she could sink right into the couch. She sits beside her grandchildren and finishes her glass of tea and resolves not to tell Lauren, or anyone, what happened. It's too embarrassing. She doesn't want them worrying.

When her drink is gone and her pulse has calmed, Helen stands. In the kitchen, she finds Lauren draining a pot of spaghetti into a colander, steam billowing around her face.

She's a lovely girl, Lauren. She doesn't deserve what she's been dealt. In the months after John died, her house had a desperate, floundering feeling, but nearly four years later, things are different. They've absorbed their new reality; this is their life now. And Lauren is still so young—too young.

"I hope you know, Lauren," Helen says, "you're too young to spend the rest of your life alone."

Lauren turns in surprise, holding a stack of plates.

"No one expects you to," Helen adds as Lauren's eyes grow teary.

"Thank you," she says. "That's very kind."

Helen nods. A blur floats near Lauren's cheek. Then a cry goes up from the living room—"Mommy!"—and Lauren sets down the plates and goes to gather the children. Helen finishes setting the table, fills the plastic cups with milk, and the four of them sit and eat. Elena recounts her day in second grade, where she learned about arachnids. Max sings the wheels on the bus song.

Then Lauren takes them upstairs for baths and Helen does the dishes, filling the sink with warm, soapy water. She sponges off the table, sweeps the floor. She goes upstairs, past the smell of sweet drained bubbles in the toy-filled bathtub, past the bedroom where her son lay in so much pain. She kisses her grandchildren, says their prayers with them. Says good night to Lauren, who is removing her earrings. "Oh, you're leaving?" she says. "Well—thank you. We'll see you soon." Then Helen eases her car out of the long driveway and drives slowly back to Apartment 16D, where she'll call Patrick first thing in the morning. For now, she writes the check for eighty dollars to "City of Philadelphia," stamps and leaves it for the mailman, puts her car keys in a drawer, and resolves never to drive again.

Cataracts, Patrick tells her. Eyedrops, pills. So it begins.

In April, baseball is back on television. At night, watching, Helen props her feet on a pillow. Her legs hurt, her knees.

The eleven o'clock news is all nothing but tragedies. Shootings, robberies, a missing baby. Helen decides that she's done watching the news.

At Easter dinner, she watches Meghan. She eats nothing while the rest of them heap their plates, but later she devours three desserts.

At Joey's high school graduation, Helen's feet hurt so badly that she has to sit when the rest of them are standing. He wins an award: Student-Athlete of the Year. She memorizes the name of it and tells everyone she sees.

Edema, the doctor says. He prescribes pills for the swelling. She takes them every day, or means to, though sometimes at the end of the week it doesn't all add up—number of pills, number of days.

Her legs still hurt, and other things. Joints, bones.

★　　★　　★

On a Sunday in early June Patrick appears at her door. Helen knows his knock, the fast tap-tap-tap. He was always the funny one, the tease. When she opens the door, the sight of him fills her with joy—she loves her son, her sons.

"Well!" she says. "This is a surprise!"

"Hey, Mom," he says, kissing her cheek.

Ten past four—not dinnertime, but close enough. He could have told her he was coming. She could have made something. A simple dinner, grilled cheese and tomato soup.

"Can I get you something?" Helen asks as Kate steps in behind him, carrying the spring air on her clothes, a hint of perfume. Kate doesn't cook. It's always saddened Helen to think of her son without warm meals to come home to. Once, she saw Kate microwave a cup of tea.

"Hi, Helen," Kate says, kissing her cheek. She looks happy, Helen thinks. She is a pretty girl, but she's always had an edge to her; the happiness makes her look softer.

"I would have made something, if I'd known you were coming—"

"That's okay, Mom," Patrick says.

"Really, Helen," says Kate, unbelting her coat, "you don't need to wait on us."

But that's where she's wrong, Helen thinks: She thinks cooking is subservient, ungratifying, something you do for others and get nothing in return.

They sit on the couch, Helen in the blue wing chair. Her son and his wife are smiling, sitting so close their knees are touching. It's good to see Patrick happy. For so long, he looked so sad. It's all she wants for him, for all of them.

"We have something to tell you," Patrick says.

They can hardly contain their joy. Looking at their faces, Helen feels a bolt of longing—she misses John. How she wishes he were here. "We wanted you to be the first to know," Kate says. Helen knows it will be good news, this time. She smiles at them, folds her hands in her lap, and waits to receive it.

Happy Face, Sad Face

Alex's girlfriend was beautiful. This wasn't subjective: The world would agree. She was tall, with high cheekbones and olive skin and long dark hair so glossy and smooth, it looked like wet paint. But what Alex liked most about Rebecca's appearance was how she wore her emotions right on the surface—eyes filling with empathy when she talked about her research subjects or one hand rising instinctively to her mouth when she was moved by a movie, cheeks flushing with excitement when they signed the lease on the apartment and moved in their things.

They had been living together at Princeton for one semester. Both of them were graduate students, but in different subjects, which Rebecca felt was good for their relationship. Alex was studying chemistry, Rebecca urban planning; for her thesis, she had interviewed dozens of homeless people in Trenton, analyzing their narratives for the social and political factors contributing to the city's demise. Rebecca had a talent for listening. She looked right into your eyes, nodding and asking thoughtful questions; she had a way of holding her face so it seemed she was mirroring just what you felt. She had a way of getting Alex to open up, too—something that, historically, he'd always had trouble doing. *You're so hard to read*, he'd heard from other girlfriends, less serious girlfriends who lasted for two or three months in college. He remembered one, Miranda, a French major, saying, *It's just that you never talk about anything*, and Alex was perplexed—didn't he talk all the time? Obviously there was some other kind of talking he wasn't doing, some layer of himself he wasn't showing. Maybe what he'd needed was a girlfriend like Rebecca to coax it out.

The vacation was Rebecca's idea, to celebrate the end of the school year. They were going to the coast of Spain, a village in the foothills of the Sierra Nevada mountains near the Mediterranean Sea. The Sierra Nevadas, the Mediterranean—Alex could hardly believe he was actually going to these places; until now they had felt purely academic, names he'd learned once for a test. He and Rebecca frequently browsed the online pictures of Hotel Plaza Lorca. A printout of their suite—the bedroom the size of their entire apartment—hung from their refrigerator door. The apartment in Princeton was less an apartment than one-quarter of a house broken into clumsy, inexact chunks. Their chunk consisted of two rooms and a wrought-iron balcony so narrow that it could fit only two people at a time. But it was only a few blocks from campus, and the library, where Alex disappeared to most nights. This had nothing to do with Rebecca; he'd always needed time alone. And he'd always loved the feeling of libraries—the quiet rustling of the pages, the conversations he knew wouldn't rise above a hush.

Rebecca was one of those people who actively avoided solitude; even her research involved people. She loved hosting dinner parties and was good at it, though not in the same way Alex's aunts and mother were. In his family, to be the host was to be unobtrusive, make sure everyone was taken care of; the goal was to disappear. But for Rebecca, hosting was a performance, part of the big dinner party show. She was always trying out new recipes, fastidiously wrapping melon in prosciutto, figs in bacon, experimenting with seasonal cocktails. She thought in advance about who would sit where and have what in common. She liked conversation, real conversation—no *empty talk*, she said. Sometimes, at the parties, as Alex's head swam with wine and he struggled to look engaged, he felt a bolt of longing for his family, their mild conversations about ordinary things, sports scores or people from their parish, and the food, which was predictable, unfussy, unpretentious: ham salads and roast beef, potatoes in hollowed-out brown skins, cobbled chunks of pickle wrapped in ham, speared with toothpicks. This was not subjective, either: The pickles tasted better than the figs.

Two nights before the Spain trip, an hour before friends are set to arrive (another dinner party), his sister Abby calls. They talk more often, since their parents' divorce.

"Mom's on an honesty kick," Abby moans when he answers. "She's telling me how their marriage was never healthy, and they never communicated really...I don't need to know all this."

"Me either," Alex says. "Stop it, please." He snatches a heel of bread from the cutting board, where Rebecca is slicing a loaf to make bruschetta.

"She feels guilty that they didn't recognize all this stuff sooner," Abby goes on. "So now she's dumping thirty years' worth on me."

Alex chews, only half listening. He doesn't point out the irony: His sister complains about their mother dumping on her, then turns around and dumps on him.

"Consider yourself lucky," Abby says. "You're the boy. Meghan's the fragile egg." She pauses then, as if sensing his inattention. "So how's this Rebecca?"

"This Rebecca is fine," Alex says. "She's good."

Rebecca waves a bread knife and calls, "Hi, sister Abby!"

"I can't believe I haven't met your girlfriend yet," Abby says.

As if Abby's so available, Alex thinks. She's always moving, always attached to some new boyfriend. He's met a few, but it doesn't seem worth the effort to really get to know them. They're usually short-lived.

"Yeah, well," he says. "We live in Princeton, New Jersey. You know where to find us." He can't resist reminding her, "Meghan's been here."

"Meghan's local," Abby says, and Alex drops the subject, even though he knows it's more than this. Meghan is also more devoted. It had been her idea to come visit them over her spring break; from their mom's house, it involved taking three trains.

"But you're going home next weekend, right?" Abby says. "Is Rebecca coming?"

"Oh," Alex says, and stops chewing, the lump of bread lodged in his cheek. Guilt engulfs him like a wave. "No. I mean—I can't." It was his fault, his idiotic oversight: When they booked the Spain tickets, it didn't occur to him that that weekend would be Uncle John's anniversary. On Saturday, the family is having a party, as they do every year: a Mass at St. Bonaventure's, a barbecue at Aunt Lauren's. "I totally forgot. I feel really badly. I just didn't think of it when we booked the tickets—"

"Oh, my God!" Abby cuts him off. "Spain!"

"Right," he says. "Spain."

"Is that now?"

"Almost. We fly out on Monday."

"Be careful, Al," she says. "There are new security regulations now, you know."

As if the entire world doesn't know. As if his mom isn't constantly reminding him, worrying about him flying so soon after the attacks.

"Yeah," he says. "I'm aware."

"Did you remember to get a passport?"

"Of course I remembered to get a passport."

From the counter, Rebecca lets out an amused chuckle.

"Are you going to propose?" Abby asks.

"What?" Alex exclaims. "No!" He lets out a startled laugh and glances at Rebecca. Propose? It hadn't even occurred to him. Was it supposed to have occurred to him? Rebecca looks over her shoulder, face crinkled—*what's so funny?*—and he rolls his eyes.

"Al?" Abby is saying. "Are you there?"

He leaves the kitchen quickly, stepping onto the balcony, where he eases the door shut and lowers his voice. "Why would you think that?"

"I don't know. I mean, you've been together over a year, you're taking her on a romantic European vacation . . . it's probably at least crossed her mind."

Alex stares at the street, the sidewalk scattered with wilted pink petals. The late May air is muggy and fragrant, tickling the back of his throat. *Taking her*—well, this wasn't quite true. Not only had the trip been Rebecca's idea, her parents were footing the bill. Alex stiffens—could her parents be expecting a proposal, too? He's never even thought about marrying Rebecca. He tries to picture what life would be like: a long march of dinner parties, an endless conversation. As his sister keeps talking—*if we learned anything from Mom and Dad*—Alex tries to imagine the proposal, kneeling on a whitewashed Spanish street, but it's like picturing a scene from a movie with other people in it.

"I mean," Abby says, "do you *want* to marry her?"

Alex looks down at the tops of people's heads moving along the sidewalk, a student headed toward the library, stooped under the weight of his enormous backpack, and wishes briefly that he were him. "I don't know," he says, which is true.

Rebecca has met both of Alex's parents—who each came out to Princeton for dinner last year, on separate occasions—and Meghan, but he's resisted taking her home to Philly and introducing her to the entire clan. He isn't sure why. Rebecca is different from his family (an atheist, for one thing), but Alex is pretty sure he isn't worried about them disapproving. (He can just imagine how his cousin Stephen would look her up and down, then mutter: *How'd you manage that, Al?*) Maybe he's worried about what Rebecca will think of them? The women sitting around the dinner table, the slow conversation about small things. *Empty talk*—it might qualify. Or maybe he just doesn't feel like stirring up all the excitement, the attention—

some adult version of the crowd snapping pictures at his senior prom—or dragging Rebecca through the aftermath of the divorce. Since last year, his dad has been renting an apartment; his mom lives in the house alone. It's just simpler without Rebecca there.

Rebecca's parents, Jane and Douglas, are still married. They live in Connecticut and have a summer house in Maine. Alex spent a weekend there last August, where they had long, boozy dinners on the deck overlooking the ocean. They talked about books and films (they were the kind of people who called movies *films*) and asked about Alex's research. He talked way more than usual, loosened by the wine and the questions. They had just returned from Africa and were astounded—borderline offended, it seemed—that Alex had never been abroad.

"Never?" Jane said. "Never left the country? Not even Europe? Oh, you need to go to Europe, Alex. Or Africa." She appealed to Douglas. "Don't you think Alex needs to see Africa?" she said, as if seeing Africa were reserved for certain kinds of people, people intellectually sophisticated enough to appreciate it.

"Watch out," Douglas said with a weary affect that seemed somehow for show. "She'll stuff you in her suitcase."

"What about your family, Alex?" Jane pressed. "Have they done much traveling?"

"Not—internationally," Alex said, thinking of the Jersey shore. "Actually, I'm not sure my parents have ever left the country, either."

"What?" Jane grabbed her face and squeezed, raking her fingers down her cheeks. She seemed a little drunk, he thought. "Well, I just don't understand it," she said. "To not go out and *see* the world. It's a problem in the whole United States."

Seeing the world costs money, Alex felt like saying. *And these are my parents, not the whole United States.* But he'd offered the information; he must have known where it would lead. He thought of his cousin Stephen, the family screwup. Their birthdays were just three weeks apart, but their lives had gone in opposite directions. Stephen, who never left Northeast Philadelphia. Stephen, who lately barely left Aunt Margie's basement. *Douchebags,* Alex imagined his cousin saying. *And what kind of asshole goes by Douglas instead of Doug?*

"I told you," said Jane. She draped a finger in Alex's direction. "This one is an *old soul.*" Her face was soft and pink, with that smug, self-satisfied expression that older people seemed to get when they were drinking. It made Alex embarrassed. His aunts might have a glass of wine or two, but they never got like this. "He's not a talker," Jane went on—which was ironic, because Alex had never talked so much in his life—"but it's always the quiet ones you have to watch out for."

"He's not always quiet," Rebecca said, and leaned over to kiss his ear.

When Alex first met Rebecca, he joked that he was just another of her research subjects. But the truth was, it felt good to tell her things. In bed—for some reason, these conversations usually happened in bed—he told her what a nerd he'd been in high school, how he used to play *D&D* and had this insane mop of hair. How he didn't kiss a girl until he was sixteen and lost his virginity to his senior prom date, Debbie. (*Oh, my God*, she said, laughing. *Such a fantastic cliché! And her name was Debbie?*)

Alex had never thought of himself as having a particularly interesting life, but Rebecca found it fascinating, especially the parts about his family. He told her about Meghan and her eating problems. How she threw away her lunches in high school and made him promise not to tell. How after it came out that she had bulimia, their parents consulted a million doctors, but it wasn't until Meghan's freshman year of college—only a few months before Alex met Rebecca—that she took a semester off and went to this outpatient rehab place. It was there that the five of them had to meet the family counselor and everything cracked open—their parents admitted they were having problems, had been having problems. They were separating. His dad was leaving. (*They never fought?* Rebecca said. *Not once?*) How Meghan had screamed and cried in the counselor's office, but shortly after, she'd finally started to get better.

"Amazing," Rebecca said, nodding knowingly. "That's what they say about bulimics. If there's some family secret, and it comes out, it gives the sufferer relief."

Sufferer—words like this made Alex uncomfortable. They sounded too grand, too elevated above his actual life.

It's seven in the morning when they touch down at Málaga Airport, though it feels like midnight in his bones. Alex read that jet lag is partly psychological—you know you're supposed to be tired, so you feel tired—but as he drives the rented Fiat down the highway, squinting into the sharp sunlight, the heaviness in his head is real. Rebecca is impossibly alert, sitting up straight and holding her blowing hair out of her face. "There's the Med!" she yells, pointing to a wrinkle of blue in the distance. "See?"

The highway is easy enough to navigate, but once they start the climb into the mountains, the road becomes narrow and twisting. Starchy white villas perch haphazardly in the foothills, as if they might go sliding right down the side. "Gorgeous," Rebecca breathes while Alex guides the car slowly around the hairpin turns, his long legs crammed into the small front seat. The road is flanked by olive trees, the live ones vertical and green and the dead ones leaning at stiff black forty-five-degree angles. He brakes hard for a goat crossing the road, an old man zipping by on a moped. A fancy-looking restaurant rises from the dust like a mirage. A mile or so later, Alex spots a hand-lettered sign for the village and follows the arrow down more steep turns. He was sure he'd recognize their hotel from the picture on their refrigerator, but Hotel Plaza Lorca looks just like every other building here—white walls, a ceramic tile sign, a bright splash of flowers. A green lizard sits like a handprint on the wall. The owner, a short, unsmiling woman, shows them to their room, where warm air drifts lazily through the screenless windows. Rebecca tips her, then sighs and kicks off her shoes. "Let's wash the plane off," she says, so they end up showering and having sex and napping off the jet lag (even though Alex read that's what you're not supposed to do). When they finally reemerge, dressed, he looks at his watch: two fifteen p.m., U.S. time.

"I'm starving," Rebecca says, hooking his elbow.

"Maybe we should ask the woman for a recommendation?"

"Nah. Let's just see what we find," she says.

Even at this hour (eight fifteen, Spain), the sun is high and warm. After nine months in a study carrel, it's good to feel the sun. They wander into the village, a jumble of sloppy hills and cobblestones. The air is thick and drowsy and smells like flowers. All the houses are white—to reflect the sun, of course—and crowded closely together, strung with colorful laundry on clotheslines. Alex cannot imagine living in such tight quarters. At least they all have balconies, infinitely nicer than their balcony in Princeton, and all of them face the sea. In fact, the entire town seems angled toward the glimpse of blue water, like thirsty flowers tilted toward the sunlight. At the crest of a hill, they see a little pink church: Saint Isidore. Alex wishes his mother could see it. He looks again at his watch—nearly three, U.S.—and pictures a Tuesday, his mother dismissing her fourth graders in their plaid uniforms, collecting her papers, driving slowly home.

"How about this," Rebecca says, and stops.

The restaurant has tables on the sidewalk and a chalkboard sign. The other diners all seem like locals, speaking in loud Spanish and smoking cigarettes. A few thin cats roam the place, rubbing people's ankles. As they take a seat, Alex is aware of how touristy they must look, with his pasty skin and their sunglasses—Rebecca's are huge and tinted green, something a celebrity would wear—but Rebecca owns her tourist status, the same way she owns everything about herself, charming their waiter by trying to chat with him in her halting Spanish. She orders for them both.

"Bella," he says, beaming, and returns minutes later with a pitcher of sangria.

Alex fills the glasses, and Rebecca proposes a toast. "To *España,"* she says, and holds her glass aloft, waiting for him to speak.

"To us," he adds, feeling corny, but Rebecca looks pleased. They clink and drink, and she tosses back her hair, expelling a deep, dreamy sigh. "I'm so glad we're here," she says, slipping off her sandals and propping her bare feet in Alex's lap. "It reminds me of how essential it is to get out of your environment every now and again."

Alex nods, sipping at his drink.

"It makes life at home seem so much smaller, doesn't it? It gives you such perspective. The world is so much bigger. Things back there just feel less important."

In truth, Alex is having just the opposite reaction. Being so far away from home makes everything there seem bigger, more important—but he doesn't feel like debating the point. He drains his glass and pours another.

"So tomorrow," Rebecca says.

"Tomorrow."

"To the beach."

"To the beach," Alex agrees.

She pushes her sunglasses on top of her head and smiles. "Is it possible we've been together over a year and I've never seen you on a beach?"

"No," he says. "You have."

"Where?"

"Maine. With your parents."

She laughs. "A beach in a *sweatshirt* doesn't count, my dear."

Alex laughs, too, just as the paella arrives in a sizzling cast-iron pan. He eats selectively, nudging the spindly shrimp antennae to the side, washing down the briny bites with more sangria. Rebecca, of course, deconstructs her shellfish like a pro. "Next dinner party," she announces, tapping her fork on the rim of the plate. "Paella. It'll be Spanish themed—we'll make our friends more jealous of us than they already are." She presses her smooth knees against his under the table, and as she beams at him, a heady feeling sweeps through his entire body, the flush of sangria, recognition of his own good luck.

For dessert, Rebecca orders churros and hot chocolate so thick they eat it with spoons. When Alex glances at his watch, he's surprised to see how long they've been here; still, he feels no pressure to leave. Everything feels slower in Spain, he thinks. Not inattentive, just unhurried. Even the sun seems to set more slowly, clinging to the sky. By the time the waiter clears the dishes, Alex is slightly drunk, and the wine has brought a deep rosy color to Rebecca's cheeks. Looking at her, in a foreign country surrounded by strangers, Alex is reminded of how beautiful she is. He puts his hand on her arm, her skin warm from the sun.

"You look pretty," he says.

She smiles and kisses him, tasting like chocolate. "I think Spain is going to be good for you," she says.

In the session with the family counselor, after his father said that he was leaving and Meghan had a meltdown, Alex started going numb. Sitting there in his chair, he felt as if he were being consumed by pins and needles, as if his whole body were falling asleep and dragging him under. *Alex?* The counselor had pinched his arm. *Can you feel that?*

"You were shutting down," Rebecca said when he described it. They were in bed, as usual, but this particular story had her sitting up, clutching a pillow in her lap. She sounded almost excited, as if seeing a species she'd only heard existed but had never seen. "You were protecting yourself."

Alex laughed uneasily. "From what?"

She looked at him with sad affection, as if his naïveté were endearing. "From the pain you were feeling in that moment," she said.

Meghan had recounted this same scene—her part in it, anyway—when she came to visit them in Princeton. *At least you were expressing how you felt*, Rebecca reassured her. Alex was listening to their voices drift in from the balcony to where he sat reading on the couch. When Meghan had arrived that afternoon, the three of them hung out together, touring the campus and getting overpriced lattes, but gradually his sister and his girlfriend formed an intense clique of two. They were a match made in heaven, Alex realized; he was surprised he hadn't anticipated this. Rebecca, the compassionate listener, and Meghan with so much to tell. Right away their conversation assumed that gentle, meaningful gravity that Alex associated with women talking (it amazed him, how quickly girls got right into things), and he knew he should be glad that they were bonding but instead felt annoyed for no reason he could discern. Having his sister around, Alex felt cast back in an old role, like the person he'd been in high school—awkward, clammed up, agitated in some vague way—while Rebecca slid easily into the part of an older sister or a cool aunt, the one you'd call if you needed to be bailed out of jail. *You've stopped purging now completely, right?* she asked Meghan, all three of them crowded in the kitchen, the girls chopping vegetables for dinner while Alex hovered unhelpfully, drinking a beer. *I don't have to police the bathroom door?* Rebecca's candor made him nervous—his family never talked to Meghan this way. But his sister answered easily, unfazed by the questions. After dinner, the two of them migrated to the balcony, wrapped in huge sweaters and sipping mojitos, while Alex sat alone inside. He longed to go to the library but knew that he should stay. Not that Meghan would care. His mother would. *My family had no idea how out of control I was,* Meghan was saying, Rebecca responding with that affirming murmur Alex had heard so often that he'd started to think of it as his. *I puked ten times after every meal,* she said. *I was puking in shoeboxes in my room*—had he known this? He pictured his sister's room, its plush rug and pink curtains, the giant, heavy-headed panda bear sagging in the corner. *When I tasted stomach acid, I knew I was done,* she said with a sad laugh. He was startled, alarmed; he was irrationally jealous. How could anything he told Rebecca now compare with this? At midnight, Alex took his book to bed but still could hear the dip and rise of their voices, clinks of their glasses, like an adult slumber party, until finally, at nearly two a.m., Rebecca climbed into bed beside him. Her cheeks were flushed, her breath sweet. A shred of mint was caught in her teeth.

"It's totally amazing you two are siblings," she said.

"Tell me about it," Alex snapped, then felt guilty. He attempted a laugh. He curled toward Rebecca, touching her shoulder experimentally, but her eyes were closed, hands pressed palm to palm beneath her cheek, breathing through her open mouth. She was already asleep.

On Wednesday, Alex and Rebecca drive in the direction of the water and end up in a town called Nerja, a strip of outdoor

restaurants and crowded beaches at the edge of the Mediterranean Sea. Alex is amazed to find the Mediterranean looks
exactly the way it does in pictures—that same bright, unreal
blue.

"Race you," Rebecca says, grinning, as they drop their stuff
on the sand. She strips down to a white bikini and runs for the
water, where she dives under immediately. Alex follows her in,
but slowly, watching his feet. The water is startlingly clear, calm
as a lake—the opposite of the ocean at the Jersey shore, foamy
and green and thick with seaweed. The sand is different, too,
more like pebbles than grains. His family would probably hate
it, he thinks.

As he wades in deeper, Alex thinks of the stir his trip must
be causing back home—surely the entire family must know his
itinerary, calling his mother for updates on where he is and
what he's doing. The same key words will be repeated over and
over, spreading through the family like a game of telephone:
*the southeast coast, the Sierra Nevadas. Yes, the actual Mediterranean
Sea!*

The water is cool, the sun burning his shoulders. Rebecca
floats a few feet away, eyes closed. Alex quietly paddles over to
her and pokes the middle of her back. "Boo."

"Oh!" Rebecca says, splashing upright. "You startled me."

He smiles at her, takes both her elbows, and places her arms
around his neck. Then he wraps his arms around her shoulders. He's starting to feel a little like a different person in Spain,
more confident and loose, almost like he's acting. But as he
leans down to kiss her, eyes level with his own wrist, he sees
that he forgot to take his watch off—it's soaked. "Shit," he says,
dropping his arms. "My watch."

Rebecca frowns. "Isn't it waterproof?"

"I don't know," he says, and wonders why he doesn't.

"Well, we'll buy you a new one," she says, and shrugs, which bugs him. The watch was a graduation gift from his dad, and he's sure it wasn't cheap. "We can haggle for it," she adds. "Have I mentioned I'm an excellent haggler?"

She is—just this morning, she bartered her way into a leather bag—but Alex turns toward the shore. "I've got to take it off," he says.

"Oh, stay," she says. "If it's ruined, it's already ruined."

The logic is sound, but Alex has to at least try to save it. "I can't."

"Of course you can't," Rebecca replies—was that an edge to her voice? If so, she corrects it instantly, smiling. "I'm going to stay in a little longer," she says.

Alex holds his arm above the water, like a limb in a cast, as he heads back toward the sand. He remembers Abby saying that traveling can underscore people's differences and thinks this might be true. Rebecca is lax with possessions, he's more careful. Rebecca is the kind of person who wanders aimlessly, while he asks for directions. But maybe these are the good kinds of differences, he thinks, the kinds that complement instead of clash.

On the sand, Alex weaves his way through the sunbathers, trying not to wince on the pebbles. The Spanish people are all darkly tan, slick with oil. Some women are topless—he averts his eyes, although he doesn't think it's required. On the towel, he unstraps his soaking watch—examining it to see if any water got in the glass; it did—and lays it in the sun. He puts his sunglasses on, picks up his book. But instead of reading, he finds himself watching Rebecca. She's the farthest person from the shore. For minutes, she swims back and forth, slow and languid, her long body skimming the horizon, dark head gleaming in the sun. When finally she comes out, Alex notices other men notice her, staring unabashedly as she saunters toward him. Watching her approach, Alex considers again what it would be like to be married to Rebecca: a life of adventure, he thinks. Of travel. Of weeks like this.

"What?" she asks, standing over him, squeezing her long wet hair in her fist.

"What?"

"You," she says, and lets the hair drizzle onto his pale chest. "You have this big goofy grin on your face."

At the end of the session with the family counselor, she recommended Alex get some therapy of his own. That was how she put it—*get some therapy*, like taking his car in for an oil change. Alex didn't want to get some therapy. Just because his family was screwed up, that automatically meant *he* was screwed up? But he went, because he always did what he was supposed to and because in some distant part of himself, he was afraid she could be right.

His therapist's name was Jocelyn, and Alex saw her a total of three times. Jocelyn was thick all over—her waist, neck, upper arms. She wore long skirts and noisy silver jewelry that rattled when she moved. As Alex talked, Jocelyn's eyelids drooped slowly, over and over, and he couldn't tell if she was dreamily listening or falling asleep in the chair. She asked about his family, his sister. She asked him to describe how he was feeling. He thought for a moment, then said, "Tired."

"But tired isn't an emotion, is it?" Jocelyn replied, with a triumphant note, as if his answer had somehow proven her right.

So Jocelyn gave him a list of emotions: a worksheet with different cartoon faces on it expressing different feelings. Happy Face, Sad Face, Angry Face. He felt as if he were in first grade. "For homework," she said, she wanted him to keep a journal. Three times a day, he was to stop and write down what he was feeling. Alex did it, because he always did his homework, but he felt ridiculous. After finishing a lab or studying for an exam—it was his second semester at Princeton—he'd find a moment alone and extract the little spiral notebook from the bottom of his backpack. He would stand very still, trying to feel what he was feeling. Finally he wrote: *Exhausted. Stressed.* Or, many times: *Don't Know.*

At the third session, Jocelyn wanted to talk about ways to express his emotions. "Little ways," she said. "For instance..." She stood up, her arms straight at her sides, to demonstrate. "Say you and your partner are waiting in line at McDonald's. You could rub your partner's back, in little circles, like this."

Jocelyn began moving her left hand in circles, pantomiming rubbing someone's back. "It's a nonverbal way to show affection," she told him. Her clump of bracelets rattled as she moved. Alex felt himself reddening. It was mortifying—being schooled on how to rub a person's back in a McDonald's, the implication that something so basic needed to be explained. There was something almost repulsive about the way she stood there, her skirt pinching at her thick waist, left hip rocking slightly. That night he left a voice mail at her office saying he wasn't coming back.

★   ★   ★

On Saturday, Uncle John's anniversary, Alex is awake before Rebecca, staring at the rotating blades of the ceiling fan. He thinks of calling home—it would be the middle of the night there, two in the morning. His mother would panic if she heard the phone. Rebecca is still asleep beside him, her hair spilling over the pillow, smelling like suntan lotion. Alex doesn't wake her; he's just as happy not to tell her where he's going. He dresses quietly and leaves. On the street, he orders a *café con leche* and starts walking through the village, but without Rebecca, he quickly feels disoriented. The streets all look familiar, nearly identical, yet somehow he recognizes nothing. He glances at his wrist from time to time, out of habit, but the watch is dead, sitting back in the hotel room, the face white and clouded over. He starts walking uphill, pretty sure the little pink church is somewhere at the top.

So do you go to church every week? Rebecca asked when they first started dating.

Not every week. He shrugged. *Just sometimes.*

Like what times?

Just when I feel like it, I guess.

So you believe in all the rules?

I don't really analyze it.

You're a scientist, Alex. A rational thinker! How can you not analyze it?

But there was no way to explain to Rebecca that, unlike science, being Catholic wasn't about facts. It wasn't even really about believing in it or not. It was something more abstract, a feeling of comfort from his childhood. A sense of ritual, an allegiance to his family. It was about his grandfather and his uncle, who, despite being a rational thinker, he believed were in heaven. One hundred percent.

As Alex keeps climbing uphill, his stomach churns from the coffee. In a few hours his family will be lining the pews at St. Bonaventure's, the church where they had Uncle John's funeral when Alex was sixteen. He remembers how worried he was, picturing his uncle's body in the coffin. How his mother didn't cry. How his cousin Stephen showed up with a black eye. When Pop died, Stephen had been sobbing, but a year later, his face was blank and bruised, as if he'd come dressed up as a tough guy.

By the time he reaches the top of the hill, Alex is sweating through his shirt, but there it is: the pink church. The doors are wide open. When he steps inside, the congregation is standing, and Alex slips into a pew in the back. Giant fans are turning, slow and languid, on the ceiling. Already his face feels cooler, his lungs more relaxed. In front of him stands a young Spanish couple with a baby, black-haired, wearing a fancy white dress. The baby is facing Alex over her mother's shoulder, white collar poking up around her ears, peering at him with liquid brown eyes. Alex smiles. The priest speaks from the altar and the people respond in unison. Alex can't understand the Mass in Spanish, but he recognizes the rhythms. He knows just where he is.

"Where did you go?" Rebecca demands. It is late morning by the time Alex gets back to their room, and she is dressed and ready, hair swept up into a high ponytail, wearing the dangly turquoise jewelry she'd bought the day before, after confidently negotiating with a street vendor.

"Church," he says.

Her eyebrows lift. "Church?"

"It's my uncle's anniversary."

"Oh," she says, and her face softens. "Oh, right."

"My whole family is getting together today. You know, sort of to commemorate it." He's talking quickly, maybe from the coffee. "It's kind of a big deal and I'm missing it."

"Why didn't you tell me?"

"I mean—we couldn't go."

"You could still tell me," she says. "We could still talk about it—"

"I don't want to talk about it," he snaps, then feels guilty. "I just mean . . . there's nothing to talk about. It's a party."

She smiles. "Party?"

"Not a *party* party. We all just get together, you know, for the anniversary."

"Really?" Her mouth remains quirked at one corner. "You don't think that's a little unorthodox?"

"Unorthodox?" Alex says, genuinely surprised. More than surprised—he feels angry. "No," he says. "I don't."

"You don't?" she says, and stops smiling, fixing him with her curious, probing gaze. "How do you see it?"

Alex's face is hot. He doesn't want to analyze his family, to defend them and explain them. It's like having to explain going to church. He shrugs and says, "You know my family. We celebrate everything," and turns to the mirror, hoping the conversation is over. But it is the moment he knows with certainty that he and Rebecca won't stay together. He doesn't know when it will end, just that it one day will, because the person he decides to marry won't be someone who thinks the party for his uncle is unorthodox or funny. She'll get it. And get that he doesn't want to dissect it. For now, though, Alex just wants to move on. They're in Spain, in a hotel in Spain—there's nowhere else to go.

Rebecca moves in closer behind him. "I'm sorry," she says. "I didn't realize this would be such a hard day for you." As she wraps her arms around his chest, Alex steps away. She drops her arms, face collapsing.

"I'm fine," he mumbles. "Let's just go out. It's our last day."

For their final night in Spain, they're going out to dinner at the fancy-looking restaurant they spotted the morning they arrived. They walk, so they don't have to worry about drinking. It's just before nine when they head out, according to their phones—Alex's watch never did recover—but the sun is still high and hot. Rebecca is wearing heeled shoes, which seems foolish, but Alex doesn't mention it. By the time they reach the restaurant, his shirt is soaked completely through. They sit at a table outside, sun beating on their faces, and order a pitcher of sangria. Alex quickly drains his first glass.

"This is strong," Rebecca says. She's wearing a dress he hasn't seen before, a dark blue strapless one she must have been saving. Her hair is pulled into a long, smooth ponytail, ironed flat, which she arranges over one shoulder as if it's on display. "Particularly strong, don't you think?"

"I guess," Alex says, fishing fruit from the bottom of his glass with two fingers. A fly is circling above Rebecca's head. "But it's not like we have to drive."

"Well. True." She runs a hand over the top of her hair, whisking the fly away. "Still," she says.

There is tension between them: It's been there ever since the conversation in the hotel room. An odd stiffness, a formal inch of distance. It's there as they spoon up their gazpacho and as they finish the pitcher and order another, picking their way through the tapas platter—fried shrimp balls, mussels and olives, green salad, slices of cheese grown soft in the sun.

"I love these longer nights, don't you?" Rebecca says.

"Kind of," he says, lifting his glass.

She turns to him with a teasing smile. Alex can see the beads of sweat on her nose. "You're telling me you prefer the freezing cold nights in New Jersey? When the sun sets at four thirty?"

He shrugs. "Sometimes I just like to be inside."

"Well...," she says, smile wavering on her face. "That's true. I guess you do."

She looks out toward the hills, the sun reflecting off the green pools of her sunglasses. Alex drains his third glass, a pile of dead fruit accumulating at the bottom. He knows he isn't being easy, but he feels weirdly detached from the moment, unable to summon the energy to care, to feel the things he should be feeling and steer himself back on course.

Then Rebecca abruptly pushes her sunglasses up onto the top of her head. She peers at him. Her skin looks soft, malleable, kind of purple. It reminds him of drunk Jane.

"What?" he says.

"You," she says, studying him with a slight smile. "What's going on with you? Are you nervous or something?"

"Am I nervous?"

She nods.

"Why? Do I seem nervous?"

"I don't know. It's just..." She shrugs. "Something."

But she's still smiling, which is weird. It's a coy, knowing kind of smile, and it occurs to Alex then that maybe Rebecca thinks he's going to propose. That what he's been interpreting all day as tension between them was really something else, some extra notch of anxiety, anticipation.

"I'm not nervous," he tells her. "I was just thinking."

"Oh," she says, and her smile falters a little. She looks as if she's about to say something else, then pushes her sunglasses back on, eyes hidden behind the seawater-green lenses, and picks up her drink. A fly is stalking the rim.

After a moment, she says, "You're really hard to read sometimes."

"I know." Then he adds, "I'm sorry." He owes her at least this. She looks away, and Alex follows her gaze, toward the road that leads back down the mountain.

They hold hands as they walk back to the hotel, hooked by just one finger. It's cooler now, the sun finally dropped out of sight. Alex can only guess at the time—eleven? midnight? More than once he looks at his wrist but finds only his bare skin, his old watch line obscured by sunburn. Rebecca is drunk, her high-heeled stride both extra careful and extra shaky. Her sunglasses perch on top of her head, new leather bag swats her hip. The tension still hangs between them. Alex wonders if this is what it felt like to be his parents. If they lived with this feeling all the time, this tick of discomfort, like an unseen fly in the room.

"I liked the gazpacho," Rebecca says. "Didn't you?"

"It was good," he says.

"I think it was my favorite gazpacho we've had."

He murmurs agreement. But it's empty talk, nothing talk,

the kind Rebecca hates. He focuses on the spot of pressure between their hands, weirdly aware of the place their fingers meet, the bend of her knuckle and smooth metal of her ring.

Then he says, "I thought maybe, tonight, you thought I was going to propose."

Rebecca stops walking and turns to face him. Strangely, the little smile is back on her face. "You did?"

"I just thought—maybe."

She looks pleased for a moment, then her expression puddles into confusion, and hurt. "Oh," she says. "Well, I didn't. It never even crossed my mind." She looks over his shoulder, eyebrows arched indifferently, but her eyes are shiny and Alex wonders if she's telling the truth.

"Sorry," he says.

"Don't be sorry."

"I just wanted to be honest with you."

She lets out a short, disbelieving laugh and looks at him with tears in her eyes. "You really don't understand anything, do you," she says, then turns and keeps on walking.

Alex follows, though Rebecca stays a few deliberate paces ahead of him. He watches her feet, the heels kicking up little puffs of dry dirt. At first he feels nothing, then the nothingness yields to a sharp sadness, sort of like homesickness, one he remembers from childhood, a mixture of loneliness and loss. At home, he thinks, it is the middle of the afternoon. The party must be in full swing by now. His family is all gathered around the pool at Aunt Lauren's, eating the burgers that Uncle Patrick grilled and the potato salad with little bits of celery and the pink fluff and pickles wrapped in ham. They're talking about Uncle John, thinking of the day he died, going through it again and again. Alex feels tears building, hot and stinging. When Rebecca stops and turns around, he stiffens, preparing for her onslaught of concern. But she says only: "What time should we leave in the morning?" The road swims up before him, olive trees blurring into the dark sky. It doesn't seem possible that Rebecca doesn't see his tears. How can he feel so much but show nothing? What more would it take? Yet she's looking right at him, waiting for his answer, unable to see what's happening on his face.

Winners

Margie has seen her story multiple times on *Dr. Phil*, enough to know that she's the one to blame. The parents drag their child (son, usually) on the show and describe how he's wasting his life, sleeping on their couch and making no plans to move out. Typically, the mother outlines the situation with eagerness and certainty, sometimes even a touch of self-righteousness, sure that Dr. Phil is going to punish the son and whip him into shape. But inevitably—have they not watched the show before?—Dr. Phil turns the tables, criticizing the parents for not making the son leave.

"He stays," Dr. Phil says, "because you *let* him stay."

The mother looks stricken, the father uneasy. The audience applauds. Margie is sure Phil is right about this, but still, she has questions: What if the mother makes her son leave and the son hates her forever? What if the son leaves but never comes back? She isn't like these mothers who go on the show and think themselves blameless. She knows that she's responsible for what Stephen's life has become. But that's just it: How, then, can she turn around and evict him? She'd rather be blamed for his staying than for his leaving and never coming back.

★   ★   ★

The numbers on the kitchen stove clock roll slowly to 12:38. Margie sits at the table, a cup of lukewarm tea in her hands. Even after midnight, Tyson Avenue is awake with all kinds of noises, rattling mufflers and thumping car stereos. But Margie knows the sounds she's waiting for: the hard, sloppy shuffle of her son's sneakers climbing the porch stairs, the whine of the front door as it bangs shut behind him, the shiver of the wooden cross on the kitchen wall. It could be two minutes or two hours. She lifts the tea, takes a sip—too bitter. She forgot to fish the teabag out.

"Sitting in the dark again?" Joe says, making her jump.

Her husband practically fills the kitchen doorway, his massive torso extending past both sides. When they started dating in their senior year of high school, Joe was broad-shouldered, bearish, a star defensive lineman for the St. Bonaventure football team; now, in his late forties, he's a man the world would officially call fat. The kind who carries his bulk as if it's a separate person, who can't fit into seats on buses and in movie theaters. When he sleeps, his snores are ragged, violent, like something struggling to the surface from the bottom of the sea.

"Just waiting," Margie says. As if he doesn't know why she's sitting there.

He looks at her for a beat, then opens his palm, revealing the crumpled Big 4. "Missed by one."

"Too bad."

"Stupid," he says, shaking his head. "Nobody ever actually wins these things."

Joe says this every night, but tomorrow he'll keep on playing. Mega Millions, Daily Number, Powerball. Margie can't bear to think what her father would say. Her father, who was always so careful—respectful—with money, having raised four children, lived through the Depression, worked at the Budd Manufacturing plant for thirty years. He always picked up pennies on the sidewalk—*five of them make a nickel*. To him, playing scratch tickets would be a sign of laziness, weakness of character. Even if Joe was right when he said, as he would inevitably tomorrow: *Somebody has to win, right?*

They do, Margie concedes, though somehow the winners always seem to have the same sad, desperate affect. Sort of like the people on *Dr. Phil*.

Joe leans over to drop the stub in the trash can—lately, even his smallest movements look like an effort—then reaches up to rummage in the kitchen cabinet for a consolation prize. He selects a bag of sour-cream-and-onion chips and pulls a Coke from the fridge. Something about the sway and hump of her husband in the darkened kitchen makes Margie's heart soften a little. Over the years, Joe has had to take on a bigger role in her family, one she knows he didn't ask for and, truthfully, isn't made for. But there was no choice: Other men disappeared. Her father. Her brother John. Her brother-in-law, Dave, after the divorce. With each man missing, a little more responsibility fell on her husband's thickening shoulders—hanging the heavy mirror in her mother's old apartment, putting up the Christmas trees, carving the turkeys. At parties, the crowd of men around the football game shrank to only Joe and her brother Patrick—almost ten years apart in age, friendly enough but never close—and the boys, whose appearances grew increasingly erratic, busy with friends and sports and then off to college, Joey on his basketball scholarship, Alex to the Ivy League. Stephen, of course, was always there.

Joe closes the fridge door and lumbers back across the kitchen, then turns in the doorway. "You okay, Marge?"

She stares, listens to his heavy breaths, the faint whistling sound in his chest. *You okay?* After twenty-six years of marriage, what do you say? More okay than some people, less okay than others. One son a constant source of fear and worry, keeping her awake nights, drowning in regret. The other happy and carefree, a graduate of the University of Maryland, great at sports and popular with girls. Fifty-fifty.

"I'm just waiting for Stephen," she says.

Joe looks at her a moment longer, then says, "Okay," and she listens to the slow creak of the floorboards as her husband ascends the stairs.

Margie and Joe have a secret, which Joe confided to her in high school after a football game one Friday night. They had been going together three and a half months. Their team had won the game (they would go on to win the Catholic League championship that season), and there was a party later on the field behind the rec center, so by the time they were alone together Joe was plenty drunk, but he didn't seem happy. Maybe that's why he told her: to unburden himself, make way for his own happiness. They were sitting in his parents' car, a tan Dodge Charger that smelled like the cigars his father smoked. When Joe started talking, Margie saw a blue vein bulging on his forehead, a single vein that forked in two.

Last summer, he said, before he met her—later, this would feel significant to Margie, as if he'd been a separate person when he did it—Joe had stolen money. Almost four thousand dollars. He took it from the safe at Lynch's Hardware, where he'd been working since sophomore year. He was closing, and the safe had been left open, the money just sitting there. He grabbed it—didn't even think, he said. He roughed the place up a little, he told her, to make it look believable. The next morning, when Mr. and Mrs. Lynch found it missing, they never suspected him; they loved him like a son. Panicking, he put the money in a shoebox and buried it—a special place only he would remember—and vowed not to touch it for five years. By then, the money would have been forgotten. When Margie asked about the special place, he shook his head firmly. He didn't want to implicate her, he said.

The entire time he spoke, Joe kept his eyes on the windshield, hands gripping the wheel, as if ready to take off at any moment. Margie rubbed at the little gold cross around her neck, her heart beating fast. This wasn't like stealing from your parents—this was a crime. Joe was a *criminal*. An act of impulse, but still—had she ever seen this potential in him before? She thought about his extra notch of jubilation—it was almost like anger—when he tackled another player on the football field. How he cut class sometimes or skipped church or drove too fast down Roosevelt Boulevard, cradling a beer between his knees. But what she saw wasn't malicious. It was almost impossible to imagine him doing what he'd described. In fact, sitting there in the Dodge, Joe in his blue jeans that were an inch too short, white gym socks peeking out, smelling like beer and mown grass, the laughter of the party in the distance, Margie felt his story had a surreal cast, like hearing the plot of a show on TV. Maybe it was this sense of unreality that made her stay with him. *I don't want to implicate you*—there was something almost genteel about it, she thought. He would protect her. He would keep her safe. Even the five-year rule struck her as appealing in its prudence. Most boys would be blowing that money on a car.

At the same time, there was an awful twisting in her gut, like a towel wrung dry. She couldn't bear to think what people would say—her father, the priests at St. Bonaventure's. Her sister, Ann, who never did anything wrong. This was more than just wrong. It was a mortal sin.

Margie looked at the windshield. The glass had grown thick with steam, as if giving them cover. "You should return it."

Joe didn't answer right away. Margie's heart was thumping. She chewed her dry lips, tasted the last of her waxy pink lipstick. "I don't know," he said. "I could get caught."

"You should confess. Apologize."

"And then what?" he said. "I'd be dead, Margie. My dad would kill me."

Margie stared at the shadows of the party on the distant field, rubbing at her cross. She was thinking of what her own father would say, how disappointed he would be.

"Plus," Joe added, "it's a lot of money," and he reached over and squeezed her hand.

It was the squeeze, the damp, complicit press of it, that brought Margie to the edge of panic. Was it fear of getting caught that was stopping Joe from doing the right thing, or was it greed? They seemed like two very different things.

"If you don't return it now," Margie said, facing him, "that's it. You can't go back for it later."

Joe kept his eyes on the windshield but squeezed her hand again, kept squeezing it, like kneading dough.

"Joe," she said, her cheeks hot, "I mean it. Do you hear me? Not in five years, not ever. You have to forget it's there."

"Okay."

"You have to promise me," she said. "You have to swear to God or—or else."

"Or else?" He looked at her and smiled, as if her tough talk were cute.

"Or else—I'll break up with you," Margie said. She was feeling flushed, slightly hysterical. She had never talked this way to him—to anyone. "I will, Joe. I mean it. I'll break up with you on the spot."

"Okay." His smile dropped, face sobered up again. "I swear."

"To God."

"I swear to God," he said, then let go of her hand. His neck slumped forward suddenly, as if it were broken. "I'm sorry," he said, and his voice cracked, and he startled Margie by laying his head in her lap. For minutes they sat there like that, inside the fogged windows, and neither of them spoke. She wondered if he could feel her racing heart. She curled one finger around the soft curve of his ear, over and over again, feeling as though she had stepped over some threshold into adulthood: This crumpled, intimate pose confirmed it. She tried to comfort herself by looking at the spot just above Joe's ear, where the barber had trimmed his hair in a neat straight line, until one of his friends shouted—*O'Brien! Don't do anything I wouldn't do!*—and Margie dropped her hand and Joe sat up and drove her home.

They never spoke of it again. For twenty-eight years, it was as though the conversation had never happened. Margie never told a living soul, so there was no one in the world to remind her. A month before graduation, Joe stopped working at Lynch's. When he proposed that summer, not even a flicker of doubt entered her mind. It was as if she'd willed that entire night out of existence, erased it, tamped it down. Joe never mentioned it, either. Maybe he'd forgotten he told her; maybe he'd forgotten it was out there.

But it was, Margie knew, somewhere, and at the five-year mark she found herself growing anxious. Carefully, she watched her husband—Stephen was small then, just two years old, and she was pregnant with Joey—looking for some sign that he'd retrieved it. Joe was the one who handled their money, but Margie started checking the accounts, looking for a surge of cash. It never came. Over the years, though, whenever money got tight she had a fresh bout of panic. *I'll figure it out*, Joe always said, and he did. She knew Joe did a little betting during football season—she grew nervous whenever the games were on, gauging the degree of emotion with which he watched the scores—but he always seemed to at least break even. Then came Joey's basketball scholarship, a small inheritance from an aunt with no children. Margie was certain these acts of mercy were her father's doing, reaching out to rescue her from beyond.

Still, as the years went by, she felt the presence of the hidden money throbbing in the body of her aging marriage. An aberration, a hairline fracture in a bone. It was something like the way Margie's mother described her cataracts—*everything normal, except this little blurred spot.* She felt its presence in church on Sundays, when she recited *forgive us our trespasses.* When her boys memorized the Ten Commandments: *Thou shalt not steal.* When the hardware store eventually went out of business, was turned into a Dunkin' Donuts, and Mr. and Mrs. Lynch were prayed for at church, listed among the sick, then the dead. *Lord, hear our prayer.* Sometimes, looking at her husband, Margie felt a silent knowledge pass between them, make their eyes lock a moment longer, a hint of shame darken his face.

I don't want to implicate you—how foolish she had been. Because she *was* implicated. The stolen money was the lie of their lives, buried beneath the old, worn ground of their marriage. As Margie drove past the ShopRite, the rectory at St. B's, she wondered where the special place might be. Under the bleachers at the school? The hill behind the rec center, the one where their boys used to go sledding? The bills would be damp by now, stuck together, maybe worm-eaten. She doubted Joe had had the foresight to wrap them in plastic—he was just a baby then. Eighteen. He couldn't have been thinking about what they'd find when they dug it up.

The zeroes on the oven clock line up with excruciating slowness: 2:00. Closing time. The hour when real nerves set in. Joe went to bed over an hour ago—it amazes Margie that he's able to sleep at all before Stephen is home safe—and the house is quiet, the kitchen gone blurry at the edges, the tea cold. There's a smell, like sweetly rotting fruit. Bananas. Margie always has bananas in the house, because Stephen likes them. *Enabling*, Dr. Phil would say. She fingers the cross at her throat, imagining where her son goes at night. The hole-in-the-wall bar on Rising Sun Avenue? The field at the

rec, strewn with smashed metal cans? He never said. He'd
come in late, reeking of beer and pot smoke and wearing
that strange smile—a smile that seems to hover just there, on
top of his face, not coming from within. The smile scared
her. It used to be, no matter what, Margie could catch a
glint of him, the old him, the real him—the discomfort or
the sheepishness, the tick of guilty conscience—the son she
knew. But lately, she had a hard time finding it. When he
was a little boy, Margie had known every inch of him. He'd
always been her favorite, which she felt guilty admitting,
but it was true: Joe's was Joey, Stephen hers. Joey had never
needed her the way Stephen did, for one thing. From the
time he could walk, her younger son was outside playing
with the neighborhood kids: She can still hear that basketball, the steadiness of the bounce, swish, bounce, swish. She
never had to worry about Joey—the ease and evenness of
that ball confirmed it. But Stephen was different; he struggled with things. He might have been good at sports but
decided early on not to care. He would never be as gifted as
his little brother—a *winner*, as Joey himself might say. Winners, losers: In high school, Joey began to classify the world
this way. The distinction, Margie gathered, wasn't about just
winning at sports, but something more abstract. Winning
at life. After her brother Patrick took Joey to a Phillies
game—luxury box seats a patient had given him—her son
said approvingly, *Uncle Patrick's a real winner*. He'd just turned
eighteen and begun referring to adults like his peers.

But for Stephen, the world was not so easy. Life got under
his skin. As a little boy, he was teased for his right eye, which
drifted when he was tired. *Bring your eye back*, Margie would

tell him, and he obeyed. He was afraid of all sorts of things—cemeteries, monsters, oceans, God. *So God knows everything?* he'd ask after church on Sundays, slumped in the car, chewing at the skin around his thumbnail. *God can see me right now? God can hear my thoughts?* When he was nine, they came home from the shore to find his fish dead, and Joe flushed them down the toilet. *But where are they now?* he asked her the next day. By the time Margie's father died, Stephen was a teenager, but he broke down sobbing in her parents' living room and stormed outside—why hadn't she gone after him? Comforted him?

Margie stares at the kitchen wall and wonders if that was her crucial misstep, or that one, or that one.

Because there are so many decisions she regrets. Naming their second-born after Joe—it should have been the first, like John and her father, or none at all. Letting Stephen move his room into the basement. Not being harder on him. Joe, especially, had always seemed more amused than angry, but they both had downplayed Stephen's problems to the family. About his trouble at school, Margie hadn't told a living soul, but it might have helped straighten him out, to be embarrassed, exposed. The shame.

Margie closes her eyes and remembers—like a penance—the spray paint incident in tenth grade. *Obscenities*, Father Malcahy told Joe on the phone, *of a religious and sexual nature*. Margie had felt sick. Where did this kind of anger come from? How did thoughts like these get inside your own son? That had been the beginning of something, the first indication of real recklessness, real fury, of her son being in the grip of something bigger than himself. But Margie hadn't handled the situation;

she couldn't handle it. John was so sick then. He died five days later. Stephen, at the funeral, with that unexplained black eye. Margie knows she should have done something. Gone to talk to the school counselor or a priest or *something*. But the spray paint had so unnerved her that she pretended it never happened. She didn't know the specifics, told Joe she didn't want to. She just wanted it all to go away. The black eye faded, the school year ended. She told herself it was a fluke. The way she'll see an ant on the kitchen counter and convince herself there's only one of them, or the way, when something new crops up in a body—the itchy red patch between her pinky and ring finger, the blurred spot in her mother's eye—she'll tell herself it doesn't mean more are coming.

Because there were other times—looking back, Margie is sure they are there—when things seemed to be turning. When Stephen got his job at Pet World—he loved that store. He fed the fish and cleaned the cages and sifted through the hermit crabs, picking out the dead ones. He came home full of stories—how the birds flew wild around the store after hours, how the mynah could sing Bruce Springsteen's "Thunder Road." Margie wasn't sure she believed it, but she loved to see her son excited about something. Then he was fired for lateness. From there, it was the same story, different versions. Sam Goody. Wawa. The Hess station on Cottman. Even the ShopRite, after Joe got him a job as a bagger—nothing stuck. He went to CCP, planned to major in engineering, but lasted only a semester and a half. There were always reasons. The teachers who hated him, the friends who goaded him into doing something that wasn't his idea. It was never his idea, but he always went along with it. Until three weeks ago, he'd had a job at the Burger King on Rising Sun, then he didn't. He never said why. Margie knew he hadn't liked working the counter, smelling like French fries and taking people's orders. It was about dignity, she supposed. But in the weeks since, he hadn't done much looking. Except for nights, he rarely left the house.

But this she knows: Her son is not bad. Probably all the mothers on *Dr. Phil* believe this, but Margie knows it's true. Life had cast her son in the role of a troublemaker, but he's a good boy. A good heart. Not like that Mark Rourke, who served jail time for assault in a bar fight, a boy truly black at the core. Look at how sweet Stephen is with his cousins, Patrick's children. Holding baby Tate, letting four-year-old Hayley serve him imaginary tea. Going to watch Max's Little League games. He stands just the way Margie's father used to watching Joey, tips of his fingers hooked loosely in the sagging wire fence. Some nights, when Stephen comes in, he pauses in the kitchen, kisses the top of her head.

But in the morning, he disappears again. Sleeps past eleven, wastes away the afternoon. *Any leads on a job, honey?* she asks him. *Working on it*, he says.

Margie watches the oven clock slide to 2:26. She doesn't care where he's been, what he's been doing, she just wants him to walk in the door. Once he's here, she can take a pill, go to bed. Tomorrow night, she'll do it all again. She fixes her eyes on the wooden cross on the wall above the toaster, rubbing at her necklace, and prays. *Hail Mary, full of grace, the Lord*— Then the phone rings and her heart stops beating. *Oh God oh God oh God.* The chair falls over in her rush to grab the receiver. "Hello?" she says. "Stephen? Hello?"

She is already crying by the time her mother speaks, her voice wondering and weak. "Margie?" she says. "Did I wake you?"

Joe grabs the coats and keys while Margie calls Ann. *She fell*, Margie reports. *The hallway.* Ann will call Patrick, who will meet them there. No sense waking Lauren, they decide, who's alone with the kids. They'll tell her in the morning.

She and Joe hurry down the front steps, crunching across the fallen leaves, Margie murmuring Hail Marys. She can't stand the thought of her mother lying there alone. She blames herself. They've known her eyesight wasn't good, that she has trouble with her swollen legs. She takes medication, but Margie has noticed once, at least once, that she forgot to take a pill. Then she stops and gasps.

"Stephen!"

Her son is slumped over on the curb, shoulders rounded, head hanging forward so his chin nearly rests on his chest. She isn't sure that he's conscious. She rushes to his side as he lifts his head, slowly, looking up at her with glassy eyes. His head seems to lean too far backward, as if loose, like a baby's on an unformed neck.

"Hey, Mom."

"What are you *doing* out here!"

Her voice is shrill, almost a scream.

"Nothing."

There's that expression again, a floating smile, almost a grimace. How long had he been sitting out here in the cold? Was he out here every night, while she sat inside worrying herself sick? Margie wants to burst into tears, collapse to the ground, and shatter into pieces. But she can't. Not now. She must prioritize: one crisis over another. Joe is somewhere behind her, awaiting instruction.

"Get in the car," she says to Stephen, her voice shaking.

He laughs. "The car?"

"Get up," she says. "Your grandmother needs help."

Impossible not to be reminded of the other time they were all summoned in the middle of the night like this, more than a decade ago, everyone in their sweatpants and winter coats and the awfulness of how her father had looked in bed. It's been almost eleven years, but Margie still misses him every day. If only she could talk to him, ask him what to do about Stephen. Would her father make him leave? Probably. But she knows that with her father in charge, it would never have come to this in the first place.

When they arrive at St. Mary's, Ann is already there, kneeling over their mother. She is on her back on the hallway floor, next to the little wooden candy table that holds the M&M's dish and phone. "I wasn't sure if I should move her," Ann says as Margie rushes through the door.

"Who's there?" Mother says, trying to turn her head.

"Me, Mother," Margie says, dropping to her knees beside her. "And Stephen. And Joe."

Her mother looks up at her, face soft without her glasses.

"Stevie's here?"

"He's right here."

"Does he want something to eat?"

"He's fine, Mother," Margie says with a short laugh.

Stephen is staring down at his grandmother, his face slack.

Margie puts a reassuring hand on his leg, feels his big kneecap beneath his dirty jeans, radiating heat. He takes a step away.

"She fell in the bathroom," Ann says to Margie. "When she couldn't get back up, she pulled herself along the floor to reach the phone."

Margie takes in her mother's nightgown, a peach flannel they gave her last Christmas. The hem is ruched up around her knees, her bare feet flopped inward. Her feet look swollen, her legs shiny and smooth, marbled with purple and blue veins.

Stephen laughs. "It's like that commercial."

Margie looks up at him, a touch nervously. "What commercial, honey?"

"You know. I've fallen and I can't get up."

Margie thinks of slapping him across the face, feels the clean tingle of it course through her palm. Heat flies like a brushfire through her cheeks.

"Is that Stevie?" Mother says.

No, Margie thinks, it isn't—one look at him and anyone can see her son isn't here, this is someone else, the smile hanging on his face, hooked loosely at the corners. At least, thank God, her mother didn't hear what he said, or didn't understand it. Margie can't bring herself to look at Ann. She looks instead at her husband, standing in the kitchenette—if he's laughing, she thinks, she'll kill him. But his face is inscrutable, his huge bulk filling the tiny kitchen, saying nothing, and resentment spikes right through her, bright and pure.

"Will someone get me up from here?" her mother asks.

"I think we should wait for Patrick," Ann murmurs, then addresses her mother in a loud, clear voice. "You're sure you're not in any pain?" In recent years, Ann has become this person, the one who will take the lead on things. All her therapy—first for Meghan's eating problems, then her divorce—has made her, if not a natural communicator, a resolute one. Margie used to grow annoyed sometimes listening to Ann talk about the problems in her marriage—their lack of intimacy, Ann's need for control—but still, she admires her sister for letting things dissolve so honestly, getting it all out in the open.

"I'm fine," Mother says. "Would everybody stop worrying about me?"

"Should we try to move her?" Ann says just as Patrick, thank God, rushes through the door.

"Hey there, gang," he says. "Fancy meeting you all here."

"Is that Patrick?" Mother says, craning her head, an uptick of joy in her voice. "Is Patrick here?"

"Hi, Mommy," Patrick says, and Margie can feel the exhalation in the room. He crouches beside her in his jeans and sneakers, red hair mussed from sleep. "What happened? Breakdancing again?"

Stephen laughs, too loudly. Patrick glances up at him, and Margie feels a deep wash of shame. Everybody knows Stephen still lives at home, has had a string of dead-end jobs, but seeing this is different. This is the Stephen only she knows, shuffling through the darkened kitchen at two in the morning, disappearing into his basement room.

"Did you bring the babies?" Mother asks. "Where are the babies?"

"No babies. They're asleep," Patrick says. He checks her vital signs, talking to her all the while—"Does anything hurt, Mom?"—while Margie and Ann look on, grateful. Their youngest brother, their funny brother. A doctor, of a kind.

Margie remembers the night their father died, how Patrick cried, slumped on the end of the couch with his pretty new wife, rendering Margie's boys sheepish and confused. Patrick was still the baby then; John was the one in charge. That's what happens in families—things shift, openings appear, roles that need filling. Patrick is now a success by all accounts—has his own practice and a big house on the Main Line—though something has hardened in his face. It's more than age; it's as if his old, easygoing personality has become an effort. His children are perfect, but it took years to make them. God knows what they went through.

"Steve," Patrick says. He looks up at her son. "Take her feet."

Joe doesn't move to help, still lurking in the kitchen, and it occurs to Margie that it's a blessing Stephen came. That Joe, with his size and his bad knees, might have been unable to get down and lift her. To do the job that needed doing. Stephen clasps his grandmother's feet, cupping them in his hands. Something about it makes Margie's eyes well up—her mother's small, swollen feet in her son's giant hands.

"One, two, three," Patrick says, and Margie prays that Stephen doesn't stumble and drop her. She holds her breath as they carry Mother across the room and settle her, gently, into the blue wingback chair. She's sitting upright, her hair disheveled. She would hate to be seen this way.

"My glasses," she says, touching her face. "Where did I put my glasses?"

"Right here, Mother," Ann says, sliding them on her face.

"Well," Mother says, and looks around. Margie notices then how bright the room is. Three in the morning and every light is turned on—the overhead, the standing lamp. The small brass lamps with the horses at the bases. When she was growing up, the lamps had sat on either end of the couch, next to her father's green glass ashtrays.

Margie looks at her son. Relieved of duty, he's standing next to the table in the hallway, eating M&M's from the dish Mother keeps filled for the kids. The night her father died, all of the grandchildren were there except Ann's oldest, away at college; tonight the only one here is Stephen. Stephen, loyal by virtue of his inertia. Looking at him, Margie is struck by how much his build is that of a young Joe—at twenty-five, the same sloping shoulders, the same shifting gait. He's turning into his father. It's never looked as plain to her as it does now.

"Where am I?" Mother says.

Margie turns. Mother is smiling, but the smile looks faint, disconnected, not so different from Stephen's.

"What do you mean, Mother?" Ann says. "You're at home."

"Home?"

"You fell."

She frowns. "I did?"

Margie and Ann exchange a quick, nervous look.

"Mom?" Patrick is still standing, studying her. "Does your left arm hurt?"

"My arm?" She glances down. "It does hurt a little, now that you say it."

Margie sees now that the arm is slightly crooked, held at an odd angle. She looks again at Ann, a jolt of alarm passing between them, and Margie wonders if it was shock that kept Mother from feeling it before or something else, something worse—a head injury, a stroke.

"Dammit," Patrick says, already moving to the candy table, picking up the phone.

"Where's Stevie?" Mother is saying, blinking. "Is Stevie here?"

"He's here, Mother," Margie says quickly. "He's right here." She looks at her son, who's rocking slightly from foot to foot as Patrick speaks firmly into the phone beside him: "She fell in her apartment. Eyes responsive, pulse normal, but possible head injury and broken bone—"

Ann sits down beside Mother, taking her hand, as Patrick spells out the address. "We're going to take care of you," Ann is saying as Mother asks again, "Has Stevie had enough to eat?"

But Stephen isn't paying any attention. He's still eating M&M's from the dish next to the phone, tossing them in his mouth like peanuts from a bowl on a bar. In the light of all these lamps, Margie can see a long brown spill down the front of his shirt. He is still swaying. His eyes are only half-open. The stink of him is unavoidable—not the smell of a few cheap beers at the corner bar, but something deeper, heavy, sweaty, as if it's seeping from his pores.

Patrick hangs up the phone, runs a palm over his hair. Then he walks into the kitchen, fills a glass of water at the tap, and wordlessly carries it back to Stephen. Margie watches as Stephen drinks it down, spilling a little on his shirt. He raises his chin—*thanks, man*—as if his uncle is just anyone, some random guy at the bar. It's the moment that breaks her: seeing her son in this light, as they wait for help to arrive.

Stephen is immediately asleep in the backseat. It's five thirty in the morning, dawn seeping into the cold October sky. Ann and Patrick followed the ambulance to Holy Redeemer. Margie will leave Joe and Stephen at home, then join them there. She urges Joe to drive quickly, more quickly. The streets are abandoned, the parking lots empty. In the backseat, Stephen is snoring. Drunk snoring, deep and ragged.

"She might not be able to live there anymore," Margie says.

Joe says nothing, just breathing, a faint wheeze from the depths of his chest. The world is quiet save for the sounds of her husband breathing, her son sleeping in the backseat.

"If something's broken, she won't be able to live on her own."

"Where will she go?"

Margie hears the real question underneath: *She won't live with us, will she?*

"I don't know," she says stiffly, looking out the window. "One of those places, probably. A home."

She watches the familiar streets pass by. The Rite Aid, the Wawa. The high school with the white-lettered sign: *Ninth Grade Dance!* She smells the dank alcohol rising from the backseat. The sound of sleeping rises with it, heavy, cut off from the world.

"Joe," Margie says. "We need to do something."

"Just wait and hear what the doctors say."

"No," she says. "I mean, about Stephen."

Joe is staring straight ahead, both hands on the wheel. It's the same way he sat in his father's car almost thirty years before, except now he is a different man, an older man. Flesh dimples the backs of his hands.

"You saw him," Margie says. "He's not going to get his life together if we—we can't keep taking care of him." She blinks back tears. "He needs to move out."

Joe stops for a red light, adjusts the defroster. She wants to slap his hand. "Joe," she says.

"I heard you."

"Well?"

He rubs his cheek hard. "I mean, where would he go?"

Margie shakes her head, teeth clenched so hard that her jaw hurts. It would have been too much, she thinks, to expect him to help her. To support her. After all this time.

"That's up to him," she says. "He has to figure that out on his own. He's an adult. That's what people do. They figure things out—"

Joe chuckles, and Margie thinks—*how dare he.*

"What?" she says.

"You can't just expect him to pull it together overnight, Marge."

"I know that," she says. "Do you think I don't know that?" She steels herself and says, "We give him thirty days."

It's what Dr. Phil would say. But her husband is unimpressed. "And then what?"

Margie feels a scream gathering, pressure building in her lungs. "It would help if you believed in him," she says tightly. "Just a little bit. You never have."

The light changes and Joe starts driving again, slowly. Past the Color Tile, the Wendy's, the deserted strip mall where the old Pet World used to be. Finally Joe says, "I'm just being realistic. What would he do for money?"

"He'll make money."

"Where?"

"A job."

"What job?"

"He'll get a job. Any job. And he'll keep it, because he has to. And he'll make money. That's what people do—"

"Who are these people you keep talking about?"

"People," she says. "Other people."

People who live their lives right, Margie thinks. Who do things the way you're supposed to. Who work hard and don't cheat and steal and cut corners. Winners. People like her father, like her brothers. *Roughed the place up a little*—the line returns to her like a blast of air to her lungs.

"You're the reason he's like this," Margie says in a whisper. "It should come from you."

Joe stops for another red light, his soft hands still gripping the wheel. On their right is the rec center—the overgrown baseball diamond, the hill where the boys used to drag their trash can lids to go sledding. Beyond it, the basketball court where Joey played pickup games, the field strewn with cigarettes and beer cans. The trees are nearly bare.

Joe clears his throat. "It isn't that simple, Margie," he says. When she turns to him, his face looks damp, distorted in the traffic light's glow. A lumpy vein bulges on his brow, like a molehill bursting through the earth. "He's in over his head," Joe says.

"I know that," Margie says. "Isn't that what I've been telling you?"

"No," he says. "Something else." He pauses, and Margie is stopped by the gravity of the pause, by the look on his face. "He made a few bad bets."

"What?" she says, as a quiet fear awakens in her gut. "What bets?"

"Through my guy," Joe says. "But I'm taking care of it. I just have to win the next few."

Blood pounds thickly in her ears as she tries to absorb what he's saying. "Football, Joe? He's betting on football?"

"Yeah." Joe wipes one finger across his upper lip, returns his hand to the wheel. "And a few poker games," he says. "Just a few."

Margie reaches for her cross. She doesn't want to imagine these poker games, which seem more sinister, dangerous somehow, than betting on football—strangers meeting in dark, seedy rooms. "How much?"

Joe clears his throat again. "It could be worse," he says.

"Oh, my God, Joe—what?"

"Five."

"Thousand?"

"It'll be okay," he says. "I told you. I'm figuring it out."

Margie pushes the point of her cross into her thumb until it hurts. Was this where Stephen disappeared to at night? Why he'd become even less motivated to find a job? *My guy*—panic spreads through her veins.

"This guy is—what, Joe? A bookie?" She looks at him, hoping he'll find the word amusing, an attempt at tough talk, but Joe just nods. She turns back to the rec center, the barren slope of the hill, her jaw tightening, eyes pooling with tears. "Is he threatening him? Threatening us? Isn't that what these people do?"

"I'm taking care of it," Joe says again. "This guy...you know. We go back."

The blood in her ears makes her feel as if she's underwater. Something has crawled out on the seat between them, ugly and stark. That her husband has a bookie, that he let their son get mixed up with him—and all of this went on without her knowing. It could be dangerous for Stephen—for all of them. Their son, in danger. Like the plot of a movie except it's real. Looking at Joe's profile, the vein branching across his brow, his eyes blinking back tears, she feels terrified and angry and also, oddly, heartbroken—her husband trying, in his way, to protect him, too.

Margie glances in the side-view mirror, to make sure Stephen is still sleeping. The snoring has grown quieter. His cheek is pressed to the window, his mouth gapes slightly. When she speaks again, she is surprised by the steadiness of her voice.

"Joe," she says. "Where is it?"

Joe goes so quiet then, she wonders if he's still breathing. For once, the whistling noise in his chest has stopped.

"Joe?"

"Yeah," he says, but a whisper. The air feels as if it could splinter into pieces.

"Did you hear what I said?"

He doesn't answer, but his hands are tight on the wheel, his knuckles white. Then he says, "You really want to know?"

Margie's eyes flood with tears—so it's true. After all these years, she didn't dream it. She wasn't crazy. It's been there all along. She feels vindicated and devastated at the same time.

"Do you?" Joe asks, and Margie knows he wants to tell her, to share the burden, but after all this time, she doesn't want to know.

She says only, "You didn't get it?"

Joe looks at her in surprise. "I didn't think you'd want me to."

The street swims up before her. The pad of her thumb is throbbing. *Hail Mary, full of grace.* Then the light turns, a watery splash of green, but the car doesn't move. Margie thinks of the old, innocent promise made in the car all those years ago. She thinks of her father—*five of them make a nickel*—and a sob escapes her chest.

"Get it," she says. "Just get it. Can you just please do that, please?"

Joe lets out a sound, like a whimper. Margie presses a hand over her mouth as the tears leak onto her lips.

"Mom?" Stephen says, rousing from his stupor and leaning forward. "What's wrong?" She feels his warm, worried breath on her neck. "Why are we just sitting here?"

At eight thirty, the call comes. Minor head injury, Ann says. Her arm is fractured in two places. Margie nods, taking this in. They talk briefly about what the next steps are. She won't be able to live at St. Mary's any longer. They'll research other places, get her on a list, and until a spot opens she can stay with Lauren, who has an extra bedroom—John's old office—and a bathroom on the first floor.

Margie hangs up and stands there, hand resting on the receiver, letting this new reality sink in. It will be difficult, complicated; it will require a lot from all of them. At the same time, she feels a determined stirring: to be on the cusp of a crisis, to rise to it, as a family. It's almost energizing, the thought of all that will need to be done.

First, she'll stop by St. Mary's to pick up some of Mother's things. Clothes and toiletries. Rosary, three kinds of pills.

For Lauren's, she'll make food. Chicken cacciatore, Mother's potato soup. The macaroni-and-cheese casserole that Max likes.

At nine, she showers and gets dressed.

At nine thirty, she stands outside Stephen's door. She knocks softly, then goes inside. His basement room is so dark that it could be night out, the windows draped with plaid flannel sheets. The old fish tank sits on the floor, empty, ringed with scum. There's a dirty baseball inside it, a magazine. Margie sits on the edge of the bed. "What?" Stephen stirs, his voice thick with sleep. Margie looks at her son's heavy face. "Stephen. I have to tell you something." And then she says what needs to be said. "By the end of the month," she tells him. Her voice is calm and steady. Thirty days. He needs to find a place. "Dad and I are going to take care of your problem," she says, and his face stiffens, eyes fixed on the ceiling. "But after that, you're on your own." Still he doesn't look at her, his face blank. "I love you," she says, her voice catching. "You have no idea how much."

At nine forty-five, Margie picks up her purse, her coat and keys. Joe is sitting on the couch—*I think it would be better coming from you,* he'd said this morning. She passes by him without a word. Outside it is cool and foggy, a skein of gray smog draped over Northeast Philadelphia. She drives to Holy Redeemer, the same hospital where they went to visit John all those terrible days and nights. In the hospital bed, her mother looks tiny, outlined beneath a thin blue sheet. "Margie?" she says. "Margie, when am I going home?" Margie neatens her mother's hair, speaks to the nurse. They're keeping her overnight for observation. Kate appears in a perfumed flurry, juggling Hayley and Tate, and Mother brightens at the baby. Lauren and her children arrive, Max with his swimmer's crew cut and Elena with her dyed black hair. Margie thanks Lauren—"It will be very temporary," she assures her—but Lauren just says, "It's the least I can do."

At four o'clock, Margie kisses her mother's forehead, tells her she'll be back in the morning. There are things she needs to do. She stops by St. Mary's and packs up the essentials. Goes to the ShopRite to get the ingredients for the casseroles, the soup. Just after six o'clock, she pulls into the church.

It isn't her parish, Resurrection, but she doesn't want a priest who might know her voice. The parking lot is nearly empty. A few people, old people, are kneeling, heads bowed. Margie steps into the confessional, hears the scrape of the little window. *O my God, I am heartily sorry.* Then she stares at the window and she confesses. Her husband's gambling. Her son's. The debt she's going to pay. *I know it's wrong—* She chokes back a sob. *But I have to help him—I have to protect my son.* The priest dispenses her penance, and Margie is certain she hears judgment in his tone. *I firmly resolve,* she thinks, hurrying back across the parking lot, *with the help of Your grace, to amend my life.*

In the car, Margie feels light and empty, too wrung out to cry. She drives home, the gray sky bruised with dark clouds, wondering what she'll find when she gets there. What her family will have become in the hours since she left. If Joe has been arrested, or Stephen has disappeared. Anything is possible. But when Margie pulls up in front of her house, it looks unchanged. The pile of dead leaves by the curb, the two lights inside: living room, basement. She carries in the groceries. Stephen is in his room, music seeping through the floor. Joe is on the couch, watching TV. He says nothing, but it's done, she can tell, by the look on his face.

Margie unpacks the food and walks up to their room. She waits on the edge of the bed until she hears Joe creaking slowly up the stairs. He enters the room and walks to the closet, wordlessly reaches onto the top shelf. When he turns, he's holding a stained white shoebox. The reality of the box itself is startling: this object from the past existing so concretely in the present. The very box in this very room, tucked among her purses and shoes. Neither of them speaks, as if the room might be bugged. He sits on the bed beside her, mattress sagging, and places the box on his wide knees. His breaths are heavy, heavier than usual, and Margie wonders what exertion was required of him to unearth it. She sees dirt under his nails. As she looks at the box, Margie has to concentrate on breathing. It smells heavy, loamy, like thirty years in the earth. The cardboard looks fragile, wet and soft, as if it might crumble in his hands. It scares her, repulses her, yet something about it is unexpectedly poignant, too—the boy's athletic shoe, Adidas, size twelve. As Joe lifts the lid, tears crawl down his cheeks. Inside the box, Margie is surprised to see the bills themselves have withstood time. He had wrapped them in plastic after all. She is surprised by the sheer number of them too, bundled tens and twenties, though it shouldn't surprise her. These are the bills from the register drawer at Lynch's; of course they would be small. She had prayed that, with time, the money might become neutral, impersonal, lose its realness. But if anything, it is only more real. These are the very same twenties from the register at the hardware store, the very same box Joe's cleats came in that winning season. The same plastic Joe wrapped them in at eighteen, like swaddling a baby. It's almost touching, the care he took.

Names

As Ann goes under, the anesthesiologist instructs her to count backward from one hundred. Instead, she recites her family, a litany. *Abby, Alex, Meghan, Margie, Patrick, John—*

When Ann wakes up, her three children are in the foreground. A needle is pinching her arm. Meghan is the first to lunge for her, teary-eyed. Alex hangs back, watching. Abby is asking questions of the nurse. Ann loves them for this, for staying always who they are.

"She'll be just fine," the nurse is saying. Abby nods. She is holding a notebook and pen. "She came through it beautifully."

Beautifully: odd word for it.

The nurse squeezes Ann's toe. "Rest," she says.

Ann closes her eyes. Vaguely she hears Abby asking about the next steps, but she knows what they are. She has the pamphlet at home. No bending, no vacuuming, no stairs. No lifting for two weeks, no driving for three. In four weeks, she'll be good as new.

One

It was a routine Pap smear, then a call from Dr. Weiss. *Irregular cells*, the doctor said. Ann knew what this meant; they all did. Their brother John had died eleven years before. The endometrial biopsy showed cancer in the uterus, but it was caught early, the earliest the doctor had seen it caught in her career. *You must have an angel watching over you*, she said.

Throughout the night, Ann hears moaning. A woman in one of the nearby rooms is in pain. For the next three days, Ann shuffles up and down the hallway holding people's elbows, practicing walking. She moves slowly past the nurses' station, dragging her IV stand. She glances at the names on the side of each door, looking for this poor woman, but never discovers which one she is.

Dr. Weiss tells her there's no need for further treatment. *We got it all*, she says. Ann thanks her, thinking: Why do some people get lucky? Why do some suffer so much and not others? Her brother John, two small children and a cancer that consumed him within a year. Or her daughter Meghan, struggling with bulimia while other women's daughters fretted over grades and boys and college applications. The normal problems, the usual problems. Why do some people endure so much?

When her body has resumed basic functioning, Ann is returned to the world. Meghan pushes the wheelchair out the hospital doors. The cold January air is a shock. The parking lot is coated thinly with ice. Alex pulls her car around, an old blue Toyota, salt crunching under the wheels. He drives them all back to the house as carefully as he's able. Abby sits in the passenger seat, anxiously chewing gum. Ann sits in the back, Meghan beside her. Her stomach bleats with pain. Ann winces when the car rolls over the lip of her driveway, fire shooting through her stapled middle—"Sorry, Mom," Alex says—but she is just relieved to be home, out of the car, to be going inside.

Two

All three children are staying in the house while she recovers. They are grown now—even Meghan is, impossibly, twenty-three—but they are all sleeping in their old rooms. Abby, her oldest, managed time away from her job at the museum in Boston, using Dave's old den as her home office for a few weeks. Alex is working on his dissertation at Princeton, teaching chemistry to freshmen; he's staying until the new semester begins. Even Meghan is staying for the first few days of Ann's recovery, even though the apartment she shares with a friend from high school is only fifteen minutes away.

You don't have to do that, Ann told her.

Oh, Mom, she clucked. *Are you* kidding? *Yes, I do.*

A bouquet arrives from school, a stack of get-well cards her fourth graders made. The same sentiments over and over, obvious prompts from the substitute teacher. *Have a speedy recovery! Get Well Soon!* Alex brings books from the library. Abby and Meghan shop for groceries. Through the haze of medication,

Ann hears them talk about dinners, chicken and lasagna and who can make what when. She struggles to listen every time Meghan speaks of food, alert to any signs of her old sadness and urgency—to not hear it is a relief. Ann imagines it always will be.

The exhaustion drapes her like lead. It's like no tiredness she's ever felt, the way the pain of childbirth is like no other pain. She takes Percocet for the throbbing in her stomach, her back and shoulder. But she can't bear to stay in bed, not with all of her children here. So she sits on the couch, holding a pillow to her lap, fading in and out among them. Meghan stays by her side. How many nights did they sit here on this very couch, Meghan curled in a ball, Ann keeping watch beside her? *Do you want something to eat, Mom?* Meghan asks now, squeezing her hand. Ann isn't hungry. She drifts on the hum and rise of her children's voices, the sound of their laughter, their casual bickering—it never stops, she thinks, no matter how old they get.

The rest of the family comes to visit, a continual revolving door of them. Somewhere on the outside, they are coordinating who goes when. Her brother Patrick, sister Margie. John's widow, Lauren, his children. Max with hair wet from swim practice, Elena with that new earring in her nose. Margie brings her older boy, Stephen, who talks mostly to Alex, shuffling his feet. The same age, the boys were destined to be best friends but couldn't be more different; but they are twenty-seven now, and cousins. The differences matter less. Ann sits on the couch while they collect and disperse and collect around her. So unusual, to not be on her feet, doing things. She is a person who does things, but now all she can do is sit and receive them. Like practice for being old.

Is this how Mother feels? However much of her daily life she even retains? Their mother has been in a nursing home for six months. Before that, she spent nine months at Lauren's—longer than any of them had expected—and they were all glad when Lauren was relieved of the responsibility. But in the home, Mother's mind has declined more quickly. Not enough stimulation, except for the hour a day one of them goes to see her. Her room is tiny, reduced to the essentials: the picture of the grandchildren, one of the old pair of brass lamps. *When am I going home?* she asks again and again. She's confined to a wheelchair now, because of the swelling in her legs; sometimes water weeps through her skin.

Ann pictures her mother's mind as a waterline rising: submerging a few more memories, and a few more after that. Leaving only the oldest layers, the ones with the deepest roots. Childhood and the old neighborhood, the house on Oxford Avenue. Sometimes she wheels herself to the doorway, peering into the hall to see what's happening on the street.

Ann remembers how Mother demurred when Meghan interviewed her for a history project back in high school—*Oh, there's nothing interesting to tell*—but now those same details have become a source of pride. Other things are lost—where she is and how she got there, the recent past, the lower tier of grandchildren: Max and below. Sometimes she forgets that John is gone.

Three

According to the pamphlet *Recovering from a Hysterectomy*, Ann should be drinking eight glasses of water each day. She does so, even though this means endless trips to the bathroom. But Ann is a person who follows instructions, like the advice from Meghan's doctors. She clung to every word. She'd thought, naïvely, that once Meghan's problem had been exposed, it would be cured. She'd had no idea the years, the complexity of it all. Psychologists, nutritional counselors, support groups. The doctors who tried to help her, the therapists Meghan liked and therapists she hated. The worry sending her off to college, thinking she was doing better, then the call from her roommate, a shy girl from Alabama whose name Ann forgets but to whom she will always be grateful—*Is this Meghan's mom?* The panicked drive to the campus in Allentown—Dave doing ninety, snapping at her when she told him to slow down—and then the conversation with the roommate, who had found her passed out in the shower stall. The meetings with the RA, the dean. *A medical leave of absence*, they agreed. Meghan would return the following fall. Then the vigilance when Meghan was at home that spring, Ann studying her like a detective, hovering beside her as Meghan struggled not to throw up, crying, sitting on her hands—it seems half of Ann's life as a mother has been spent sitting, watchful and worried, by Meghan's side—then that summer and the outpatient clinic where, finally, things began to turn.

Meghan has returned to sleeping in her apartment but calls every day. She insists on being the one to drive Ann to her follow-up appointment and arrives bearing gifts: a pound cake from Stock's, a bunch of flowers. As they zip along to the office in Meghan's little car, Ann can't help remembering the other appointments: sitting with Dave in the front seat, an ocean of fear between them, Meghan huddled in the back. Now Meghan chatters brightly as she drives—about her weekly support group, the kindergartners she teaches at a private school in Center City, the new guy she's seeing, a movie date, a text message, an excited swirl of details—and Ann's heart clutches, a reflex. For so long, Ann's life was an extension of her daughter's. Hoping that she was okay, that she didn't get hurt. She reminds herself what her own therapist used to tell her: *She has to learn to manage her own life, Ann.* In the office, Meghan hovers over Ann as the staples are removed. *Healing beautifully*, Dr. Weiss says. Beautiful: odd again. Especially as there is a garish purple scar down her middle. Dr. Weiss prescribes hormone replacement pills and tells her she should be fine to drive next week. *Just short distances, Mom*, Meghan says, and pats her knee.

Ann is in no hurry to start driving again. She's always been nervous behind the wheel, but lately it's intensified. She doesn't like driving during rush hour, on highways, in rain or snow or darkness. When she was married, Dave drove them everywhere. One more of the adjustments of divorce: the small but significant transformations, the reimaginings of yourself. A little over a year ago, when they were cleaning out Mother's apartment at St. Mary's, Ann discovered a canceled check to the city—a traffic violation, eighty dollars, dated around the time she stopped driving. Mother had never mentioned the ticket. Ann respected her wishes and kept it to herself.

*   *   *

She decides to tell Mother about her surgery. Now that it's over and there's no reason to worry, she doesn't want Mother wondering why she hasn't been to visit. Ann makes the call when she knows Margie is there to coordinate phone to ear, make sure the receiver returns to the cradle.

"Hello, Mother," she says. "It's Ann." She tells her that she had an operation, but it's fine, she's fine.

"Operation? What operation?" Mother snaps. Lately, she can sound curt sometimes, which is startling. Their mother was always a model of decorum. But she's lost this, too: her restraint, her filter. She'll devour an entire box of chocolates if somebody isn't there to watch.

"A hysterectomy," Ann says. She pauses, hears her mother breathing, listening. "They found cancer, but it's gone. I'm fine. Just resting. But I can't drive yet. I just wanted you to know why I haven't been to see you."

"Cancer?" her mother says, and Ann hears the abrupt swell of feeling in her voice. Maybe it had been wrong to tell her. Later, Margie reports that for the next hour it is all Mother asks about. Ann had hoped she would hear it and then forget it, but still there are certain things that stick—that go inside and stay there, get traction on what ground is left. Something wrong with her child. It burrowed right inside.

In bed at night, Ann listens to the traffic on Spry Boulevard. For thirty years, she's listened to these same sounds: the stream of cars rushing by, the pounding beat of a stereo, the gravelly grind of a truck's wheels. Theirs has always been a corner prone to accidents, the intersection of a quiet street and a busy one. Before the age of cell phones, theirs was the house strangers would run to, asking to make a call. Ann thinks of Abby and Alex asleep in their old rooms, wonders if they're listening. Growing up, they'd all become accustomed to the long, sudden squeal of skidding tires—looking up from dinner or TV, pausing, jaw frozen midchew, bracing themselves for the sound of a crash or, more often, the eerie quiet, the smell of burnt rubber, the world picking up and moving on.

Now that the fog isn't so thick, Ann is convinced that something is bothering Alex. When he's typing on the laptop, his eyes sometimes glaze over and wander off the screen. Ann feels guilty now for not paying more attention to her son when he was younger, for assuming he was fine just because he never said he wasn't, because Meghan always needed her more. The day before he's leaving, Ann decides to ask. It's a deal she's made with herself since the divorce: to be more honest. Even though it requires a breath, a steadying of her chest.

"Al," she says, "is everything okay?"

He glances up from the laptop propped on his knees. His face still contains the shyness it did in childhood, the tendency to drop his eyes, his chin; but beneath his cropped hair, his handsome features are exposed now, a dark hint of stubble on his jaw.

"What do you mean?"

"It just seems like something might be bothering you."

She waits. Even now, at twenty-seven, Alex might be reluctant to confide in her; maybe it's the surgery that makes him speak. He looks at the curtains, situates his glasses more firmly on his face. "Rebecca and I broke up."

"Oh!" Ann says, truly surprised. Alex and Rebecca had been dating for a long time—they lived together in Princeton, took that trip to Spain—though Alex rarely brought her home. "When?"

"About a month ago."

"Oh," she says again, stung—a month. Then she says, "I'm sorry," and she is, though it's something of a relief. Ann had thought they might get married—Rebecca seemed the kind to go after what she wanted, Alex the kind to get carried along—but Rebecca always struck her as a little too uppity, proprietary. The first time the three of them went to dinner, Rebecca had regarded Ann with a knowing air, as if fitting together the pieces of a puzzle, causing Ann to wonder exactly what she'd been told.

Now she looks into her son's face, checking him for damage, but with Alex it's always hard to tell. She remembers the session with the family therapist at Meghan's outpatient clinic. How the therapist pinched his skin: *Alex, can you feel this?*

She asks him, "How are you doing? Are you okay?"

"I'm okay," Alex says. He takes his glasses off, holds them by one arm. "I think it's the right thing."

"Who was it who..." She tries to be tactful, then just asks. "Who ended it?"

"Both of us, sort of. But mostly me, I guess. I'd been thinking it for a while." He rubs the skin between his eyes, a gesture that seems strikingly adult. "I just couldn't see her being the mother of my children," he says, and Ann is surprised by the sentiment, the sensitivity of it, surprised and touched.

★   ★   ★

The day with the family therapist, the day Dave told the children he was leaving, was the worst and best day of Ann's life.
The best because it marked the true beginning of Meghan's recovery, the worst because of the scene itself. Ann will never
forget that image of her three children. Meghan crying so hard
that she gasped for air. Abby with her arms crossed, staring at
the window, the look of leaving in her eyes. And Alex disappearing, going numb before them. *Alex, can you feel this? Can
you hear me?* the therapist asked him as Ann's thoughts spun
wildly—*We caused this, we're causing this*—and she watched him
recede, the color draining from his face. She is most like him,
she thinks.

Four

In the months after Dave moved out, alone in the house for
the first time, Ann had been committed to her independence.
She painted her bedroom, rearranged the living room furni-
ture, cleaned the gutters, and learned to mow the lawn. At
first she hadn't wanted Dave to leave, but gradually, she began
to feel happier. Not happier, maybe. More comfortable. More
like herself.

During that time, she read every self-help book she could
get her hands on. *When Your Child Has an Eating Disorder. Eating Disorders: A Parents' Guide. When Things Fall Apart.* She
found some comfort in it, reading books that identified her situation, that recognized what she was going through.

And she told Abby things—things she was learning in therapy, things she'd read in her magazines and books. Ann was in

a cloud of panic then, saturated with new self-awareness, desperate to keep her children from repeating her mistakes. She told Abby how she and Dave had never learned to communicate. How, when they got married, they hadn't known each other very well. They'd never slept together—it wasn't like today. How even on her wedding day, she hadn't felt completely sure.

This was inconceivable to Abby, almost offensive: *How could you not be sure?*

Abby was inexplicably annoyed by these confidences. Maybe Ann told her too much? Abby has had many boyfriends, enough that Ann finds it mildly disconcerting (probably she and Dave were to blame for this, too). On this visit, though, Abby seems calmer. For the first time in a long time, it's just the two of them alone in the house. Ann remembers when Abby was a newborn, rocking her at night, humming into her dark hair, acclimating to her new identity: *mother*. She absorbed it like a second skin.

They talk about Abby's job at the museum, which she seems to be liking, and Alex's breakup—*a good move*, Abby concurs. They talk about Joey, who's getting married this summer; he's twenty-five and his fiancée is only Meghan's age.

"Well, that explains the honeymoon at Disney World," Abby says.

"I guess," Ann says, then smiles and shakes her head.

"What?"

"Nothing." She pauses. "I was just thinking of our honeymoon, me and Dad's." Hesitantly, she tells Abby about when she and Dave arrived in California. How as they buckled into the rental car, Ann had looked at him sitting there—the side of his face, the large freckle by his ear—and was suddenly sure she'd never seen that freckle before. And then the hand—the one wearing the gold band. Whose hand was that? Who *was* this person? There was a complete stranger behind the wheel.

Two years ago, the story might have sparked impatience in Abby, but now she laughs. Ann is relieved. "God, how weird," she says, lines fanning around her eyes. In the last year, she's cut her hair to the shoulders, let a few of her old earring holes close over. Her brown hair shows glints of premature gray. She turned thirty last year, which doesn't seem possible. Her child? Thirty? Ann supposes every mother in the world thinks this.

The night before Abby is leaving, they watch a sad movie. Sad movies are Ann's favorite kind. She doesn't think she's morbid, or likes to be depressed. Just the opposite—these stories seem to get at some truth about people, life, that makes her feel connected. She's always had trouble expressing her emotions. *Rigid*—that was the word Dave once used. But the truth is, Ann feels so much that it leaves her paralyzed. Watching movies, she lets other people's feelings move through her, flood her; tonight, a documentary about the children of prostitutes in India moves her to tears. She sometimes has the same reaction to strangers, a teenage girl in a restaurant pushing food around a plate, a pained look on her mother's face. Or one of her students, nine years old but already clearly different, needy or anxious, marked for a difficult road. Ann always pays these children extra attention. She is drawn to sad things, leans into them. Empathy, but something else. A sense of kinship, a comfort.

★   ★   ★

When Abby's car pulls away, Ann stands waving on the back porch. The sadness swells up from her stitched belly, threatening to split her apart. She's reminded of a night when Abby was twenty-one, home for spring break, and drove to Florida with three friends from college—a plan she and Dave had only reluctantly agreed to—then forgot to call when she arrived. Ann had been beside herself, trying to track down the other girls' families, calling hospitals in major cities from Richmond to Fort Lauderdale. She waves until Abby's car is out of sight.

Then she steps back inside the house. She hears the tick of the oven clock, the refrigerator's drone. Her children are all gone; she is back to being alone. She'd grown accustomed to this after Dave left, but having had the house full again, she now finds the solitude palpable. She thinks briefly of all the things she should be attending to: library books that need returning, bills that need to be paid. Her mother in a nursing home, wondering why she hasn't been to see her. The car sitting cold in the driveway. For now, she shuts the door.

Five

Ann had had plans for her convalescence: things to do around the house, boxes from the attic to sift through, the children's old things to get rid of, donate, organize. Things that, in the interest of other, more pressing things, she never has the time to do. Before Alex went back to Princeton, he brought the boxes down from the attic, but they remain stacked in the

dining room, untouched. Alone again, Ann can't seem to mo-
tivate. *After three weeks, most women can resume driving and light
chores*, the pamphlet says. But once Ann lets herself succumb to
the heaviness, ease into it, it's difficult to lift herself back out.
To be inside her mind, self-contained, a wall between herself
and the world—in a way, she thinks, it is her natural state.

Kate comes to visit, like a small tornado. The children, and
all the children's things. Kate and Patrick have astounding
amounts of things. Hayley perches beside Ann on the couch,
chatting a mile a minute. She's verbal, funny, a little comedi-
enne. Six years old, but her affect is older, like one of those
mature child actors. She's wearing a backpack and shoes with
little heels—heels, at six? Tate, almost two, races in circles
around the room. (Ann had a playpen for her kids, but they've
fallen out of favor. The bars, she supposes. Miniprisons.) Kate
chases after the baby, talking all the while, relaying her latest
funny stories of domestic dishevelment—the peanut butter in
the DVD player, the vomit all over the car. *What a scene!* Kate
sighs, and Ann smiles obligingly. She's happy for Kate, who
jumped through hoops to get pregnant. A relief, when it happened. A shock when it happened again. *My gynecologist actually
laughed!* Kate told them. But Ann knows these stories are partly
for show, proof of how much work her life is. There's something naïve about them, too. Because the truth, Ann thinks,
is that when they're young, it's easy. The part that seems so
exhausting, so unrelenting—nap schedules and middle-of-the-
night feedings, potty training and ear infections—is actually
nothing. When they get older, the problems are intangible, invisible. This is the true hard: the kind that makes your marriage

age and stoop and split open. The kind that makes you panic as you listen to them close their bedroom doors. All those nights sitting beside Meghan, helplessly tracking the fluctuations in her mood, as if just by being near her, Ann could stave off whatever was happening to her. The sound of Alex thundering upstairs—he was always so quiet, but how he stomped and pounded and scraped his chair back from the kitchen table, needing a release. Watching them drive away, horns beeping as the cars disappeared around corners, waiting for the call that they arrived safely on the other side, unable to sleep until it came. *I just forgot, okay?* they might say, heaving a sigh, annoyed—annoyed!—by her worry. If she could, she would warn Kate, warn all the young mothers: Your life is no longer just your own. You will feel their every feeling. You will live two lives.

That evening, after Kate leaves, Ann sinks into the quiet. The sun is setting by five fifteen, the undersides of the low, long clouds glowing pink—the kind of thing Ann now has the luxury of noticing. She turns on a lamp and wanders her empty house. She watches a show about an obsessive detective, the first five minutes of the ten o'clock news. *More frigid temps on the way!* There's a numbness in her belly, radiating around the incision, spreading to the tops of her thighs. She goes to bed early, listening to the cars pass by.

A hysterectomy represents an end to your childbearing years, says the pamphlet. *Even women with children may experience a sense of loss.*

*   ★   ★   ★

Every day, a phone call from Margie. She talks mostly about Joey's wedding—flowers, dresses, the reception at Dugan's Banquet Hall. She rarely mentions Joe. Ann has wondered if everything is right with them, knows that Margie would never say. It took years for her to admit there was any trouble with Stephen, even when it was plain to everyone around him. Ann remembers the night Mother fell in her apartment, how troubled her nephew seemed, drunk or maybe on drugs. But she knows, too, how easy it can be not to see what's right in front of your face.

"Mother's been asking for you," Margie tells her.

"I know."

"Are you driving yet?"

"Not quite," Ann admits. "I will. Soon."

Regular walks are encouraged, says the pamphlet, but it's too cold to go outside. Ann does a few laps around the first floor. She picks things up and sets them down, as if looking for something she's misplaced. In the driveway, the car has begun to look bigger, some sort of hibernating creature hunkered down by the garage. The trunk seems wider, the nose longer, the blue of it the color of winter itself. The driveway looks icy, too, and the occasional noise from Spry confirms it—a long screech of brakes, the squeal of sliding tires. Ann cringes each time, fear sweeping through her like a wave.

Saturday: Joey and Amy's engagement party. Ann knows she should be there but can't bring herself to leave the house. Not in the dark, in this deep cold. *Avoiding stress and anxiety is important to your recovery*, the pamphlet affirms. She tells Margie she's not up to it, endures her sister's unhappy beat of silence. Around nine, Patrick's giant SUV pulls up out front and Hayley runs a plate to the door.

Dave stops by after work, a Tuesday. Ann is sure that he waited a while out of politeness, giving her privacy during the weeks that were most raw. "A beer?" she offers—strange, in his own house. The drink, the knocking. He says no to the beer but accepts a glass of iced tea. While she pours it, she notices him gazing toward the back deck; it was always his favorite place.

"You're feeling good?" he asks her when they're settled in the living room. He's sitting in the rocking chair, a chair he never used to sit in.

"Much better, thanks."

"And you're getting around?"

"Oh, yes." She doesn't admit she hasn't driven yet, that she called school and told them she needed another week. Instead, they talk about the children. About Abby, who seems happy in Boston; after twelve years, they've resigned themselves to the fact that she isn't coming home. About Alex and Rebecca's breakup—sounds like the right thing, they agree. In a way, it's as it always was: Come together, talk about the children, then go their separate ways. Except now they're older; they are observing from a distance.

"And Meghan seems good," Dave says. Always, they have to confirm, about Meghan. They were in the dark together once before.

"She does," Ann says, and prays that this is true.

*   *   *

Once, when Abby was in third grade, she had a homework assignment that required her to check the newspaper each night for a month and record the times of the sunrise and sunset. The time inched one minute later each day, occasionally two. Dave hadn't seen the point of this exercise (and more than once, exasperated, had had to run out to 7-Eleven for the paper after he was settled in the den), but Ann had liked it. It wasn't the kind of homework she would ever assign (*old school*, Alex calls her), but there was something to it, she thought, pausing to note that small change each day.

Ann feels guilty for being so idle. Though the longer it goes on, the easier it is. When she called the school, they were nothing but sympathetic—*Take all the time you need.* The children were good, they assured her, the sub working out fine. Ann imagines a woman younger, cooler, than her. For the first time in her life, there is nothing tugging at her, needing her. Nothing demanding her presence. She has stepped out of life's current, and life rolls on without her. It's both freeing and disconcerting. Is this how Mother felt? How she feels?

A call from the nursing home: Mother escaped. She made for the exit, forgetting where she was. She wheeled herself onto the elevator and out the door, and one of the nurses found her sitting in the courtyard. Now she has to wear an anklet to alert the nurses if she tries to leave again. *She's like a celebrity in rehab!* Meghan jokes on the phone.

"Do you need anything, Mom?" she asks before hanging up. "You're good, right? You're driving?"

"Oh, yes," Ann says.

She tries, because she feels guilty for lying to Meghan. But when she steps outside, she is instantly overwhelmed—the sun so bright it makes her eyes water, the sharp smell of the cold. Her incision stings, her nose hairs freeze. As she walks toward the car, the grass crunches beneath her feet, hard and white, blanched with frost. The basketball net looks gray and frozen. She sees an odd shine on the driveway—black ice? Her eyes film with tears. It is all too much. She turns and goes back inside.

That night, it snows. True snow, wet and heavy. Eight inches, ten. It buries the car, blankets the roads. It climbs all the way past the porch.

Six

One of her books said that it isn't good to name things because it limits their identity. So instead of *That's a blue jay*, say: *That's called a blue jay.* Ann finds this idea appealing. Otherwise, it's easy to reduce a person to just one thing. She remembers, when they arrived for the session with the family therapist, overhearing the doctor on her office phone: *I'll have to call you back. I have a family here in crisis.* Ann had glanced into the waiting room, looking for these poor people, then realized with a start: *That's us.*

★   ★   ★

Awake in bed, Ann listens to the plows churn slowly up and down Spry Boulevard. She watches the splash of headlights move across her bedroom wall. The neighborhood is quiet, the kind of quiet that befalls a place only after a storm. By morning, the street will be alive with scrapers and shovels and bundled children—children Ann no longer knows, the children of young families—dragging their sleds and saucers up the street.

The next day, she picks through the boxes Alex brought down from the attic. Old clothes and toys. Meghan's collection of stuffed panda bears. Abby's books, *Anastasia Krupnik* and *Harriet the Spy*. Trapper Keepers and diaries, Legos with half-built helicopters and hospitals. Enough here to feel sad for, Ann could implode. She folds the clothes, puts them into piles. *Donate, Trash, Keep.* She gives away most of the clothes, holds on to everything else. In one box, she finds an envelope filled with pictures she'd forgotten. There's John with his Fu Manchu mustache. John, cradling Max in his lap, just days before he died.

The house is cold, so Ann turns the heat up five degrees. A needless expense, but for once she has an excuse to do it. She's never felt so warm, so cozy, in her own home. Never heard such lively humming in the pipes. The phone rings—experimentally, she lets the machine pick up. *Ann? It's Margie.* A pause. *Ann? Are you there?* She takes a long warm bath, the tub filled halfway up the side, submerging her scar, her knees.

★　　★　　★

Ann pictures the inside of her body as a shell. As a room, quiet, with pulsing walls, beating like lungs, the pale pink color like the smooth inside of a conch. A place she could live inside.

When Margie shows up after church on Sunday, it takes Ann by surprise. Margie usually calls first. Ann is becoming one of those people, she thinks, like Lauren after John died: someone people drop in on with no warning.

"How were the roads?" Ann asks.

"Fine," Margie says, shaking off her boots and coat. As Ann puts on water for tea, she is embarrassed by the state of things. Dust has settled on the baseboards, dishes piled in the sink. The kitchen tablecloth, the red snowflake one that's been on since Christmas, has visible stains. And the heat—the house feels extravagantly, wastefully, warm. When they were children, they walked around indoors with cold hands and noses. She's sure Margie will confront her about it, all of it.

They sit at the table as the kettle simmers. Ann knows the determined look on her sister's face. For all her anxieties, Margie is capable of such moments: doing what needs to be done.

"Well," Ann says.

Margie's eyes are on the window, her mouth set in a hard, thin line. Her entire face looks hard, Ann thinks: the blunt cheekbones, the deep wrinkles stitched permanently across her brow. While Ann has grown a little rounder over the years, Margie has grown smaller, sharper, worry paring down her soft corners like a whittled stick. She reaches for her cross, her nervous habit ever since she got the locket for confirmation in eighth grade. "I haven't told you this," she says. "I haven't told anyone. Joe and I have been having some problems."

Ann is surprised—that the problem has nothing to do with her, and that Margie would admit to it. She tries to remember the way her therapist would react to things: never under, never over. As if nothing is too strange or insurmountable.

"I'm sorry," Ann says. "What kind of problems?"

"Money," Margie says. She knots her hands on the tablecloth. The kettle on the stove begins to shake. "And other things."

Ann nods, not pushing it. She knows they've struggled with Stephen, knows well how a child in trouble can take a toll. Once she saw a prescription bottle in Margie's medicine cabinet, something for anxiety or sleep.

Margie meets Ann's eyes, presses her lips together. "He's a weak man, I think," she says. Then she looks away, mouth twitching as if she's trying to keep from crying. She blinks quickly into the cold spill of sunlight through the window. The kettle is on the verge of whistling. "And Stephen," Margie says, and her eyes flood with tears.

Ann reaches instinctively for her sister's clasped hands, bracing herself. Stephen—it could be anything.

"There's a girl," Margie says just as the kettle starts to shriek. Ann stands to pull it off the burner, fills two cups. When she sits back down, Margie's face looks pale, but composed. "The girl, she's pregnant."

"Oh, Margie," Ann breathes.

Margie quickly shakes her head, as if to an unasked question. "We barely know her. We've never even met her. They're not . . . you know." She folds her hands again, knuckles straining against her freckled skin. "She wants him to do a test."

Ann's first impulse is to empathize: acknowledge the disappointment and the shock of it, the shame. This is not the kind of thing that happens in a family like theirs, not the kind of thing they imagine for their children—and so public. But as Ann picks up her teacup, senses her sister waiting, hands clenched on the table before her, she forces a firm note into her voice.

"Well," Ann says. "It's disappointing. But there's not much you can do, is there. Stephen has to manage his own life."

It's the wrong thing—Margie looks instantly annoyed, a quick V sinking between her eyes. "I know that," she says, reaching abruptly for her cup. "I was just telling you. I'm going to tell you, aren't I?"

At least her anger has unfrozen her, jarred her out of her contrite pose. Margie takes a sip of tea, and Ann does the same. As the warmth slides down her throat, blooming through her middle, Ann ventures: "I think he'd make a good father."

Margie says nothing, staring at the table, but her face seems to uncloud a little.

"And a new baby," Ann reminds her.

"That's true." Margie's chin is down, hands wrapped around her cup. "I guess all we can do now is wait," she says, and Ann nods, thinking: How much of life is spent doing just this. A call from a doctor, result of a test. Some sign of progress, forward movement—some small but crucial, hopeful change. "That's all you can do," Ann says, and then they talk of other things. Joey's future mother-in-law, who has funny ideas about the bridal shower. A woman from Margie's parish diagnosed with chronic fatigue. Mother, the security anklet. When the tea is gone, Margie stands, puts on her coat and boots, and tells Ann that her boys will be over soon to shovel her out.

Names

Ann stares at the car. The driveway is clear now—Stephen and Joey showed up, as promised—and the temperature is well into the forties, the old snow dripping from the eaves. Just past three thirty—she needs to leave now in order to get to the nursing home before Mother's dinner. Ann takes a breath, then starts carefully across the deck. Her scar tingles in the cold, tracing a faint line up and down her middle. She makes her way across the grass, which is slightly muddy, giving softly beneath her boots. She pulls hard at the door handle, grown stiff with the cold, but the door comes unglued. Inside, Ann turns the key—nothing. A blast of hope. Maybe the car's been off so long, it won't turn on again without a call to the mechanic, a jump start. Another day. But when she tries again, the engine catches. Sluggish at first, but it holds. Ann sits and waits as the car warms up. It's 3:45 by the clock on the dashboard. The sun won't set tonight until at least five thirty. Ann looks at the trees, bare and white against the feathery gray sky. She surveys the front seat, evidence of the last time the car was driven, the ride home from the hospital with her three children. A gum wrapper, a crumpled white bag from the pharmacy. A pink hair elastic knotted with a single long brown strand. A copy of *Recovering* on the rubber mat beneath the gas pedal, marked with Alex's size thirteen shoe. But Ann isn't thinking of her children, or her mother. She's thinking about the woman from the hospital, the one in so much pain. All night she moaned, but Ann never heard her in the daytime, never figured out her name. As she puts the car in reverse and starts backing slowly down the driveway, it occurs to her to wonder whether that woman was real or if, alone in the dark, she made her up.

Two Houses

D addy?"

Patrick is standing in his front yard, looking up at his new picture windows. Custom-fit, with state-of-the-art crown moldings, fluted exterior trim.

"Daddy? Dad?"

He is thinking, for some reason, about their old apartment on Spruce Street. The worn brown couch, the galley kitchen, the coffee mugs hanging from hooks nailed to the ceiling—the entire apartment was the size of what was now their master bedroom suite. But it was cozy, that apartment, and you couldn't beat the location. It would have been impossible back then to imagine Kate ever not living in the city, critical as she was of anyone who didn't.

"Patrick!" his daughter shouts, and finally he turns. His nine-year-old is standing by the minivan, next to the sign staked in his freshly mowed lawn: CARLSON LUXURY WINDOWS & DOORS. She is clasping the bowl she made at her friend's birthday party, one of those make-your-own-pottery ones. They had clowns, too, and face paint. Hayley's face is painted like the puppy Kate won't let her have, black and white with a bright pink tongue hanging from one side.

"Hi, sweetheart."

"Are you *ready*?"

She manages to look exasperated, even with the paint. "I was born ready," Patrick says, and they buckle into the car and go.

Since his brother John died fourteen years ago, Patrick has been determined to take away some life lessons from what happened: the suddenness of the cancer, the two small kids left behind. He's concluded, among other things, that to plan for anything is pointless. There's no telling what life will become. The only things worth planning are in the short term: playdates, meetings, birthday parties, trips to the Jersey shore.

Patrick has been doing some version of this trip his entire life—even the year John died, the entire family went, the absence unbearable, the baby crying. Today he is headed to his house in Ocean City, where Kate and their five-year-old, Tate, went this morning. Hayley stayed behind for the birthday party, and Patrick picked her up after work this afternoon. *See you next week*, he said to his assistant as he was hurrying out the door. Louise is Irish, true Irish—not the kind that Patrick was championed as on Saint Patty's Day pub crawls, a red-haired mascot to his drunk college friends, but actually from Ireland, with pale arms and soft shoulders, a brogue he finds strangely soothing. That afternoon, he'd overheard her talking to Mrs. Swift about her glaucoma in a voice so gentle and lyrical, Patrick could have closed his eyes and slept.

Enjoy your holiday, Dr. B, Louise replied. *And don't think I'm not jealous.* Something about the way she pronounced it—*jay*lous—gave Patrick an almost visceral jolt.

"Earth to Dad!" Hayley is saying from the backseat. This is one of her new lines, acquired at her private elementary school and delivered dipped in sarcasm. Patrick is not a fan.

"Yes, Hay."

"How much longer?"

"Jeez, Hay, we just left——"

But when he glances at her in the rearview mirror, he sees that her painted-on puppy mouth is smiling. She knows she's being funny. Hayley has always had this in her——a streak of humor that makes her seem more adult, more aware, than other kids her age. Her mother's child, Patrick thinks: hyperverbal, social, with that same pin-straight blond hair. Tate was born a redhead, as if sensing his father's allegiance even in the womb. Hayley, the one they fought for. Tate, the surprise. Patrick remembers that first healthy ultrasound, how Kate broke down in the doctor's office, crying with relief. She had been driven, desperate, to have that baby, after all the drugs and two attempts at IVF that didn't take. But four years later, it was a different sort of crying, quiet and helpless, leaning her knuckles against the marble sink in the master bathroom, the plastic stick sitting among the toothbrushes and face creams. Hayley was calling from the living room, Kate biting her lip, eyes brimming. Then she had turned to Patrick and said: *Maybe one is enough.* At first Patrick wasn't sure if she was joking——sometimes his wife was being funny, sometimes she only thought she was being funny——but then he saw the doubt on her face. Was she fucking kidding? It was against his religion, for one thing, but it wasn't the only thing. It was a child. *Their* child——and after all they'd gone through for Hayley. He turned and left the room and walked downstairs. She didn't mention it again.

Patrick pulls onto 76, where the traffic is thickening, heading toward the Walt Whitman Bridge. In hindsight, he thinks, Kate's hesitation shouldn't have been such a surprise. Despite her desperation to get pregnant the first time, Patrick has realized that his wife is not a natural mother. She isn't one of those women—like his sisters or his brother's wife, Lauren— for whom mothering is just inborn. She'd wanted to go back to work when Hayley started kindergarten—a plan now on hold indefinitely. In its stead, motherhood has become Kate's career. She knows all the terms and trends—Ferberizing, tummy time—but often seems resentful of her role. *I don't know who I'm supposed to be anymore*, she'll snap. *Is this really all I am?*

In these moments, Patrick feels like shouting: *You have a healthy family.*

Or: *Are you just determined to be unhappy?*

Or: *Look at Lauren! She never complains, after all she's been through!*

Look at himself, for that matter, working insanely long hours so she can have shore houses and state-of-the-art windows, hours that will stretch endlessly into the future (because he's learned: Once you live at a certain level, there's no going back).

But Patrick can't say these things, so instead he asks: *Want to trade?* A joke, but not really a joke, and they both know it. The potential argument simmers between them, until eventually one of them backs down. They have sex, usually. Despite all the injections, the long scar from the C-section, the years of rote *procreating*—Kate's word for it—their sex life is still good, and can make other things feel less looming, less tempting.

★   ★   ★

Hayley pushes her foot against the back of Patrick's seat. They are inching across the bridge, past the gauzy Philadelphia skyline. It's boiling outside—the windows are up and the air conditioner on full blast. When Patrick was a kid, there were hot days, but not this sweltering, summer-long heat. Twenty-first-century heat. It is unbearably muggy, even at six thirty, but there will be relief once they get to the shore.

Patrick glances in the rearview mirror, at Hayley staring dully at a handheld video game. As if sensing his look, she says, "How much longer?"

"Five minutes less than the last time you asked," he says.

Without looking up, she rolls her eyes. *Fresh*—it was the quality Patrick's parents disliked most. He reaches for the radio, tuning in the Phillies pregame, and Hayley sighs, a disconcertingly adult-sounding sigh. "I'm so bored."

If you're bored, you're boring, Patrick thinks, fiddling with the knob. On his childhood drives to the shore, he and his siblings were barely containable in their excitement, pressed into the backseat, itching to get to the cramped, shabby, week-long rental that was all his parents could afford. The drive was made of rituals: the license plate game, the suitcase game, the stop for cones at Jerzee Freeze. When finally they crossed the Ninth Street Bridge, Patrick would race to be the first to roll down his window and shout: *Smell the ocean!* The first whiff of salt water, confirming they were truly out of the city and away from home—the relief of space and air.

In the mirror, he sees the video game abandoned on his daughter's lap. She looks listless, painted-on pink tongue drooping from the corner of her mouth. Patrick turns the radio down. "Okay," he says. "Let's play a game."

"What game?"

"The license plate game."

Hayley frowns, wary. "What's the license plate game?"

He explains the rules, and she is engaged for half a minute, sitting up to peer down from the window of their tricked-out minivan—"Delaware, New York, New Jersey, Pennsylvania." A pause. "Delaware."

"You already said Delaware," he tells her.

"So?"

"So that's not how the game works."

She lapses into a bored slump again. Is his daughter becoming spoiled? Entitled? Lately, fearfully, Patrick catches glimpses of the teenager Hayley will become—the knowing tone of voice, the sarcasm that is more mean than funny. Despite the big house and the fancy private school, Patrick is determined that his kids stay grounded—if they don't get something and cry about it, fine. It's how he was raised. How John's kids were raised. As they creep past the tolls toward the Atlantic City Expressway, Harry Kalas is announcing the starting lineup. He glances in the mirror at Hayley, chewing absently on her hair.

"Did you know, Hay," he says, "we're having a barbecue tonight?"

"Why?"

"Why?" he repeats, wondering where she gets it—has she picked up on some of Kate's resistance to his family? "What do you mean, why? We don't need a reason to have the family over."

She considers this argument and, finding it sound, asks, "Who's coming?"

"All the usual suspects."

"What are all the usual suspects?"

He chuckles, glancing at her in the mirror. "You know, the usual crowd. Alex and Meg and Aunt Ann. Aunt Margie and Uncle Joe. Joey and Amy and—"

She sits upright. "Is baby Joey coming?"

"Yup." He nods. "Baby Joey in the house." Hayley loves babies; this one is just two months old. "And Stephen," he adds.

"And Faith?"

"I doubt it, honey." Poor kid, Stephen. For years, Patrick's nephew had had a rough time—drinking, maybe depression—but recently he'd turned things around. He got an apartment near the old rec center, a job as a security guard at Circuit City. It was a life, Patrick thought. Then Stephen got a girl pregnant; he has a daughter now he sees maybe once a month. Patrick feels for the kid. He knows what it's like to be the other brother. Knows how, when you're dealing with your own stuff, sometimes being around the family, all that normalcy, makes it harder.

"Dad!" Hayley is saying. She is leaning forward as far as her seat belt will allow, breathing in his ear. *"Is. Elena. Coming,"* she says, stressing every syllable, having evidently asked multiple times already.

"Elena." Patrick bobs his head. "Sure is."

"Awesome," Hayley breathes, and flops backward in her seat.

"In fact, you better get in some QT with her, Hay," Patrick says. "She's leaving soon. For college."

"Okay." His daughter nods, taking this assignment seriously. Patrick can't help smiling. His little girl has always adored

John's daughter. Hayley has no memory of John, of course, except the picture of him she was trained to point to as a baby and say his name, but whenever Elena's around, Hayley is glued to her side. In June, Elena graduated from high school, the Catholic school John had instructed that she go to the night he took Patrick into his office and closed the door. They sat on either side of his desk, as if it were a business meeting, John gaunt in his bathrobe, explaining his family's financial future: retirement accounts, stocks, bonds, school tuitions. He died eight hours later.

It was when he and Kate were living in the Spruce Street apartment that John bought his house. A grown-up house, Patrick thought admiringly. A *real* house. It seemed like a palace at the time. Big by any standard, but compared with his and Kate's fourth-floor walk-up—or the cramped, three-bedroom Northeast Philly row home they had all grown up in—it was monstrous.

Patrick's house now—both houses—are bigger than John's. The house at the shore they bought three years ago, when Hayley was six and Tate two and Kate was *going cuckoo for Cocoa Puffs*, as she said. She took up all kinds of hobbies. Yoga—*marijuana for grown-ups*, she called it—Reiki and Pilates. She joined the neighborhood co-op and made phone calls for the DNC. But she was always itching for the next thing, as if she had something more to prove. The shore house became her project. She obsessively scoured the real estate listings and drove back and forth on weekends, walking through empty, sunlit rooms. Patrick liked the idea of a shore house, in theory—someplace relaxed, uncluttered, an alternative to life at home—though Kate would only consider houses built in the last decade, which meant they didn't feel like shore houses; they didn't have the feeling of salt water seeped into their joints. She insisted that buying new was the smart way, the only way. *I used to work in market research*, she liked to remind him.

The house she fell in love with was twenty-eight hundred square feet and squatted right on Third Street Beach. Patrick sent up a halfhearted protest about being on the water—too pretentious—but lost that point, too. It had six bedrooms, a master bath with whirlpool, a two-car garage. It was more space than they needed—than anyone did—but the fact was this: His wife had grown up with money. Over time, Patrick had learned this was more than just a fact of your upbringing; it was part of your core.

It was the sort of thing he couldn't have known when he and Kate first met, though in retrospect, the signs were there. Planning their wedding (paid for by her father, who also helped with their down payment), Kate obsessed over pointless minutiae like the cut of the wineglasses and precise yellow of the groomsmen's ties. Patrick figured this was what all grooms went through, and kind of liked being cast in the role—the hapless husband with the beautiful, funny, opinionated wife. But it's impossible to look ahead and know how much these things will matter, like the fact that his wife isn't really Catholic—*raised Catholic*, she says. He had liked this, too, at the time. It hadn't occurred to him what it would mean later: that she wouldn't want the kids going to Catholic school, wouldn't want any mention of God at their wedding, wouldn't want the babies baptized. Patrick was sure this worried his parents, even though they never said it.

And it hadn't bothered him then that Kate hated cooking, but this feels different now, too. He's forty-four. He's tired. He works long hours and comes home wiped out at the end of the day. Sometimes he just wants a warm meal on a plate—the kind of life his father had. The life his mother made. Roast beef, green beans, twice-baked potatoes. But if he voiced this to Kate, there would be hell to pay. Sixteen years and two kids later, his wife still associates cooking with a domestic role she finds reductive, as if the minute she makes a turkey on Thanksgiving, she's compromised in some fundamental way (a graduate of Bryn Mawr—Patrick had underestimated this, too).

You said you didn't want that kind of marriage, Kate reminds him.

But was he still accountable for something he said twenty years ago? It might have been a moment of rebellion, of being blinded by his libido, by Kate's willingness to have sex in public places. A life that was different from his family's—hell, why not? Who doesn't want that at twenty-five?

Patrick has learned this, too: The older you get, the more you revert to what you came from.

Once they've fought their way across the Walt Whitman, the road widens, and the congestion lightens. A half hour later, the sky is a lazy blue, the city smog burned off behind them. After exiting the Garden State Parkway heading toward Ocean City, Patrick swerves into the parking lot of Jerzee Freeze.

"Hey!" Hayley demands, sitting up straight. "Where are we going?"

"Detour," Patrick says.

"What detour?"

"Ice cream," he says, jerking the car into a spot. "Best in the world."

She frowns. "Does Mom know?"

Christ, he thinks. But she isn't wrong; Kate doesn't like the kids having too much sugar. "Mom doesn't need to know," he says with a pinch of guilt, but he proceeds, getting out and opening the child-locked back door. "It's our little secret, Hay. You and me."

He takes her hand as she jumps down from the car. The air is still warm but less humid, tinged with salt; the ocean is getting close. As they head across the parking lot, the proximity to ice cream makes her complicit. "Do they have strawberry?" she says, keeping her hand in his.

"You bet," Patrick says. "World-class strawberry."

They stand in line, cars turning into the traffic circle behind them. He can feel Hayley's alertness, concentrating on her order. When she gets to the counter, she speaks in a single breath: "One strawberry ice cream that's all please thank you."

"Aw, how cute!" says the ice-cream girl, leaning over the counter. She has the tan of a kid who's worked at the shore all summer, a shiny brown ponytail and frosted pink lips, the striped straps of her bathing suit peeking beneath her Jerzee Freeze T-shirt. "Are you a clown?" she says, smiling at Hayley's painted face.

"No," Hayley replies. She looks suddenly embarrassed. Maybe it's being singled out, or singled out by a cool older girl. "I'm a puppy," she says.

"Oh, a puppy!" The girl nods faux seriously. "I have a Doberman."

"Well, I'm a husky."

"A husky!" She laughs, grabbing a scooper.

Hayley adds, "I want to get a puppy, actually, but my mom won't let me."

"Oh, really? That's too bad." She smiles, glancing at Patrick as she digs into the strawberry carton. "She's adorable."

"Shameless, too," Patrick says. "Playing the puppy sympathy card just to get an extra scoop."

Laughing, the girl hands Hayley a massive cone. She takes it carefully in two hands. "What about you, Dad?"

"Chocolate with sprinkles. Rainbow, please."

"Rainbow sprinkles coming right up," she says.

The ice-cream girl looks nothing like Louise—in fact, she is much prettier and certainly sexier—but they have something in common. It's the laughing, Patrick thinks. Louise is always laughing. It's part of why he likes to be around her, because she thinks he's funny—talking to her, Patrick *is* funny. As if she taps into some shut-down part of himself, his old sense of humor coming back to life.

"Eight oh two," the girl says.

Patrick checks his thoughts, feeling guilty again. He smiles and pays, jamming the change in the tip jar. Then he and Hayley walk over to a picnic table and sit side by side on one of the peeling red benches, her feet dangling an inch above the hot cement.

"Good, huh?"

She nods, focusing intently on catching the drips with her tongue as they roll down the sides. They sit in silence, facing the traffic circle, licking their cones. Patrick watches the shore-bound cars slow down before them, wending their way

into the on-deck circle and waiting for their opening. He lets
his mind wander back to Louise, to their conversation this afternoon as he was leaving. Patrick has wondered sometimes if
Louise flirts with him (somehow the accent makes it harder to
tell), but today he was almost sure. *And don't think I'm not jealous*, she'd said, sighing. *Think of me back here in Philly, melting in
my flat.*

No A/C?

Uh-uh, she'd said. When she smiled, her cheeks bunched
and softened like plums. *I would kill to be at the beach.*

Patrick had paused in the doorway. *To be honest with you,
Louise, I sort of wish I wasn't going.*

Why's that?

I need a break from my life.

Her face had registered surprise, but she'd recovered quickly
and leaned forward slightly, the cross around her neck dipping
forward, voice dropping to a conspiratorial whisper. *Shall I call
you back with a work emergency, then?*

He'd grinned at her and whispered back, *Please do.*

It had all happened so quickly, glibly. Surely they had just
been kidding—hadn't they? Patrick stares at the rotary, the
sun beating on his brow. Either way, it wasn't appropriate. He
shouldn't have implied there were any problems in his personal
life, betrayed any hint of his unhappiness at home—was *unhappiness* even the word?

Patrick hears the buzz of a text message. He pulls his phone
from his shirt pocket. Kate, as if sensing his thoughts.

R u close?

He squints at the phone, then looks at Hayley, who is working her way studiously around the lip of her cone. He drops

the phone back in his pocket as guilt needles him again. Guilt: It is his baseline.

When they were at home in Philadelphia, he and John lived largely independent lives—in school, they were a critical four years apart—but they were inseparable at the shore. They spent all day on the beach together, playing paddleball and building elaborate castles, digging holes to China and burying each other in the sand. In the ocean, they played a game where they named the waves after different creatures, depending on their size and strength. *A cheetah! No, a lion! A T. rex!* They rode the waves, arms straight out and heads down, salt water rushing up their mouths and noses, tossing them on the sand. As the afternoon softened and purpled into evening—for Patrick, the most unbearable part of each day—they started the long trudge back to their rental, six blocks from the beach. Their bedroom in the rental wasn't much smaller than the one they shared at home, but somehow the novelty of bunk beds made them stay up late talking, stifling laughter in their pillows. John would drift off eventually, but Patrick lay awake, watching the dip in the mattress moving, squeaking faintly as his brother breathed.

In the months after John died, Patrick worried that what got his brother would get him, too. He felt pains and aches. He woke at night drenched in sweat. He worried it was cancer, worried it was other things. He was in his third year of med school, clinical rotations. Disease was everywhere. And his paranoia felt justified, because if John had been checked sooner, might not things have turned out differently? Patrick resolved to be less stubborn. To extract some wisdom. *What doesn't kill you makes you stronger. God has a plan.* But if he said these things to Kate, she raised an eyebrow, so he started keeping them to himself. He started taking Lexapro, too, which helped his nerves but killed his sex drive. He felt flattened all the time—drugs? grief? After a while, it was hard to say.

Now, Patrick is no longer afraid of dying. He feels the pressure of being alive. To do right by his family. Be a good father, a good husband, a good uncle to John's children. To be responsible and right. He wonders sometimes if his anxiety simmers elsewhere in the family—did John wrestle with it, too? Patrick doubts it, though sometimes he considers asking Lauren. Back when his brother started dating her—it seems like a million years ago—Patrick thought Lauren was a little boring, a little plain. But over the years he's come to admire her more and more. The way she keeps her house, the way she puts her kids first. She's actually become prettier with age; it looks natural on her, not as forced as lots of Kate's Main Line friends. And her loyalty to their family has never wavered. After their mother fell and broke her arm, she lived at Lauren's for almost a year—longer than any of them had expected—but Lauren never once complained. Patrick doesn't want to know what Kate would have said if put in that position but their house, for all its tricks, didn't have a full bath on the first floor, so thankfully, it never came up.

Patrick can see the shore approaching, the top of the Ferris wheel emerging from the haze. The Phillies are up two in the fourth, with a man on. Suddenly he feels a blast of wind from the backseat. "Smell the ocean!" Hayley yells.

Ninth Street Bridge. Patrick hadn't even been paying attention. He feels the rumble under their wheels, the whine of the metal grid.

"Dad!" Hayley shouts, leaning her face out the window. "Smell the ocean!"

"Good girl, Hay," he says with a laugh. "Beat me to it." It makes him smile, makes him ache—his daughter and these old traditions, passed down.

The bridge ends, and they are coasting down Ninth Street. He tastes salt on his lips. They drive past people pedaling bikes slowly down the sidewalk, wearing bathing suits, towels slung over shoulders. Past the Food Mart, the cheap turquoise motel, the subpar Italian restaurant they loved when they were kids.

"What time is the barbecue?" Hayley is asking. She is sitting forward now, bouncing with excitement or sugar.

"Soon."

"Who's staying?"

"Let's see," Patrick says. "Joey and Amy and the baby, I think." It's one of the advantages of having such a big house—between the three extra bedrooms and the covered porch, there's room for people to stay overnight. Joey can't afford his own rental, especially now, with the baby. Patrick is sure this bugs Kate, but it makes him feel better: Their house may be obscene, but at least they can share it with the family.

They pull onto Third Street, heading toward the ocean, and the roof of their house comes into view. It's the biggest, most ostentatious house on the block, a modern behemoth at the end of a row of old, gently worn duplexes with rainbow wind socks and Phillies flags flying from their porches. Patrick winces as he pulls into the driveway, little stones crunching beneath his wheels. The moment he turns the engine off,

Hayley flings open the door and goes running inside. For a long minute, Patrick just sits there, his hands on the wheel. As kids, he and John always envied the people with houses right on the beach. Dragging themselves home in the evenings, they would loiter in the shaggy grass of the dunes just beyond the big picture windows, squinting to make out the people inside. Patrick would be briefly impressed, then distracted by hunger or mosquitoes or some sudden, paralyzing nostalgia for the day that was ending, but John would regard those houses like a problem to solve, a skill to master: *Who do you think lives in places like those?*

Patrick closes his eyes and draws a deep breath of ocean, lets the salt air flood his lungs. When he looks again at his house, he reminds himself: Money doesn't buy happiness. That one's easy, but still it feels surprising every time, how deeply true it is.

He steps out of the car and into the cool breeze. Slowly he collects the suitcases and the pottery bowl and crunches across the small white stones. The deck is stocked and ready for a party—coolers of ice, cases of soda, top-of-the-line grill—but when Patrick steps inside, the place is chaos. The living room floor is covered with Tate's toys, the kitchen counter a mess of potato-chip bags and soda bottles, torn-open packages of cookies and store-bought cupcakes—and a few puddles of jewelry, pearls and pendants that Kate must have tried on and discarded.

Then his wife strides into the kitchen, looking perfect: sunglasses, hair, nails. She is wearing a red bathing suit under a silky flowered cover-up. "Are you late?"

"Hello to you, too," Patrick replies, setting Hayley's bowl on the counter. "The drive was fine, thanks."

"Hi, Dad!" Tate yells from the next room, where he's parked in front of the TV.

"Hey, bud," Patrick says. At least someone is happy to see him. "What are you watching on television on this beautiful summer evening?"

"*SpongeBob*," he replies as Kate scoops the jewelry off the counter and into her palm.

"I was expecting you an hour ago, wasn't I?" she says.

"We hit traffic," Patrick replies, and heads for the stairs, carrying the suitcases.

"Oh?" She trails him, sounding skeptical. Maybe she's already seen Hayley's face, the evidence of strawberry on her mouth.

"And we stopped for ten minutes," he adds. "We got ice cream."

"Ice cream? Didn't she have a sugar infusion at the party?"

"I don't know what she had at the party."

"You didn't ask?"

"We were driving to the shore, Kate," he says, dumping Hayley's suitcase inside her bedroom doorway. "The ice-cream place was there. She was bored. I was nostalgic. We had a moment." Patrick turns into their bedroom and tosses his duffel on the bed.

"Just for the record," Kate says, her voice tight. "I really needed you here sooner."

"Yeah. I got that."

"I'm not kidding, Patrick."

"I didn't think you were."

He turns to face her. It's dangerous, he thinks, two funny people; humor can so easily turn cruel.

"I've been here since nine this morning," she says, arms folded over her chest. "I've spent the last eight hours shopping and cleaning for your family."

Your family—after all this time.

Patrick looks at her. Was he wrong to hope things might be different? He resists the urge to mention that the living room looks as if a cyclone hit it, yet she had time to deal with her nails and hair. Because he hates the trading of responsibilities, the contests over who's done more, worked harder, but he can't help adding: "I worked all day, too, you know."

From downstairs, the kitchen door slams and Hayley shouts, "Hi, Aunt Lauren! Hi, Max!" He hears Lauren's effusive greeting and the mumbled hello from his nephew, John's son, now sixteen. The door slams again and Hayley yells with furious, possibly sugar-addled, excitement, "Elena! Check out my face!"

Patrick's head is pounding. He feels suddenly as if he could implode—with love for his family, frustration with his wife, the two parts of his life that he's always struggled to reconcile, like having two close friends who just don't click.

Kate closes her eyes in a long, decisive blink. When she opens them, she smiles. "I'm sorry," she says. "I'm sure you're wiped out, too." Patrick can see the effort behind it as she tries to relax her face. Then she takes a step toward him, touching his wrist—an invitation. They could have a quickie right now, her look says, a furtive session like in the old days. Sidestep the tension between them, smooth things over.

"There are people downstairs," Patrick says.

"And?"

A glitter in her eye—flirty and willing, but something else, too, a streak of vulnerability. Patrick can see how hurt she will be if he rejects her. Because what he knows about Kate, that most people don't, is how insecure she can be. How her bold personality is a front for her fear of failure. She's tormented by her looks disappearing—the wrinkles around her eyes, the scar from the babies. He should give in, to spare her feelings, but suddenly all he wants in the world is to get outside.

He loosens his arm from hers. "I'll be back."

"What?"

"I need to take a walk."

"A walk?" She sounds incredulous.

"Mom!" Tate calls.

"Just a quick one," Patrick says.

"But you just got here."

"It'll just be a minute," he says, starting for the door.

"But there are *people* downstairs," Kate calls after him, pointedly.

Patrick keeps moving, loosening his tie. From downstairs, Tate keeps yelling. "Mommy! *Mom!*"

"You're kidding me, right?" Kate shouts after him, and he hears a tremble of fury in her voice but continues down the back stairs, feeling weirdly buoyant, out the side door, and onto the beach.

On the sand, Patrick slides off his shoes and peels off his socks. The sand beneath his bare feet feels so cool and smooth, he could weep. He leaves his shoes on the dunes and stuffs his socks into one pocket, tie in the other. The beach is nearly empty, a few stragglers still hanging on to the end of the afternoon. Two sunburned boys whacking a paddleball, a girl sitting on the lifeguard stand with her sweatshirt pulled over her knees. A decent sand castle, adorned with sticks and shells, stands just out of the tide's reach, the foamy waves curling to a stop at the edge of the moat.

Patrick walks down to the ocean, keeps walking up to his ankles, not caring that the bottoms of his pants get soaked. He squints at the horizon, the first glimmers of pink and gold. Of all the hours on the beach, this is the one that makes him most wistful. As a kid, he was always painfully aware of the hours ticking down each afternoon, the number of vacation days remaining, the pleasure of the week so tinged with impending loss it was almost impossible to enjoy. He's sure John never let himself get caught up in thoughts like these—or did he? Did he feel this way, when he knew that time was running out?

A lump wells in his throat and rises to his eyes. He notices a few people glancing over at him. Maybe they recognize him—the eye doctor, the guy who lives in the giant house. Patrick almost doesn't recognize himself. That he ended up as any kind of doctor still mystifies him completely. As a kid, he made middling grades in science. Needles made him squirm. Whenever he tries to retrace the steps he took to get here, he can hardly recall when and why he made those pivotal decisions—unlike his brother, who set goals and achieved them, life just carried Patrick along. It was Kate who pushed for med school: *You have such a good bedside manner.* As with many things, she was teasing but she wasn't. Kate wanted him to be a doctor, wanted the life that came with it. He applied, mostly to make her happy; it was only after John died that he began to take it seriously. A rotation, an internship. A supervisor who remarked: *You have the right personality for eyes.* The ability to put people at ease, to make patients relax and trust him—it was one of the reasons he'd hired Louise. Because people are funny about their eyes. It's a delicate business, and also weirdly intimate—how close you sit to someone's face, staring into their eyes in the darkened office, an inch between your face and theirs, so close you can feel their breath. Sometimes he has the urge to kiss them, just because it would be so easy.

A shore plane flies overhead, trailing an advertising ribbon—EAT AT O'MALLEY'S! BEST CLAMS AT THE SHORE! The waves are crashing hard, thumping against the ocean floor. *It's a lion!* Patrick thinks. *It's a T. rex!* The foam rushes around his ankles, a tangle of seaweed wrapping around his big toe. He lets the sand suck his heels under, one inch and another, until his feet are encased comfortably in cement. It occurs to him that his whole life has been shaped by other people—the guilt of surviving his brother, the need to placate his wife. What would his life be if it were up to him? Can he even tell anymore?

His phone buzzes in his shirt pocket. *Jesus Christ, Kate.* He pulls it out and reads the text.

There's an emergency at work. :)

Patrick's lips go dry. He stares at the phone. He considers writing back, something witty. He considers hurling the phone into the surf. He drops it back in his pocket and peers out at the sunset, the sky reddening behind the clouds, his face damp with spray. Then he pries his feet from the wet sand. As he heads back up the beach, he hears a wave crash behind him and watches it sprawl up the sand, far enough to reach the castle, filling the moat and causing one section to collapse gently. He looks up at his house, the grand house on the beach, the bright shapes moving behind the windows.

★   ★   ★

Back on the highway, driving with the windows down, Patrick cranks the radio as loud as it will go. The game is tied in the seventh. The Phils have two outs, men on first and third. His cell phone is silenced, sitting in the cup holder. The traffic is creeping along, barely moving, but it's intoxicating being on the highway alone.

A work emergency? Kate had repeated.

I'll just run back, he'd said.

She had looked at him in disbelief. *There isn't someone else who can handle it?*

Like who? he'd said. *She was in this afternoon. She has glaucoma. She's old.*

Patrick, Kate had said, patiently, as if he were a child.

I'll be back as soon as I can.

You'll miss the entire party.

I'll miss three hours. Four, tops.

Exactly, Kate had said. She'd looked furious, but with the family around she couldn't make a scene. Instead she'd asked: *Who's going to cook?*

Steve, he'd said, pointing at his nephew. *Right, Steve?*

Kate had looked skeptical, which had pissed Patrick off even more. *Here you go*, he'd said, handing his nephew a spatula and clapping his thick shoulder. *The passing of the torch.*

Remembering the moment, Patrick feels indignant all over again. On the radio, a crack of a bat, the swelling cheer. Rollins hit a double; two runners score. Patrick yells out loud and thumps the wheel. A woman in the next car glances over. He smiles at her apologetically, inches the car forward another foot.

Pitching change. Commercial. He gazes out at the highway, the billboards for casinos and concerts in Atlantic City, the shimmering sea of license plates. Alaska—they would have never seen an Alaska thirty years ago, he thinks. He lets his mind wander up the road to Philadelphia, his huge house sitting empty in the suburbs. To Louise's stifling city apartment—her *flat*. It must be somewhere near the office; he's heard her mention riding her bike to work. Patrick imagines a walk-up with a small, bright kitchen, a careworn sofa—then realizes he's picturing his and Kate's old place on Spruce Street. Louise's apartment is probably nicer, actually, more domestic. Last Monday, she'd brought cupcakes into the office for no reason—*I just had the urge to bake*, she'd said with a shrug of her soft shoulders. Each one was carefully frosted, transported in one of those Tupperware holders made specifically for cupcakes. It was the kind of thing that, if Patrick had it all to do over again, might just win him over, suggest a certain kind of life.

Ridiculous, he thinks. Meaningless.

The traffic is still barely moving. The mass of bumpers simmers in the heat. If he doesn't turn back now, Kate will be vindicated, for he really will miss the entire party. He could get off at the next exit and turn around, make up one more lie about poor Mrs. Swift and her glaucoma. Or he could keep going and spend the night at home. One night, apart from real life. One night with no consequences.

But Patrick has learned this: Everything has consequences.

And this: He's tired of learning things.

It is nearly nine when Patrick crosses back over the Walt Whitman. The skyline is a dense, dirty gray. The car windows are rolled up tight, the air conditioner cranked. The Phillies won in extra innings and the crowd from the new stadium is spilling onto 95. The old stadium, the one he and John used to go to, is gone now, demolished. The skyline is changed, too, the tall buildings clustered in the distance twice as many as when he was a boy.

Patrick creeps across the bridge. Nearby cars thump and rattle, stereos blaring, unleashing pent-up excitement from the game. As a kid, riding home from the shore and glimpsing the city, Patrick used to feel deflated, sick with the thought of normal life resuming, of having to wait another year. Tonight, though, as the city grows nearer, there is quicksand in his gut, a muddle of giddiness and nerves. He gazes out at the dark, humid city and lets himself imagine tracking down Louise's address, showing up at her apartment door—

Fantasies are harmless, Kate used to say, but surely this isn't what she meant.

When he exits 76, the traffic lightens, and he quickly reaches the wealthy Main Line suburb that has become his home. When he pulls into the driveway, the sky is dark, but the house glows like a castle, gold lampposts flanking the flagstone path on either side. As he walks toward the door, the backs of his wingtips chafing against his still-sockless feet, he can just make out the sign in his lawn: CARLSON LUXURY WINDOWS & DOORS. It strikes him fully then: There will always be some project, some upgrade or improvement. The work will never end.

Patrick yanks the sign from the lawn—it's wedged in good, and he stumbles a little before muscling it out—then crams it under one arm and walks up to the porch, punching in the code. Inside, the empty house yawns around him. He drops his keys on the foyer table, flicking on the lights. Alone, the house feels huge and oddly unfamiliar. That lamp with the glass base—has he ever seen that lamp before? He walks through the foyer with its vaulted ceiling and marble tiles, vases filled with artful flowers. The place is air-conditioned within an inch of its life—it feels like the inside of a florist's refrigerator—and smells clean, professionally clean, which is somehow fundamentally different from the clean of Patrick's house growing up, a smell made of grainy Ajax, soapy water, work, and grit.

He walks past the formal living room, the one they almost never use, and into the ironic joke of a kitchen—the double oven, the fancy espresso machine. Patrick folds the sign in two and crams it into the trash can. Then he rummages in the fridge, finding nothing but juice boxes and leftover SpaghettiOs. He pulls out a beer. Standing at the counter, he gazes out the new state-of-the-art kitchen windows, but with the lights on and the darkness outside, he can see nothing but his own murky reflection in the glass.

He slugs the beer and takes his phone from his pocket. As he powers it back up—two missed text messages, three voice mails—his heart leaps like a kid.

They are all Kate, of course.

The first text: *ETA?*

The second: *r u there???*

The voice mails are Kate, too. Patrick doesn't bother listening. He drains the beer, then sets aside the empty bottle and picks up the phone and dials.

"Hello?"

"Hey," he says. "Is this Louise?"

A pause. "Dr. B?"

The title alone is almost enough to stop him, to remind him who he is. But he presses on, keeping his voice light. "Yeah," he says. "Hey there, Louise." He can feel her waiting. "Listen—I'm calling because I hear there's a work emergency?"

"Oh," she says. "Oh, right." She sounds confused, and a little nervous, and Patrick wonders if he's misread this entire thing. If sending the text wasn't Louise flirting but merely following his instructions. "There was no emergency, really, though . . . ," she says, and then Patrick understands that she's just worried that he took her message seriously.

"You're *kidding* me, Louise," he says, thick with sarcasm. "There *isn't?*"

She exhales a laugh, a puff of relief. "For a second I thought you believed me!" Then she sighs, an oddly long, contented sigh. "Was that okay, then? Sending it?"

Like that, it's as if they're conspiring already. Competing twinges of guilt and nerves fire off in his gut. "Well, sure," he says, staring at the granite countertop. "Of course it was." He adds, "I'm glad you did, Louise."

"Oh?" He can hear the pleasure in her voice, pictures her pink cheeks bunching. He sees himself standing in the ocean, letting the sand grip his heels.

"Well, so . . . ," Louise says. Her voice has a new edge, eager, slightly flustered. "How's the beach? Sounds pretty tame there, have to say."

"That would be because I'm not at the beach."

"No?"

"I'm home." He adds, "But my wife isn't."

"Oh," she says, and his feet get sucked in to the ankles. A

thin sweat has broken on his brow, despite the air-conditioning blasting from the kitchen's every pore. Sweetly, she asks, "You decided not to go, then?"

Patrick stares hard at the counter, at the empty beer bottle, the sign jammed awkwardly in the trash can. He looks up at the darkened window, and he makes a decision. "I went," he says. "But when I got your text, I came back."

She laughs again, a different laugh, more like a giggle, and it is then that Patrick knows for sure he hasn't misread anything. He knows, too, that this would be easy. To be charming and funny, to meet up with Louise in the city, sleep with Louise in her small, sweltering apartment with the cupcake carriers. He can see it all, the ease of it all; it breaks his heart, how easy it would be.

"Well, then . . . ," she says. She's hoping that he'll jump in to steer the conversation, as he should. He's a prick for letting her just hang there, but suddenly he can't bring himself to speak. "What are you doing tonight?" Louise says.

Patrick stares hard at the refrigerator door: a watercolor that Tate made at school. *Mommy, Daddy, Hayley, Me.* It isn't a co-incidence, the picture—he could look anywhere and find a reason not to go through with this. The framed family photos, the fridge filled with juice boxes, his wife's hand lotion on the edge of the kitchen sink.

Then he thinks of John. This, he knows, is something his brother would never do. But is that even true? Does he know that for sure? Or has his brother become so sanitized in his memory, so sanctified, that he can do no wrong? It's been fourteen years—who can say?

As he stares at the window, the truth settles over him, and

he knows he won't do anything. He'll ease off the phone, without hurting Louise's feelings. He'll call his wife and apologize and go to bed alone in his strange, glowing house. In the morning, he'll drive back to the shore, to his family. Whether that's who he really is, or who he's decided he has to be, it hardly matters.

"Dr. B?"

"What's that, Louise? I think my phone cut out for a sec," Patrick says with another guilty stab.

"I said, um, what are you doing? Later tonight?"

He summons up his most self-deprecating tone. "Well, let's see," he says. "Sadly, Louise, since I'm an unhip old fogy, I'll probably hit the sack around nine thirty."

"Oh?" She manages a confused laugh. "You will?"

"Ten, tops," Patrick says. He knows he should just be honest with her. He should say: *I'm tempted, Louise, but I have to do the right thing here.* But he can't—it would make work too complicated. What he needs is to make her think it was all a shared joke, end the call without any injury to her self-esteem. Be funny. Put her at ease.

"When you're out having fun tonight, think of me," he says. "I'll probably be doing the crossword puzzle."

She laughs uncertainly. "That's sad, Dr. Blessing."

"Maybe watching a little TV," he says. "*Masterpiece Theatre. Murder, She Wrote.*"

"Maybe we should have you fitted for bifocals," she says, playing along, and Patrick laughs overly hard in appreciation. In the office, he thinks sadly, things will be fine. "Good night, Louise," he says, and then hangs up the phone. The silent house throbs around him. He looks at his kitchen, all the glossy chrome and granite, the fridge door covered with the kids' pictures. He has no right to be so unhappy, he thinks.

When he walks into the living room, Patrick kicks off his shoes and then stretches out on the white couch, the one the kids aren't allowed to sit on. His feet are still a little sandy, but he props them on the opposite arm. He stares at the ceiling, an ornate chandelier, and remembers the day he and Kate moved out of the apartment on Spruce Street. He'd just finished med school and was starting his residency, and they were moving into a bigger, nicer apartment in West Philly. Still, they couldn't afford movers, so they did it all themselves. They carried armfuls of stuff down four narrow flights of stairs, bloated trash bags and cheap lamps and books packed in liquor store boxes, tossing them in the Budget truck double-parked outside. At the end of two hours, they were exhausted and sweaty and a little giddy. The only thing left to go was the couch. It was brown and sunken, a relic from Patrick's college dorm room. They each picked up one end, then Kate insisted they have sex on it in the old apartment one last time. *It deserves a proper send-off*, she said.

So they did, which left them feeling loopy and unmotivated, and hungry, so they ordered a pizza and split a bottle of wine. When they picked up the couch again, it seemed to have grown heavier. They shoved it through the apartment doorway, then spent ten minutes trying to maneuver it around a tight corner of the stairwell between the third and fourth floors. Kate stood on the landing holding one end, while Patrick perched a few steps below her, bracing the other with his chest. Then Kate stopped pushing. "This isn't working," she said. "It's stuck." She looked at Patrick across the sagging brown cushions, her damp blond bangs plastered to her brow, and she smiled, a familiar streak of mischief on her face. Without discussion, they both dropped it. The couch hurtled fantastically down the stairs, bouncing between the wall and railing, crashing into pieces at the bottom, a cheap wooden arm, a splintered foot. The railing snapped in two.

It was a feeling he'll never know again, Patrick thinks, staring at the ceiling. Because now he could never be so reckless. He no longer has the sort of life where you just let things break. It isn't just the things he owns, it's the person he's become. But he can still remember how good it felt, trying so hard to hold on to that old couch and then just letting go.

Flight

Elena is always stopped by security in airports. She has "a look," her brother Max says. A big baggy green coat, hair shaved on one side and long on the other. She wears lots of layers. Coat, hoodie, T-shirt, and, sandwiched in the middle, her dad's blue button-down shirt, the soft denim one with the sleeves that hang an inch past her fingers. Maybe it's the layers that look suspicious—she could be hiding anything in there.

"The shirt was my dad's," she says to the security guard as she's jamming her feet back into her Chucks. She isn't trying to be fresh. She blurts things out when she's nervous. The guard looks at her without expression, then waves her through.

Elena knows that children of dead parents sometimes construct fake memories, idyllic scenes that never really took place. She has only a few memories of her dad, but she's pretty sure they're real. They *feel* real. In one she's standing in her crib as he walks in, holding a baby. In another she's in the car beside him, a stuffed owl in her lap. Supposedly memories don't form before the age of five, but Elena is sure she remembers the time she ran into the pool and her mother jumped in to save her.

She wasn't even four yet, but her mom can corroborate the story, and Aunt Kate. *That was a very difficult summer,* her mom says whenever it comes up, as if in defense of something. *Daddy dying was the first really hard thing that ever happened to me.*

Mostly, though, what Elena knows about her dad—or thinks she knows—she has constructed from negative space. In his absence, he's become a way to explain all the things about herself she doesn't understand, all the things that are so totally different from her mother. Her mom is traditional, conservative; she still goes to church every Sunday. Elena is a creative. She wants to adopt kids, to travel the world. Physically, she takes after her mother—nobody in her dad's family has their dark skin and hair—but her height is her dad's, and her nose, both things she happens to like about herself. She used to despise her name until her grandmother once said offhandedly, "Your father loved the name Elena." She realized the hypocrisy but couldn't help it. After that she loved it, too.

Elena can't reminisce with Max about their father; he was too young to remember anything about him, not even the possibly shadow memories that Elena has. But Max has his looks, and his personality, apparently—*There's John's confidence,* her family says at his swim meets, when Max has the poise to wait on the starting block until the very last second—unlike Elena, who gets so rattled by everything. Elena has her memories, though, and in that way she guesses that she's lucky. Max has only things. A green Eagles hat. A heavy gold pen. Elena has things, too, like the denim button-down, which she wears when she needs luck, or comfort, like for a midterm or a ride on a plane.

She walks down the aisle, messenger bag hitched to her

shoulder, and spots her seat—a window. Her stomach tightens up. She wouldn't have chosen the window, wouldn't have chosen to fly at all (had it been up to her, she would have gone by train). But the trip to Boston had been a graduation present from her cousin Abby—more like an aunt than a cousin, really. They're almost twenty years apart, but they've always been close. Abby babysat when her dad was in the hospital (though Elena has no memories of this, either). She's spent the past two days in the South End of Boston, in an apartment Abby shares with her boyfriend, Charlie. "Boyfriend," Abby said, frowning. "Such a weird term at my age."

"Kind of a weird term at any age," Elena agreed.

On her first night, over wine and lasagna, Abby and Charlie told Elena they were getting engaged. "That's awesome," Elena said. It came out sounding childish, but she meant it. She thought it made sense to wait until you're older, thirty-five, at least—her mother was twenty-two when she got married (the same age Elena is now, which is insane)—and she likes Charlie, who is arty but in a genuine way. He asked her lots of questions about her photography. Yesterday, they took her to the Museum of Fine Arts and to the ICA, where Abby works.

"We're going to move back," Abby told her, dipping a piece of bread in the lasagna. "To Philly. This summer, most likely."

Elena was surprised. Abby hadn't lived at home since she left for college; since then, a lot had changed. Her parents got divorced, her sister Meghan had a serious eating disorder—things such a part of the fabric of the family story that it was almost weird to think there was a time before them. When Meghan was in high school, she used to babysit a lot for Max and Elena; she was already bulimic, though nobody knew it yet. Later, of course, Elena would know tons of girls with eating disorders and recognize the symptoms—in old pictures, she can see Meghan's weight fluctuated in weird ways—but she doesn't remember her cousin as skinny, or chubby, or sad. What she remembers mostly is a night that Meghan was babysitting and let her stay up past ten, confiding in her about a boy she liked as they took turns dipping the same spoon into an ice-cream tub—like a slumber party in a movie—then made Elena brush her teeth and promise not to tell. It was one of the best nights of her life.

"It was when my mom got sick," Abby said, and her eyes grew briefly teary. Then she shrugged. "That was it. I knew then I would move back someday." She tapped the back of Charlie's hand. "It just took a few years to get all my ducks in a row."

Elena nodded as Charlie topped off their wineglasses. When she was in high school, her aunt Ann had had surgery because the doctor found cancer. Luckily, it was caught early; her dad's had been caught late.

"It's strange," Abby continued, shaking her head. "You hear how people's priorities change and eventually they go back to where they came from, like some kind of homing instinct. And you think it won't happen to you, but then something changes, and there you are."

Elena understood moments like this: where a thing just clicks and the world looks different—*crux moments*, she called them in her Artist Statement. *When the world looks suddenly, irrevocably changed.* Like the time she was nine and her mom apologized for yelling and it occurred to Elena for the first time that grown-ups could be wrong. Or her sophomore year of high school, when she was going out with Paul Dow, who was doting but clingy, and she realized you didn't have to like people back just because they were nice.

"I'm glad I lived other places first, though," Abby told her.

"Definitely," Elena said, adding, "Actually, I'm taking next year to travel."

"Oh, yeah?" Charlie said. "Where to?"

"I'm not sure yet," she admitted sheepishly, but they both nodded, undeterred by her lack of a plan. The truth was, she wasn't really planless; there were just so many things she wanted to see that she couldn't decide—she was less interested in whole places than in details. Brunelleschi's doors in Florence. Monet's gardens. In Geneva, the longest bench in the world—she can already imagine trying to take a picture of it, to capture the paradox, the sense of intimacy and endlessness at the same time.

"Europe, mostly, I guess," she said.

"You should talk to Alex about Spain," Abby said, lifting her wineglass. "He went there once with that girl Rebecca."

Elena had never met her cousin's old girlfriend, but Alex had recently caused a stir in the family, marrying a woman he taught with at Columbia, a biology professor named Cynthia. They eloped without telling anyone, which Elena had thought was pretty cool, although her aunts were upset they hadn't been there.

"I forget where exactly," Abby said. She frowned, took a sip. "But ask him. It was near Seville, I think."

"I definitely will," Elena said. She was grateful for Abby's faith in her travel plan. When Elena told her mother about it, she had freaked out, predictably. Her dad would have been more open-minded, Elena was sure. But her mother was a worrier and had never gone anywhere, never left the country except for their honeymoon to Bermuda. In retrospect, Elena hadn't helped her cause by the way she'd broached the subject: *Mom, I'm taking a year to see the world.*

The world? her mother had pounced.

Well, not the world, she'd said. *Just parts of it.*

Elena rummages in her messenger bag, digging out her iPod as a woman takes the aisle seat beside her. Elena can tell right away this woman is from Philadelphia. Something about her unfussy sweater, her salt-and-pepper hair, the gold earrings shaped like little shells. She looks as though she could be friends with Aunt Ann or Aunt Margie, though why exactly is hard to explain.

"Hello," the woman says.

Philadelphia—the "o" sound confirms it.

"Hey," Elena says.

The attendant walks by, clicking shut the overhead compartments, and Elena feels a catch in her throat. She leans her head back, sliding her thick silver ring back and forth over her knuckle. She's always hated flying, even before the World Trade Center, but that was when her fears intensified. She was almost eleven then, and Max nine, and somehow his being two years younger—or not having yet gone through those particular, nine- and ten-year-old years—was enough to keep Max relatively unaffected, or unaware. It was the same with their father dying: Elena was just old enough to remember what life was like before, Max just young enough not to know anything different.

Flight

For weeks after the attacks, Elena had nightmares. Fathers jumping from buildings and bridges, fathers drowning, melting in fires. She dreamed about those signs with the missing people on them plastered all over New York and woke up crying in the middle of the night. It got so she was afraid to fall asleep. That was when her mother found Gail, a children's grief counselor, and Elena started seeing her every week. She told Gail about her nightmares, and about her father, what few things she remembered. In high school, she talked about her growing annoyance with her mother. They disagreed about everything back then—what Elena was wearing, who she was hanging out with, the fact that she was being forced to go to Catholic school. Then, in her junior year, her mom decided to go back to college. It drove Elena insane. Not because she had to help more around the house, or even the weirdness of both of them having homework to do, but the way her mother transformed—the new haircut, the new cool clothes. The morning of her first day, Elena caught her turning in circles in front of the mirror, wearing a pair of skinny jeans with the tags still on. Her mom had never finished college, because she dropped out when she got married. *I can't believe Dad was okay with that*, Elena once said.

Her mother looked hurt, but only for a second. *It was what we both wanted*, she said, then added, *You don't really know him. You only know a version of him.*

Elena guessed this was true, but still, it wasn't what she remembered. It's not the sense of him she gets from pictures, either, and she understands pictures. The way a certain light or angle can capture the essence of a person: something not immediately visible, something the person may not even realize can be seen. In one of Elena's favorite pictures of her dad, he's sitting by the pool, in the shadow of the house, with the sun lighting half his face. The light falls in a diagonal line, one eye bright and one in shadow. He is looking right at the camera, his expression focused, attentive, as if whoever's taking the picture is the most important person in the world.

The flight attendant is giving the safety spiel about the flotation devices and oxygen masks and Elena is quietly freaking out. She knows these safety procedures by heart yet feels compelled to listen every time, afraid that by not listening she may jinx herself and plummet to her death. She kneads her hands inside the shirtsleeves, squeezing fistfuls of cotton, and tries to visualize being back in Philadelphia, the plane coasting to a stop on the runway. She reminds herself that the flight is less than an hour—the length of an art history lecture or a show on TV.

Elena realizes the woman next to her is saying something. She yanks her earbud out. "Sorry?"

"Would you like one?" She is offering her a mint. "They help me relax."

"Thanks," Elena says, and takes one, adding, "I have an irrational fear of flying."

"I've never liked it either," the woman says, dropping the mints back in her purse.

The engine is revving now, the plane moving slowly down the tarmac. Elena's stomach is in knots. "Were you in Boston on vacation?" the woman asks. Maybe she's asking because she's interested, maybe to distract her; whatever the reason, Elena is thankful.

"Yeah. I was visiting my cousin. She lives in the South

End. With her boyfriend. He's cool. He's an artist. They told me they're getting married, which is cool, because they're older. I definitely want to wait until I'm older." She knows she's babbling but can't stop. "It was a present for my college graduation—the trip, I mean. Because my cousin couldn't get to my show—I majored in photography, and all the seniors have this final show—" The engine is louder now, almost shrieking, as the plane gains speed. "I have to get used to this," Elena whispers, gripping the arms of her seat. "I want to travel next year."

"Oh?" the woman says. "Where are you going?"

"Europe," she says. "Geneva. Italy. Spain. Seville, maybe," she says as the plane lifts into the air.

Sometimes, Elena has trouble imagining her parents together. She wonders what would have become of them if her father were still alive—would they still be married? She suspects this isn't a question you're supposed to ask. You're supposed to think they would be in love forever, but Elena is a realist. More than half her friends have parents who are divorced. She knows things end, people change and grow apart—even people you wouldn't expect, like Aunt Ann and Uncle Dave.

Her mom never dated anybody after her dad died, not that Elena knew of, but last summer she decided to go on Match—*I think seventeen years is long enough to wait, don't you?* Her mom sounded nervous, telling her, but Elena was happy she was trying it. She had a job as a paralegal, had finished her degree. Max was away at college. Elena didn't like thinking of her mom being alone. When Gran died last year, her mom was so sad; even though Gran was living in a nursing home and had dementia, the two of them had always been close. Gran was over a lot when they were little; after she broke her arm, she'd lived with them for almost a year. The family had always seemed apologetic about that, but her mom had never seemed to mind—*I owe her a lot*, she always said.

When her mom called to say she had a date, Elena was happy for her, but the guy sounded lame. Divorced, which was fine. But a car salesman. His online name was OldFashionedGent. In his profile, which Elena's mom read to her over the phone, he talked about treating ladies right. "Ugh," Elena groaned. "Nobody who says 'ladies.'"

But her mom found this inexplicably charming. "I don't know," she said. "Your dad was a gentleman, you know. He was kind of old-fashioned, actually."

It was exactly the kind of thing Elena found impossible to fathom, but this time she kept her mouth shut.

When her mom came home from the date, she called Elena in her dorm. Elena could tell right away that her heart wasn't in it. *He was fine*, she said airily. *There was nothing wrong with him.*

Not exactly a ringing endorsement, Elena said.

Her mother laughed, but sadly. She was maybe a little tipsy. Then she started talking about her dad. She told a story Elena had never heard before, from before they were married, when they were at a wedding and some guy was hitting on her. Her dad stepped up to him and said: *I see you like looking at my wife?*

Oh, my God! Elena said. She was on her bedroom floor, pressing the phone to her ear, trying to block out the sounds of her roommates in the kitchen. *Really? That's like out of a movie.*

I know, her mother said. She sounded almost giddy. *It was.*

She offered a few more morsels and Elena gobbled them

down—how the guy apologized and her dad ended up shaking his hand, refreshing his drink, and then her parents left—her young parents, a fancy hotel on a cold night in Philadelphia, just a few months before their own wedding—and then her voice seemed to close, like a curtain drawn, and Elena was abruptly aware of all she didn't know. The fact that her mom had had a relationship with her dad that was private, that was theirs alone. It made Elena feel jealous of her and sorry for her at the same time.

The next weekend, Elena went home and convinced her mom to let her look at her profile. SingleMom2—the name alone made her feel a groundswell of sadness. But as she read on, she felt better. The description was nice; it sounded like her. *I am a proud mother of a beautiful daughter and a wonderful son*, it began. Reading it, Elena teared up. Her profile picture was one Elena had taken last August, at Uncle Patrick and Aunt Kate's shore house. She has a dark tan, the way she always did by August, and she's smiling and looking away from the camera, one hand holding her hair. Elena tweaked her profile to be a little more boastful, changing *average* to *slender* and adding that she was pretty (she was). Then they browsed through other people's profiles, checking out the guys who had e-mailed and winked at her, and by the time they had waded through all the cheeseballs and bodybuilders and weirdos they were laughing so hard they were crying.

The plane is in the air. Elena pulls the shade down, but only halfway, in case the woman beside her wants to see. She closes her eyes, focusing on the sound of the woman turning the pages of her magazine. She tries not to think about where she is, but she can't help picturing what could happen—the plane falling, an engine failing, the bottoming out in her stomach, the pieces crashing, her mother picking through her room. Elena has always braced herself for tragedies, had the ability to instantly summon them in gruesome detail. For her, these awful things always seemed possible. Gail told her it was understandable, her feeling this way, because she'd had a formative experience with loss. She compared it with being in a car accident and tensing up every time you went around a sharp corner. *Muscle memory*, she said. *You learned at a very young age that things can disappear.*

"Drink?" says the flight attendant.

"Oh. Yeah—um, ginger ale, please."

The pop and hiss of the can lid makes her feel a little calmer. The woman next to her unlatches the little tray and opens a cranberry juice.

"So," the woman says. "Did you say you're a photographer?"

"Oh—yeah. Well, I mean, I majored in photography."

"Photography." The woman nods. "That's different."

Elena smiles—it is so much like her family. *That's different*, they said, about the stud in her nose, the variously colored streaks in her hair.

"What do you take pictures of?" the woman asks.

"Um, well, it's kind of weird. It's photography, but mixed with found objects. So it's more like photo-collage," Elena says. She wants to explain it in a way that's clear and unpretentious. She hates when the kids in her class are deliberately obscure. "The subject is my family, mostly. It's about these contradictions"—*the dualities of family life*, she called them in her Artist

Statement—"having this identity as part of a big family but also this part of yourself that's separate, dealing with your own private stuff, that they never really know. Or dealing with the same stuff, just differently."

Elena frequently hears her friends complain about their families, but she's never been that stupid. She knows how lucky she is to have the family she does. As different as they are—her cousins Joe and Hayley, who she hangs out with at parties, are a jock and a cool girl—she's always loved being near them, all of them. It makes her feel as though her dad is still around. She loves hearing the old stories, sitting around the table after dinner, some worn thread picked up as casually as a comment about the weather or the food. *That reminds me of one time John . . . gosh, I think John was about seventeen . . .* handing off the baton. Listening, Elena feels drowsy, all her fears seeping out of her. She could curl up at their feet.

Most of the stories and pictures of him Elena has memorized, but occasionally something new turns up. When Aunt Ann was home recovering from her surgery, she cleaned out her attic and found a bunch of photos she'd forgotten that she had. For Elena, it was a treasure chest—all these images of her father she didn't already know by heart, new details she could add to her pile. In a few he has this insane mustache, but beneath it his face looks just like Max's. In another, he's wearing the blue shirt she has on now, holding her in the crook of one arm. She's laughing, looking up at his face.

Aunt Ann said she could have them, and some of them ended up in her senior thesis: *Where We Live.* The project was dioramas, done in shoeboxes, like in elementary school. In the boxes she created scenes of family, domesticity, rooms assembled from a combination of photos and found things. A slice of fabric from the inside lining of the blue shirt became a runner on a miniature dining room table; a newspaper headline about the Twin Towers, copied over and over, turned into wallpaper in the kitchen. She used photographs for the people, a combination of old pictures she found and new ones she took—a pair of folded, freckled hands; Max's face, half-submerged in bright blue pool water; the little gold cross her aunt Margie always wore. An old Sears portrait of the grandchildren taken before Max was born. Her parents' wedding picture—crazy, how young her mom looked—and the one of her dad's face, half-lit. Elena doesn't mean for the work to be depressing; she thinks it's lame, the kids who believe that only dark stuff qualifies as serious art. For her, it's about both feelings. *My work is about a paradox*, she wrote. *The moments when everything you know is suddenly different, but everything is the same.*

There is a spot of turbulence and the plane dips. Elena's stomach balloons into her throat. She closes her eyes, feels a sharp prick of sweat under one arm. Another abrupt sway, the rattle of soda cans in the attendant's cart, and the seat belt light blinks on. "We can expect a little turbulence, folks," the captain says. *Oh God. Oh no.* Elena squeezes her eyes shut and digs her nails into her palms. She became an agnostic when she got to college, but right now she prays. *Please don't let this plane crash, okay?* She tries to breathe in through her nose and out through her mouth, the way Gail taught her. She visualizes the airport in Philadelphia. Visualizes her brother strolling through the terminal in the nylon WIDENER SWIMMING jacket he always wears. She focuses on the woman beside her, the calm rustling of her magazine, how she licks her fingertip between each page, the way Gran used to when she read them stories. In a few minutes, the turbulence has passed.

For her final show, Elena's entire family showed up. She hadn't told anyone about it but her mother, who spread the word to everybody else. Elena was one of the few kids who had any family members there at all, much less eighteen of them. She wasn't surprised—her family came to everything, especially anything involving her and Max, forever making up for what was missing—but she was touched all the same, by them all being there, by their unease among the art kids with their pierced lips and dyed hair. Aunt Ann circled the room slowly, pausing before every photograph, as if giving each equal attention. Aunt Margie fidgeted nervously with her necklace, but this didn't mean anything; she always did. Alex and Cynthia walked through the exhibit slowly, talking with their heads bent toward each other, his hand on her back. Her cousin Joe and his wife focused on keeping their kids from screaming or touching things, four-year-old Joey III and Caitlyn, the newborn, wearing a flowered headband that practically engulfed her tiny head.

Aunt Kate and Uncle Patrick showed up late, as usual, as if blowing in from a storm. Uncle Patrick was in his doctor's coat and Kate was dressed as fashionably as a college student, in leggings and knee-high boots. Hayley and Tate moved in a techno-trance, absorbed in games on their parents' cell phones. Uncle Joe was there, too, squeezing his huge body through the narrow aisles. He did a brief walk-through and then stepped aside, puffing slightly, and talked to Uncle Dave, who had come even though he wasn't married to Aunt Ann anymore. Meghan scooped up baby Caitlyn—she was always glued to the babies—and swept past the photos, effusive about everything, then stood beside her dad. Of all of them, her cousin Stephen looked the least comfortable, hands in pockets, shifting from foot to foot. Maybe he felt awkward around college students—he'd gone to college for only a semester and a half. Elena knew that Stephen struggled with things, not exactly like the things she struggled with, but she'd always felt a connection to him all the same. He had a daughter now, a six-year-old, Faith, and around her Stephen was the happiest she'd ever seen him. "Cool stuff," he told Elena, then ducked outside to smoke. When Elena's father died, Stephen was in high school, so he was a reliable source of information there. Once he told her, *He took you seriously, even if you were saying something really fucking stupid*, and Elena remembered that picture with the half-lit expression and thought this sounded true.

At the show, her family took pictures—pictures of her pictures, like tourists in art museums. "Get in," they told Elena, which meant that her head or shoulder was blocking some part of the work in every shot. But her family liked pictures with people in them, so Elena stood next to each of her photos, smiling over and over, sometimes grabbing Max or Tate or Hayley and making them get in, too.

Toward the end of the show, Elena noticed her mother looking at one of the dioramas. *(Dis)comfort.* This one was done in layers, five shoeboxes stacked on top of one another like the floors of a tall, unwieldy house. On some floors, people sat alone in rooms; on others, the same people were all grouped together. She was trying to get at this feeling of being separate and together, belonging and not belonging at the same time. Her mom had been stopped in front of it for minutes, holding her fingers to her lips.

"What do you think?" Elena said, coming up beside her, and to her surprise, her mom hugged her.

By the time she's finished her ginger ale, Elena doesn't feel quite so scared. For minutes at a time, she can actually forget she's in the air. This is good practice for next year—she'll have to fly to get over to Europe, even if she'll be mostly riding trains once she gets there. She loves the idea of trains, rolling through different countries, watching the scenery slide by the window, staying in hostels in random towns. Surely the experience will be filled with those *crux moments*—the world, altered slightly. She knows they aren't the kind of thing you can go looking for, but she can at least get in position.

"It's a pleasant seventy-six degrees in Philly, folks," says the captain's voice. "We are preparing for our descent." He sounds so confident already—thanking them for flying, projecting to a future where they've already landed safely in Philadelphia— that Elena starts to believe they'll make it down intact.

"Nice weather," the woman says. "I hear it's going to be nice all week."

"That's good," she says. "My mom's having a party for me tomorrow. For my graduation."

"It sounds like you have a very nice family," the woman says.

Elena nudges the window shade up a little. It *is* kind of cool, seeing the clouds up close, if she can manage not to focus on falling. The clouds look so tangible, so textured, it's hard to believe touching them would feel like nothing. This one is fat and bulging, like one of Raphael's angel paintings. That one is a blanket of ripples, like a Van Gogh field. *Hi, Dad*, she thinks, only partly joking. She believes he's up here somewhere, which she admits is not very agnostic of her, or very realist either.

They are down below the clouds, and Philadelphia is in sight. The cluster of tall buildings, the blinking lights, and the great gray sprawl on either side—easy to forget how huge the city is, the endless grid of it. The smoke from the factories near the airport turns the sky a kind of unearthly blue. As the city draws closer, Elena feels something relax in her chest. She pictures her family, their own little corner of the city, a fortress. Her mom and Max have probably already cleaned the pool, getting it ready for tomorrow. Her cousin Joe will play lifeguard, holding little Joey in his bubbled water wings. Tate and Hayley will splash in the five-foot end, while Stephen mans the grill. There will be all the usual foods—macaroni salad, potato salad, pink fluff—plus cheesecake that Alex and Cynthia bring from New York. The Phillies game will be on in the living room and Uncle Patrick will wander in and out, reporting on the score. Aunt Ann and Aunt Margie will make sure everyone is taken care of, refilling drinks and clearing dishes. As the plane starts down, and Elena's heart begins to pound, she visualizes everybody gathered around the table after dinner, the way the kids will grow tired, wrapped in towels but fighting sleep, and the family will tell stories, grazing over the desserts, as the night turns cool, and the new baby is passed from lap to lap, arms to arms. She can picture it already.

Acknowledgments

Thank you to Katherine Fausset at Curtis Brown, for her wise and steadfast guidance, and to Emily Griffin and all of her colleagues at Grand Central, for their passion and hard work on behalf of this book. It could not have been in better hands.

Thank you to Laura Miller, Clark Knowles, Kerry Reilly, Amanda Strachan, and Gina Pierce, for their thoughtful advice on the book in various stages. Thank you to Bob and Jolanda de Levie, who provided the ideal Maine hideaway in which to write it.

Thank you to Dolores Juska, Phil Juska, and Sally Juska, who have always supported my writing without question or exception.

To the entire Pierce family, who have taught me about courage, resilience, and the importance of the little things.

And to Jake, who makes me feel so lucky.

About the Author

Elise Juska's fiction and nonfiction have appeared in *Ploughshares*, the *Gettysburg Review*, the *Missouri Review, Good Housekeeping*, the *Hudson Review, Harvard Review*, and many other publications. She is the recipient of the Alice Hoffman Prize for Fiction from *Ploughshares* and her work has been cited in *The Best American Short Stories*. She lives in Philadelphia, where she is the director of the undergraduate creative writing program at the University of the Arts.

Reading Group Guide

the
Blessings

by

Elise Juska

A Conversation
with the Author

What inspired you to write a novel about a family?

In a way, I feel as though as I've been writing this novel, or some version of it, for a long time. When I was in college and graduate school, I wrote several short stories about close extended families, always with this central image—the aunts around the dining room table, the uncles gathered around the TV, the quiet emphasis on food and children.

I grew up in a big family, one of sixteen cousins on my mother's side, and as I've gotten older, I've thought a lot about what the particular experience of being from a big family means. For me, and I imagine this is fairly common, the family—the beliefs and traditions, that long shared history—is a crucial part of who I am. At the same time, there are parts of my life that remain separate, and private, that the family couldn't or wouldn't know. Figuring out how to write the story I'd been circling since college was probably in part a matter of maturity—approaching the subject with more experience and (hopefully) more insight—and finding the right form in which to tell it.

You grew up in Philadelphia and still live there. Is The Blessings *autobiographical or otherwise informed by your experiences there?*

The characters in *The Blessings* are fictional, but the rhythms and rituals of this close family were certainly influenced by my own. Like the Blessings, my relatives on my mother's side are based in Philadelphia. They've dealt with devastating loss, and they're the strongest, most grounded people I know.

In "real life," two of my uncles died quite young, and both had young children. These deaths occurred about ten years apart, but they have shaped our family history. Though the events of this book are invented, that absence has loomed large in my life, and in my writing. The multiple perspectives provided a way to show the long ripple effect of such a loss, the way the family grieves both separately and together.

How did you come up with the title for the book?

Naming the book was largely about naming the family, which was surprisingly difficult. Ultimately, the name Blessing was chosen for a few reasons. It's an Irish-Catholic surname, one I'd heard in Philadelphia; it's also, in the context of this story, a name that has dimension. At first I hesitated about choosing a name with an extra layer of meaning, but the meaning of this word, a *blessing*, felt so right for this family. It's not pretentious or grand. It's an abstract concept, but still rather everyday. It's a word I can imagine Helen using. To me, it speaks of small things, ordinary joys, and a fundamental inclination toward what is good.

Though the novel starts with a chapter from the point of view of a young woman, you are able to evoke the voices and experiences of a range of different characters—a middle-aged man, an elderly grandmother, a teenage boy, and more. Which of these was hardest to write? Why did you choose to set up the book this way?

Writing linked chapters from multiple perspectives enabled me to capture that relationship between the individual and the clan, and to explore the experience of a big family from several different angles. In writing Lauren, for instance, I imagined what it would feel like to be a sister-in-law from a small family, unaccustomed to the constant togetherness of big family life. In Alex's story, I wanted to explore geography, to think about what a close-knit, intensely local family feels like when you're far away from home for the first time.

I enjoyed writing each one of these characters. I suppose the most difficult to write was Helen, not for reasons of craft, but because my grandmother died while I was writing the book. They weren't the same person, yet there is something at the core of Helen that reminds me very much of my grandmother. After she died, it was difficult to go back to that chapter; it took me a while to get through it.

The chapter that came easiest was probably Elena's, though that must have been partly a function of how I wrote it: in a little cottage in Maine during Hurricane Irene, the trees thrashing wildly, bracing myself for one of them to come crashing onto the roof or my power to go out—I'm sure that some of my own anxiety was in the mix as Elena waited for her plane to take off.

Do you plan out the whole novel in advance? If not, did anything surprise you as you wrote?

I didn't have much of a plan when I started writing, but as the families began taking shape and the relationships falling into place, there were certain characters' perspectives I naturally gravitated towards. As I wrote their stories, many moments came unexpectedly—in "Two Houses," for instance, the fact that Patrick was contemplating infidelity—but the one that surprised me most was when Stephen started beating up the old man in the parking lot at Wendy's. It was one of those scenes that sort of appeared on the page, and part of me wished it hadn't, though I knew that it felt true to Stephen, who wasn't a violent person but just didn't know how to handle his anger and sadness.

You currently teach college students at an arts-focused university. What about late adolescence interests you, and what did you want to convey through Abby, Alex, and Elena, the three characters who are college-aged in their chapters?

Going to college seems to me a moment when you begin to define yourself as an individual in a number of ways—to make independent decisions, separate yourself from your family, see your life at home with more objectivity. I clearly remember going to college and, like Abby, being surprised to find that not all kids had families like mine. It was the first time I understood that it might not be the norm to see your first cousins on a weekly basis and to have fifteen relatives watching you go to the prom!

Abby, Alex and Elena all find themselves at similar junctures. For Alex, away at grad school, traveling abroad with his girlfriend causes him to confront how he is (and isn't) like his family, to evaluate his values and priorities. Abby's and Elena's stories I see as bookends to the novel and parallels in various ways, both in terms of plot—both are eighteen years old, one is leaving and the other coming home—and insight, as Abby is realizing that she's not just like her family, while Elena is coming to appreciate the ways that, despite their differences, she and her family are alike.

If you were to write a follow-up to The Blessings, *which character's story would you be the most excited to expand or bring into the future?*

I loved living with these people so much, I felt as though I could have gone on writing them forever. But if there's one family I feel particularly compelled to return to, it's Margie and Joe and Joey and Stephen. Specifically, I'm interested in Amy's experience after she marries former high school basketball star Joey and how it might not end up being quite what she'd expected. I'm also curious about Stephen's daughter, Faith, and what would it be like for her—the daughter of a dad with very partial custody, parents who were never married to each other and are no longer together—to be part of a close extended family like this one. What is her mother's family like, and how does she reconcile the two? I wonder how the dynamics of the Blessing family might change, in general, as the grandchildren get older and have families of their own. Maybe I'll check in with them in ten years or so to find out.

Questions for Further Discussion

1. There are many departures and arrivals at different points in THE BLESSINGS, both literal (like Abby leaving to go back to college) and metaphorical (the deaths of two family members). The Blessing family creates rituals around all of them—does your family do the same? Why or why not? Do you think it's more important to recognize happy occasions and events or sad ones?

2. Do you come from a big family or a small one? Which characters in the book do you identify with the most?

3. Food is not just a means of sustenance in the novel; it can also be a gift, an obligation, and a means of coming together. In Meghan's case, it is part of her illness. What do you think that the author is trying to express about families and food?

4. In "Her Last Great Act," Helen feels awkward about becoming part of Meghan's social studies project. Do we risk marginalizing the older generations as we try to honor them?

5. The chapter "Happy Face, Sad Face" deals with a couple who come from two very different kinds of families. Do you think that Alex and Rebecca's relationship was doomed to fail? What common threads might have made the difference?

6. In "Two Houses," Patrick experiences a moment on the beach that brings back his childhood in ways that are both comforting and difficult. Have you ever had a similar experience? Does the ocean evoke nostalgia in you?

7. When Elena's art show reunites the Blessings, many of their lives have taken surprising trajectories. What surprised you the most about where the characters are at the end of the novel? What do you think is next for them?